# Penance

## Teen Heroes Unleashed Book One

## Paula Richey

OtherRealm Studio

*To Jimmy and Meri Lyn*

# Contents


1. About to Drop   1
   United States of America, Planet Earth

2. Ambitious   8
   Great Desert, Planet Hylinek

3. Crossroads   24
   Alley, United States, Earth

4. Incoming Storm   32
   Location: Planetary Justice Headquarters, Earth

5. The Plunge   38
   Salvage Break, Great Desert, Hylinek

6. The Big Game   49
   Stadium, United States, Earth

7. A Hero's Welcome   65
   Enormous Plasma Bomb Filled with Hostages, Earth

8. First Impressions   71
   Trouble, USA

9. Lab Animal   78
   Undisclosed

10. Out Past Curfew   90
    Unauthorized

11. Far From Home   95
    The Dunes, Great Desert, Hylinek

12. Free for All   102
    Prison Mine, Great Desert, Hylinek

13. Death's Door     115
Seventh Level, Prison Mines, Hylinek

14. Busted     120
Serious Trouble, Planetary Justice Headquarters, Earth

15. Salvage Operation     127
Planetary Justice Headquarters, United States of America, Earth

16. First Aid and Abetting     136
Civilian Home, United States of America, Earth

17. Soldier Out of the Desert     143
Location: Undisclosed, the Sequel

18. Getting Out     158
Civilian Home, United States, Earth

19. New From Old     172
Undisclosed 3: Junky Barn, Earth

20. Path     181
The Home for Inconvenient People and Convalescents, Earth

21. Last Ditch     188
Interstate, United States, Earth

22. No More Hiding     191
Home for Inconvenient People and Convalescents, Earth

23. Road Trip     201
Departing Home for Inconvenient People and Convalescents

24. Close     205
Interstate, United States, Earth

25. Final Connection     222
Outside Nuclear Facility, United States, Earth

Epilogue: Penance's Diary     225

Epilogue: Kail's Records     230

To My Wonderful Readers     233

About the Author     235

Who Is Thomas Plutarch?     236

# About to Drop

## UNITED STATES OF AMERICA, PLANET EARTH

*I'm gonna explode*, Penance thought. Her arms prickled with pent-up electricity.

The fluorescent lights of the crowded grocery store buzzed unbearably overhead.

Two children discovered they had static-charged fingers and chased each other around their mother's cart, zapping each other and giggling. The mother recoiled as a static arc from the metal shelf stung her fingers. Another arc flicked with a small, audible crack from the aluminum edging on the butcher's display to a nearby cart.

Penance slowed her breathing in an effort to damp down the energy before someone noticed that it came from her. *Calm down, girl, you haven't exploded for real during one of these spells*, she told herself. *Yet.*

Until the spell passed, the maddening sense of every electrical pulse nearby would thrum in her blood, from the wiring in the walls to the bioelectricity of bystanders' brains, and her own energy field would ripple out and surge along anything conductive in range.

*I can't stand it in here much longer.*

Quickly palming an apple into the sleeve of her jacket, she glanced across the rows of produce. None of the shoppers milling about paid any mind, so she moved on to lean against an endcap display and slipped a packet from it up the back of her shirt. On the next aisle, she bypassed the canned drinks and slid the first plastic bottle she found up her other sleeve.

A fresh prickle ran up her spine and echoed in the sudden flickering of the lights above. *A Prime? Here?* In the next instant she pegged him. A middle-aged man in plainclothes, who walked straight to customer service with a flyer in his hand.

Penance's field didn't react to every sort of superhuman that existed, but she could sense the ones who affected electricity, even in the midst of a sensory crisis. This guy didn't come in for groceries, so she'd rather not stick around in case he'd come for her. Abandoning the rest of her shopping, she walked out without even a curious glance back at the newcomer.

*After all, how stupid would it be to get busted for shoplifting right before a big job?* In spite of the sullen weight of the yet-to-drop storm overhead, her tension eased. She wouldn't explode today – she'd been laying low too long, and tomorrow's gig would give her an outlet. Penance sauntered a few blocks away from the store before eating her apple, eyeing the blackening sky. *I should scrounge up a change of clothes before I turn in for the night. Before this storm drops.*

The bottom dropped out of the sky before Penance made it inside. She hugged the lumpy bundle of her finds to her stomach and bumped the front door of the mill with her hip. It didn't budge from the swollen doorframe.

An icy stream dripped from the eaves down her neck and she swore. The last of her patience lost, she kicked the door in. It pitched open and banged against the inside wall, setting off echoes. Sheepishly, Penance edged in. The door, cracked off one hinge now, wouldn't fit back in the frame all the way. With no way to fix it without dropping her stuff, she wedged it shut as far as she could.

The rotted places in the floor filled with water from the leaks. Penance picked her way through the puddles and climbed the creaking metal stairs. The best room, she knew, was in the far corner. Maybe one day the old mill would be made into expensive loft apartments, like had happened with some of her old haunts, but until then, the rent cost exactly what she had to spend - nothing. It was almost funny to think about.

The room waited, undisturbed; empty except for a broken chair. She dropped her armload of stuff on the floor and sorted it by the weak yellow light coming from the streetlight outside. The bundle's outer layer was a puffy winter coat, ugly as all get out, but good to sleep on. A packet of microwave popcorn and a warm bottle of sports drink – she set those aside. A T-shirt, good condition, with a picture of a goofy green alien. It made her smile. With all the Primes and villains and super-mega-ultra battles that went on in places like Serenity City, she felt better thinking that there were still some things left in the world that were too crazy to be real. A lightweight gray hoodie, smelled a little smoky. A couple things looked like they'd be too small after all. A pair of jeans turned out to be chopped up so no dumpster-divers could get any use out of them. She made a disgusted snort. She hadn't really hoped that she'd found an intact pair of jeans. They were clean, though, so she toweled her hair with them. Rain had soaked her thin shirt, so she peeled it off and draped it over the broken chair. Her athletic tank top was wet too, but she'd rather shiver to death than remove it, whether anyone could see her or not.

Time for dinner. Penance unwrapped the packet of popcorn and held it between her palms as she searched her mind for the right frequency to generate. Energy slid smoothly over the insulating oils in her skin and radiated from her fingertips. The bag warmed in her hands.

*Pop pop popopopop!* Kernels ricocheted around the bag, expanding it as she shook it gently to get every last kernel to pop before ripping it open. Steam scorched her fingers as she shoved a handful of popcorn in her mouth, savoring the warmth before it dissipated. Too soon, the chill overtook her again. Her drink tasted too sweet and too salty, especially after popcorn. *If I'd just held out a bit longer in the store and paid attention to what I picked instead of getting spooked by that Prime...* Her thin shoulders jerked involuntarily. Acid would know she'd let herself get caught to get out of the big job he had lined up. That wasn't a trick she'd pull again.

Penance bunched the pile of rags into a nest on the splintered floor and curled up in it. The storm outside thundered and flashed, shaking off all the fury it had built up during the day. Rain slammed the roof and windows in heavy sheets, splattering into puddles under leaks, but not in this corner of the abandoned mill. It was almost cozy. If she could only slow down the anxious spiral of her thoughts and sleep, it'd be a pretty nice spot. She couldn't afford to be tired in the morning.

When had she last slept in a house? She was so tired. Not so much from training or lack of food, but the thought of getting up again in the morning – or ever – was almost more than she could stand. *Just sleep*, she thought. *Get through one more night.*

*The silver cross spun in the darkness.*

*Green eyes, trying to hide fear, coaxing her out of the darkness. Mama's smile, a little tight, her hand outstretched.*

*The pounding grew louder.*

*Little Penny let Mama take her from her hiding place in the cabinet.*

*Mama ran with Penny, threw aside the chair blocking the door and fought with the locks. Penny dashed back into the cabinet to hide from the man.*

*Step, scuff. Step, scuff.*

*Wait, Penny thought, confused. That isn't right.*

*Mama screamed.*

*A thud, then silence.*

*Little Penny crawled from her cabinet to Mama's side. Mama's breathing stopped and started again, raspy, burbling.*

*"Jesus..." Mama said. "Save my baby."*

*No, Mama! Penny screamed, but she couldn't make a sound. It didn't happen like this. I had... I had...It was my... I'm dreaming...*

*The man's shadow fell over Penny.*

*Step, scuff.*

A shadow fell over Penance, and an acrid smell filled her nose.

Hair. Her hair was burning.

She jerked awake and yanked the strand of hair away from her boss, Acid. He stood, his fingers still smoking from his acidic skin reacting with her hair.

"Get up," he said. "You have a date with Justice."

Penance glanced at the window. A few stray raindrops, lit by the dirty yellow streetlight, streaked the glass. "What time is it?" She could swear she'd only just shut her eyes.

He wasn't looking at her. His teeth clenched, and he wrung the paper bag in his hands.

"Sir?" Penance asked, carefully respectful. She watched him for a sign of today's mood.

Staring intently at nothing, he spoke rapidly. "Got new info on him. Natural force field. Bulletproof. Makes him land soft, too. Jumped down thirty stories once. I saw him." He began to pace,  his stiff left leg slowing him slightly.

Step, scuff. Step, scuff. The same sound that had invaded her dreams.

Penance grabbed her new t-shirt and pulled it on.  She felt better with the tattoo on the back of her right shoulder covered, where Acid had put his name on her long ago. She considered the "new info." Why did Acid think she had to know this? He always told her to avoid Primes. Justice was cool at a distance, though, even if he was sort of a cop. He had his own thing, like most of them, and didn't bother with petty thieves like her.

When the thefts weren't so petty, well. Acid lined up major gigs sometimes, hiring her out to get through high-level security systems. As long as she followed his instructions and stayed on task, she always got out clean and well ahead of any Primes.

Acid didn't make a habit of giving her too much info, though, and that made her suspicious.

Penance combed her fingers through her hair and pulled it to the side to braid it. "Energy field like mine?" she mused. It wasn't such a stretch. If Justice could surround himself with energy to repel attack – or slow down the ground coming at him from thirty stories below – maybe she could, too. She could use some new tricks. Could she study Justice and learn how to copy the frequencies he put out, like she copied electronic keys and alarm system codes? Imagine what she could do with even a weak copy of some Prime abilities and a decent head start.

She slid her gaze furtively to her boss as he paced the room. What could she learn, and how far could she get? Bulletproof would be useful. *Acid*-proof was what she needed, though.

Acid's restless eyes found the window and his pacing led him to it. He stared out at the clearing sky and the pink beginning of dawn. "He's out there now. Watching the route. Gotta hold him up today, all day." He paused. "You get Justice to come to you."

*What?!* Penance clenched the ends of the braid. Purposely break the rule and get close to a Prime? There could only be one way to do that and get back out again."A *hit*? On *Justice*?"

Acid stopped wringing the paper bag. Absently, his fingers traced the veins standing out from his arm. They ended in an ugly, pulsing blotch inside his elbow. "It's paid for," he said softly. He rustled the paper bag.

A fast-food biscuit wrapped in greasy paper plopped to the floor in front of Penance. She finished her braid and picked it up. It warmed her cold hands. This time he'd bought one instead of digging it out of the trash. He never allowed her to hold enough money to buy her own, and the one time she'd been *caught* with money... The smell of bread and sausage hammered against her hunger, making her lightheaded even as her stomach roiled, too nervous to settle and let her eat it. "I'm taking on *the Justice*?" she muttered.

Acid shoved away from the window, on her before she could even flinch. He grabbed her shirt and yanked her up to his face. "I said it's paid for!" he shouted, and dropped her, muttering, "You were *made* for this," as he stalked away.

Step, scuff. Step, scuff.

Penance scowled at her t-shirt. The cute alien graphic now had a smoking hole through his green head. Acid hadn't touched her skin, so the oils her skin naturally produced still covered her entirely, insulating her from her own energy pulses. He still intended for her to take the gig.

*Guess he already knows it's gonna be a tough one if he doesn't want to send me out hungry and hobbled.*

At least he didn't stomp on her biscuit, though. She pulled on her gray hoodie and took her breakfast outside.

She leaned on the wall beside the service door and choked down dry bites of biscuit.

From the darkness inside the mill, Acid hissed, "Bonus if you kill him."

The door clicked shut.

Penance swallowed with difficulty. *I'm an electronic lockpicker, and sometimes an enforcer, but not an assassin!* Acid did the actual killing jobs. Though he *had* been training her.

She sighed. It had to come up sometime. She couldn't escape it – sooner or later she'd have to grow up and take serious gigs. It wasn't a future she'd picked, but after she'd helped destroy the one place that took in dangerous freak kids like her, she'd permanently screwed her chances for anything else. It didn't matter that she hadn't meant to cause trouble. Hangman House was gone.

And Acid would never stop hunting her.

Acid had a claim on her, as plain and permanent as his prison-tat mark on the back of her shoulder. Her abilities were just too useful to let be, and if it wasn't him, it'd be somebody else. He was the devil himself, especially while "switched" high on his drug, but he was the devil she knew.

Out of the corner of her eye, a slim cat approached, sniffing the odor of greasy biscuit in the air. A bony and dirty cat, but still optimistic enough to hop up to the stoop beside her and wind around her ankles. Its tiny chest vibrated with purrs.

Another purr caught her attention, far away and getting closer, picking through the maze of alleys near the docks. The timbre of the engine noise and the speed of the approach gave it away long before she saw it. *Motorcycle. There's my ride.*

She sighed and pushed off the wall. "Don't make friends with me, cat." She set the remains of the biscuit down for the cat anyway. "It ain't worth it."

The motorcycle pulled up at the other end of the alley and the rider, a lanky guy wearing a bandanna on his head and mirrored sunglasses, called out. "Hey, excited about the audition?"

*They're still luring girls in with the acting gig story? They must want pretty ones then*, she thought. *Tall Guy must be half blind to think that I'm one of them, though.*

Penance shrugged. "Something like that."

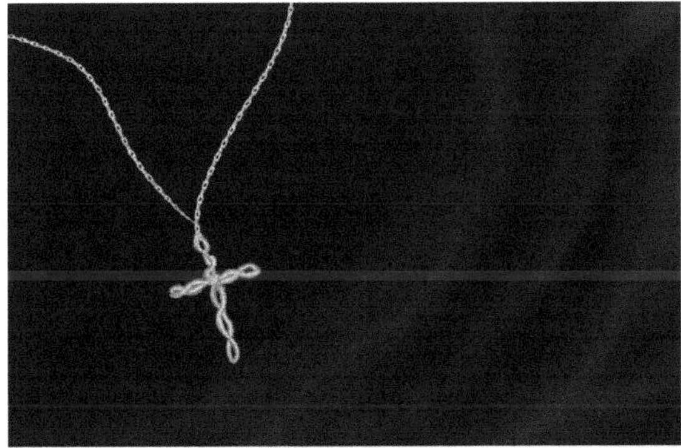

# Ambitious

## GREAT DESERT, PLANET HYLINEK

Kail crept down the familiar desert path in the darkness, an hour before dawn. His foot slipped and sent a pebble bouncing down the cliff to the fence that surrounded the compound. Somewhere in the cave-pocked cliffs, a fox yipped twice and fell silent. The soldier paused and switched off the alien transmission he'd been listening to over the augmented helmet comm. He couldn't afford distractions so close to his destination.

Reaching the gate, he let himself in cautiously and prowled toward the main building of the compound. Ahead, a small shadow slipped around the corner of the building and out of sight. Low to the ground, someone breathed, sniffling slightly in the dust. Kail paused, mid-stride, and glanced down.

"The giant! Get him!" a small soldier howled, and the yard erupted in whoops and shrill battle cries as boys leaped up from their hiding places of shallow trenches and camouflage sheets to attack. One sprang up from where Kail had been about to step, shoving the "giant's" leg with all his might to try to throw him off balance – an admirable effort, but ultimately useless. Others pelted him with dirt clods and pebbles, which only bounced off his armor.

Kail strode forward, unhindered by the small army's efforts.

Reinforcements arrived, attracted by the ruckus, and a fresh troop mustered and rushed the big soldier. A dozen boys tackled him, hanging on to his arms and legs, and the first troop clambered on top of them to weigh him down. The first child, who had signaled the ambush, took a running start and leaped up to grab around Kail's neck.

The giant soldier stumbled, falling to his knees and pitching forward to crawl ahead in spite of the attack. The boy hung around his neck with one arm and pounded his helmet. "Surrender or meet Death!"

Kail couldn't hold back laughter any longer. He shrugged the army of children off his back and stood. The one around his neck hung on stubbornly.

*"Daik ni, ko ibak,"* Kail told him, laughing as he set the child down. *I look forward to meeting him, but your rank is too low to introduce us.*

With the game over, the rest of the children dispersed, running off to finish interrupted chores before breakfast. But their stubborn leader, Jearn, stayed.

"Is the caretaker-general in his quarters?" Kail asked him.

"Yes, sir." The boy reached up and brushed the big soldier's wrist with the outside of his own as they walked – at six years old and in level one, Jearn was considered too old to grasp hands for reassurance. "Supply Officer Kail? Will you stay with us? As the new caretaker-general?"

Kail shook his head. "No, I've already been assigned a mission. I'm lucky that my route brought me close enough to visit today." At the door to Caretaker-General Baos' quarters, he glanced down at the small boy. "Here, hold this for me." He removed his helmet and set it on Jearn's head. "Tell me if my unit calls."

"Yes sir!" Jearn saluted, staggering a little under the weight of the huge helmet. He listened to the transmission for a moment, puzzled. "Are they aliens?"

"Not that channel. I'm learning a new language on that one. Here." Kail adjusted the channel and turned to tap the door, but it opened before he touched it. He snapped a salute, a reflex born of years of respect to the man inside.

"Come in, 'Giant,'" Caretaker-General Baos said dryly. "The boys are excited to see you again."

The big soldier ducked through the doorway to the small, sparsely furnished room. Plain gray walls, a bed, a box for a carefully folded spare uniform, and a desk were all it contained for the needs of the Caretaker-General. "It's good to see them. My little barracks-brothers have grown so much in two years!"

Baos looked up at Kail and shook his head slowly, the ghost of a smile at the corner of his lips. "Fortunately, none quite as much as you. Are you taller?"

Kail shrugged. "Only a little." His sensitive nose caught the scent of blood and disinfectant. "How are you? I heard there was an accident."

Baos sighed and turned his hands up – or rather, one hand and a bandaged stump. "Most of me is fine, but my right hand couldn't be retrieved. Last day of landmine removal, one of the boys slipped. He'll recover."

"But you -"

"I've received my compensation credits." Baos flipped open the credit document on his desk. "You remember Greer, don't you? Graduated six years ago? He expedited my claim."

It would be rude to lean over to read the document, but Kail's height made it easy to glance at it politely. His eyes widened as he calculated the sum represented. "Permission to speak, sir?"

The older man chuckled. "You outrank me now. But yes, granted."

"This is enough to buy a name, a home, a wife even. You could have sons of your own blood."

Baos bowed his head. For the first time, Kail noticed the gray streaked through his hair, and the loss of muscle through the caretaker-general's once-powerful shoulders.

"That's a young man's dream," Baos said at last. He glanced up at Kail. "I wouldn't recommend this method of earning it."

The big soldier shrugged. "A right hand for that isn't such a bad deal."

"True, you're left-handed." Baos' sly jab reassured Kail that the man who had raised him – and countless other *ibak* boys – would be fine. "But," he continued, "I've had many years to build this credit. Becoming crippled so early in your career would put your debt beyond hope of repaying. You're on your way to your first mission, aren't you?"

A frantic tapping at the door interrupted them. "Supply Officer Kail!" Jearn called. The boy stumbled in, hefting the helmet toward Kail. "They need you! A rival unit is robbing Salvage Break!"

Salvage Break was the first town on Kail's requisitions route. Named for the site of a spaceship crash that had cracked open a cliff, exposing valuable minerals deep within, the town barely sustained the people who lived there.

*There won't be enough supplies to meet quota for* two *units.*

Kail scooped up the helmet, nodding goodbye to Baos and Jearn on his way out the door. His long strides ate the distance to the tall gate, and he vaulted smoothly over rather than waste the time to unlatch it. His boots hit the ground on the other side with hardly a stumble as he picked up the pace again.

"I'm on my way," he told the convoy as soon as he'd clipped his helmet in place. "Don't wait – I can catch up."

Supply Technician Deyn's voice came through the comm. "Good, none of these *inek* want to wait for you."

Kail cursed and picked up speed. *Always, I have to prove myself to these* inek *soldiers,* he thought grimly. "I'll remember their insubordination when *they* apply for a half-day's leave."

As Supply Officer, he'd been permitted to choose a second-in-command, and he'd chosen Deyn, a friend he'd grown up with. Blunt, unthinking honesty characterized the technician's personality, and Kail could be certain of his loyalty as well as his competence. He couldn't say the same for the rest of the unit, but he'd build them into decent soldiers eventually.

He crested the ridge at the top of the path as the first light of dawn struck, and sighted the tail end of his convoy in the distance. Taking a running start, he leaped from the ledge and rolled as he hit the ground, bouncing up to his feet in an instant to resume his sprint across the sandy valley. "Is the rival unit still in sight?"

"Yes. They appear to be moving out," Deyn said. "I think it's Rorcon's unit."

Kail didn't waste breath cursing Rorcon – with any luck, they'd catch up to the rival convoy and then he could finish the fight that high-born low-brained fool had started a week ago at graduation. As he opened his mouth to give the order to pursue, Deyn's voice broke in. "Sir? There's smoke over Salvage Break."

*That triply-cursed excrement of a cave lizard!!!* "Increase speed to Salvage Break," Kail growled. "Prepare to put out fires and contain whatever other damage Rorcon's unit has done." *Revenge will have to wait – but at least there'll be less reason to hold back when the time comes.*

Ahead, his convoy turned west, and as he gained ground he could see the smoke rising from beyond the next cliffs. To the north, a plume of dust trailed behind the rival unit as they made their escape. *I hope they burn through their fuel allowance before they make it to their* own *supply route.*

As the convoy met the cliffs at the edge of the valley, the vehicles had to maneuver through the roads and switchbacks carved into the cliffs. Kail cut across country, watchful for mines and traps as always, even though it had been a decade since the last rebels had been exterminated in this region. Old, over-looked mines still existed – evidenced by the caretaker-general's experience. The hard ground on top of the cliffs couldn't conceal mines, however, so once he scaled the first, he was safe enough to leap across the narrow chasms cut for the road.

Fortunately, the day had hardly begun. Soon the sun's heat would turn deadly.

He caught up and then some, crossing to the next switchback before clicking the comm on again. "I'm back, recon's clear, dropping in on Vehicle Two." *Disappointing that they didn't notice me. Whoever is on watch is in trouble.*

"Did he say Vehicle Two?" one of the soldiers muttered in the background. "I was looking *behind* us!"

A thud on the armored roof answered him. Kail swung open the hatch and dropped inside. "Nothing's behind you but your own crap, Vorak," the big soldier said before opening the comm signal to the rest of the convoy. "Keep a lookout ahead and prepare for damage control at Salvage Break."

The rival unit, in their vendetta against Kail, had left the town in terrible condition. The partially gutted spacecraft the town was famous for hadn't sustained any new damage, but entire homes had been crushed under tank treads. Several outbuildings and the main storage building, identifiable by the raised loading dock, blazed to rival the desert sun. The people of Salvage Break panicked at the sight of a second unit of soldiers driving up to the town, abandoning their firefighting efforts and sending the women and children into hiding.

"Vorak, Jarin, find the governor and bring him to me. Deyn, take a crew to put out the fires. Use water if you have to. The rest of you, start setting up camp."

The soldiers grumbled as they dispersed reluctantly to labor in the heat of the day. Kail fetched his own kit – he was the only one strong enough to carry his pack, and he didn't trust the other soldiers with it. He set the posts for the corners and doorway of his quarters one-handed in the hard earth, attracting stares from the townspeople as well as his own men.

The soldiers glared at him as he easily assembled his quarters while they sweated and strained for each post they planted in the rapidly increasing heat. Their hostility meant nothing to Kail, so long as they obeyed him. He'd dealt with resentment from his fellow soldiers all his life.

As for the desert, he had grown up here. The burning onslaught of ultraviolet rays during the day and the sudden deathly cold of night had little effect on him. Where others had died of exposure to the elements, he had grown tall and strong – massive in fact. He literally stood head and shoulders above them all.

Except they weren't *ibak*. He didn't care that these men chose the military, rather than be abandoned to it from infancy. That they had names and fathers who had paid the tax on their births, instead of leaving them with debt to be worked off during a lifetime of service.

Kail pushed the thought from his mind, tuning his comm to the alien language again to resume learning as he worked on his living space. Most of the soldiers in officer training had no interest in decoding alien tongues, but Kail enjoyed the mental exercise of translation. He already had a decent grasp of one of the more popular languages from a planet that had come into range of the portal relay only six months ago.

Jarin and Vorak returned, hauling a man about the same age as Baos between them. They threw the man at Kail's feet, pleased with themselves.

The giant supply officer folded his arms and stared at the soldiers until they belatedly remembered to salute. "I don't need anyone treated roughly today. Go assist Deyn's crew in putting out the last fire." He looked down at the man on the ground before him. "You must be the governor. I am Supply Officer Kail *ip ibak*. I'm sure you didn't intend for Salvage Break to be unprepared for the supply run."

The governor stared after the soldiers who had brought him, and the crew engaged in putting out the fire on the main storage building in the town. The men had a hose running from the reservoir now."No, not the water!" he gasped.

Kail bent and offered the man the outside of his wrist to help him stand. "The fire must be extinguished before it can spread to the homes," he said gently.

The governor turned to him, desperation and horror plain on his face. "We have nothing – nothing! Not even water to offer now, nothing left for ourselves. The first unit that came..." He faltered and fell silent.

Deyn had already informed Kail via the comm that all the food had been confiscated by Rorcon's unit, and the meager water supply severely depleted. The people of Salvage Break would have nothing left for themselves for the scarce season, but that had not been a concern for the rival supply officer.

"We will help you in the time we are here," Kail offered, and the governor flinched.

*Doubtless he's had enough "help" from soldiers today.* The big soldier sighed. "Inform your people that no one is to be punished and they may salvage and rebuild what they can. You may return to your home, if it still stands. I'll confer with my technician, and I will meet you later to discuss what may be done."

Deyn returned, covered in soot. The rest of his crew had used more of the town's water to wash before they came to camp. They were within their rights, as it was part of the town's responsibility to host the Emperor's military, but the desert-bred *ibak* didn't take water for granted.

Kail invited the technician in to his newly assembled quarters and opened a seat for him. "Is there anything at all of interest here?"

Deyn shook his head. "Only the spacecraft. I'd like to get a closer look at it."

Kail laughed. "You would. We weren't allowed when Caretaker-General Baos brought us here for the endurance hike."

"I'm serious. Most of it is still there. This town has only miners and farmers. No one has touched the solar arrays or the plasmic reactor or the portal drive. It may even function!" Deyn removed a small ring from his pocket. "I found the portal focus device on the ground below the ship. It's the most difficult to manufacture, and it seems to be intact."

Kail rubbed the bridge of his nose. "That's interesting to you, Deyn, but if the Emperor's military needed a scavenged portal drive, they would have come to get it already. What can help us meet quota on the supply list?"

A tap at the door interrupted the discussion. The two men looked at each other quizzically.

Kail rose from his seat and opened the door.

A veiled girl glanced up – far up – at him and dropped to her knees, trembling. With shaking hands, she held up a small basket containing a few small, carefully wrapped portions of food and a bottle of alcohol.

The supply officer stared down at her for a moment, registering the gold thread edging the fine, transparent veil, and the arrangement of the folds of the outer robe, fallen open to expose the girl's delicate shoulders. He stepped back and slammed the door, blushing furiously.

"Who is it?" Deyn asked.

"The governor has a daughter," Kail said. "I'd guess about twelve years old."

"Really? Why is she here?"

Kail shot the technician a critical look. Deyn could be remarkably obtuse at times.

From outside, a male voice said, "Are you lost, little girl?"

*Vorak.* Kail grabbed his helmet from the stand and opened the door again, resigned. "Go back to your post, Vorak. I could almost believe you *want* your credits docked." He looked down at the girl, self-consciously tugging her outer robe back over her shoulders. "And *you* are going home. Come, I'll take you."

The girl staggered to her feet, still weak with fear. She offered him the basket again.

"Keep it," he said. When she reached for his arm as though he was a proper escort, he stepped aside, hands at rest behind his back, and nodded for her to precede him. "Aren't you aware that I am *ibak?*"

She nodded, hesitantly, and then shook her head. "It can't be true, though?" she asked, glancing up at him shyly as she assumed the lead. "How could you possibly be inferior?"

Kail shrugged, falling in behind her. "It is the Emperor's decree."

*Just my luck*, he thought. *The first female I've spoken to is a timid, confused child. I've heard all females are, though, so perhaps it's to be expected.*

Some men liked girls this young and even younger, but Kail didn't see the appeal. He was already freakishly huge – the last thing he needed was a tiny, underage female.

She led him to a house slightly larger than the rest and tapped on the door. A moment later, the governor opened it. Behind him, his wife muffled a shriek and reached for her daughter, pulling her inside and behind her. The governor hushed her and gestured the supply officer inside.

Kail ducked through the doorway and ignored the offered seat. "Governor, while your daughter is very... thoughtful, it is much too early to assume I would want this sort of gift," he said. He raised an eyebrow at the girl. "Several years too early."

Behind the girl and her mother, a door cracked open, revealing a fourth member of the family. Kail glimpsed disheveled dark hair and one swollen, purpled eye as the girl he had escorted and the mother slipped into the other room. The whiff of air as the door closed bore an odor of blood and pain.

*When I find Rorcon, I'll kill him. It'll be worth the fine.*

"My apologies, Supply Officer Kail *ip ibak*. I did not send her; I did not realize that she had gone to you." The governor bowed his head. His shoulders twitched involuntarily, giving way to waves of shudders.

Kail cursed his own sensitive hearing as he picked up far too much of the conversation between the females in the other room. "I don't need your other daughter for anything either. Don't allow anyone else to disturb me until I send for you." He left, switching on his comm to distract himself from the mortifying walk back through the watchful town.

He didn't care for the alien music transmitted through the portal relays, but he'd found a frequency dedicated to the discussion of sports on that distant planet. Ignorant of the Emperor, the wealthiest of the population gathered to witness the championship of a game called football.

Soon, a fleet of spacecraft such as the one embedded in the cliff above would dominate those alien skies to subjugate and civilize the world in the name of the Emperor of Hylinek. Before then, he had to meet a quota of supplies to send with those ships, and all he had to work with was this picked-clean carcass of a town and a junk spacecraft. He could move on and attempt to make it up on his next stop, but that wouldn't help the civilians here.

His steps slowed as he gazed up at the wrecked spacecraft, the alien channel crackling in his ear about the food and drink available at one of the many places that sold meals.

The various pieces of his problems slid together, aligned like the solution to an encoded map.

The sun flared hot and orange, hanging low across the desert as its rays blazed through the high rocky cliffs, glinting off the long panel arrays and dusty black cables. Teams of soldiers worked to catch the last rays of sun on the arrays, angling them manually since the dust blown in the constant wind had jammed the motors. Interrupting their midday rest for more backbreaking work had caused more animosity, but Kail didn't care.

By this time tomorrow, none of that would matter. His idea was so huge, so daring, that they'd never doubt his place again. A mission that would set him on a path to pay his debt and buy any name he wanted. And then any future could be his.

"I don't like this." Deyn interrupted his daydreaming. Kail glanced down at the Supply Technician.

Kail shrugged. "Don't be so nervous. It's just a supply run."

"On a planet that isn't ours." Deyn fiddled with the control panel for the array and checked the stability of the salvaged plasmic reactor again. It would provide the bulk of the power needed, once the energy from the solar array revived it.

"Supply raid, then." Kail grinned. Where else would he get provisions for the army set to launch in twenty days? The town of Salvage Break was too small and poor. The civilians couldn't possibly meet the demand. This rich planet had recently come in portal-range, and the six months prior of eavesdropping on transmissions had taught him the language. The hobby others considered odd would be his ticket to freedom. It wasn't a waste of time after all.

"It's a violation of interstellar law to attack foreign civilians," Deyn said. "Retaliation..."

"Will take months," Kail interrupted. "People are starving now. Our civilians have nothing to requisition for the military. These civilians do." He shook his head. From the luxuries advertised, basic goods like food and water must be plentiful. And many of the wealthiest civilians would be gathered together in one easily-contained space, ripe for ransom...

"I still don't like it. We have very little intel on the Justice for Earth."

Kail put his helmet back on and switched on his headset. An update on the upcoming championship game came through, followed by an advertisement for a luxury land vehicle. He smirked. Next would be an example of their "breakthrough technology" - maybe another unimpressive communication device to record images and play little games on. "I'm not concerned about a rookie Justice on a primitive planet. I'll eliminate him myself."

Penance scanned the rooftops from the back of the motorcycle as the tall guy zipped through the alleys. His speed suggested he'd taken countless girls down this route before.

She saw no one else.

Had she missed Justice? Maybe he kept surveillance from an alley? No. Rooftops had a good view and little chance of being seen. If Acid was to be believed, Justice could hop down whenever he wanted, so he had no reason not to be up there.

Unless he knew about the trap.

*No.* Dread crawled up her spine and nestled in her throat. She swallowed it back down.

Acid kept things quiet. That's how he worked. That's how he survived with his crippled leg. So Justice – unless he could read minds too – would have no idea.

But still. It wasn't like Acid to take on a high-profile job. He stayed below the Primes' notice and left them to their hero versus villain battles. He kept quiet at all costs – and not even she knew where he hid the bodies.

What if Justice wasn't keeping watch? What if she came to the end of the route and vanished, just like the other girls? The tattoo on the back of her shoulder prickled. Acid marked all the girls he sold.

What if he'd sold her, too?

She looked up – and there on a rooftop stood a dark figure silhouetted against the early dawn.

Sunlight glinted from the lenses of his binoculars.

Penance had never been so happy to see a mark in her life.

*All right, time to get him down.* No telling if he'd watched other girls go by to make sure he had the evidence. She needed to be irresistible bait.

She shoved against Tall Guy, nearly causing him to run the motorcycle off the road. "No!" she screamed, leaning back as far as she could without falling off. "I don't want to go!"

Penance kicked and scraped the bike with her boots and scored a long nail scratch in his leather jacket, shrieking. She had pegged Tall Guy as somebody who liked his bike and gear pristine. His ears turned red and he skidded to a stop in a deserted alley.

She scrambled off the bike, clumsy-on-purpose, and let him elbow her hard in the gut. Tall Guy didn't play around – he knocked her breath out for real. It was a little much to fall down and crawl, but she did that too. He easily caught her braid and hauled her to her feet. She screamed and flailed the whole time like she couldn't simply turn and stomp his face to a pulp.

Tall Guy laughed, casually punching her head. "Not going anywhere, baby. Nobody can hear you."

He spun her against a brick wall and pressed his knee into her back. He wasn't acting, but he hadn't yet managed to do more than toss her around. Her natural strength and toughness didn't affect her weight. His free hand crawled over the front of her shapeless gray hoodie and squeezed... *Ewww*. Penance jerked her head. The back of her skull connected with his nose and glasses with a satisfying crunch.

*Where is Justice? I'm flopping like a fish here!* Fake tears spilled down her cheeks as she strained to look over her shoulder, looking for Justice. "Let me go!" she whimpered, as if she was in real pain. Taking the beating stung her pride more than it hurt for real. She'd had worse on any ordinary day of the week with Acid. *Justice had better be watching this*, she thought grimly. *This is the freakin' performance of my life.*

At least Tall Guy bought it. He grinned like she had appeared straight out of his favorite daydream.

*I swear*, she thought, *if he starts humping me, I'm gonna forget to wait on Justice.* Her fingers curled into a fist. *No. I can't. I have to see it through or Acid'll give me a* real *beating.*

Tall Guy yanked her braid again, pulling her to his chest. "See?" he said. "Nobody cares. Nobody's gonna come save you. Make this easy on yourself."

*It's taking too long.*

A hiccuping sob escaped her throat and she shuddered for real, her fingernails digging into the crumbling bricks of the wall. Was that really Justice on the rooftop? Or had Acid tricked her?

*It's the kind of sick thing he'd do.*

Had he sold her after all?

A sudden, overwhelming wave of static rolled through the alley like thick fur, startling her out of the fearful spiral of her thoughts and making her hair stand on end.

"Is this person bothering you, miss?" a stern voice said.

Penance looked up. A man in body armor stood in the one patch of daylight that fell in the alley, his fists on his hips in the classic power pose.

"Justice!" Penance gasped with real relief – no acting necessary this time.

*This is it.* She focused the way Acid had taught her. For every advantage, a disadvantage. For every strength, a sacrifice. The Justice's armor sacrificed protection for ease of concealment. He probably wore it under his regular clothes. A soft close-fitting shell hood covered his head but left his face exposed. Only his eyes were hidden behind a visor.

Tall Guy threw her down and ran. He didn't even bother to get on his bike. The Justice nodded to Penance and ran after him.

His path would take him right past her.

The chest plate of his armor didn't cover his sides.

He crossed in front of her, his side wide open.

Penance launched into him, her energy field rising and wrapping hot around her. It met his energy field with a sharp electric *crack!* Her left fist burned through and connected with his gut.

Her fists blazed with crackling arcs as she slammed his exposed face – right and then left again, before he regained his balance. Penance jumped back lightly, eyeing him over her left forearm, her right fist ready to strike again. She could do this all day.

"I don't know what they've told you...," the Justice said.

Penance swung a kick at his head, but he blocked it easily, jarring her. "But I'm not the enemy," he continued, calmly. Like she hadn't just slammed him with enough force to break bones. Like he could do this all day, too.

*I'm not an idiot*, Penance thought. *Great big patronizing...* His fist whistled – actually *whistled* - past her face and she barely dodged in time. Scared now, she sped up her strikes, falling into a sequence she'd trained on. He dodged everything she threw at him, moving closer and closer, walking right up in her space. Maybe she'd wasted her first surprise hit. Maybe she couldn't defeat him. *Hell, he ain't even swinging and I can't hold him off.*

Her form deteriorated from MMA to Panicked Hellcat.

"Please stop fighting me," he said, his tone polite and reasonable.

They might as well have been having a chat over lunch.

"If I wanted to hurt you, I would have already," he pointed out. "I am not your enemy."

His fist flashed and stopped a fraction of an inch in front of her face.

Her mind blanked with terror – and then anger boiled up in the next split second. Nobody – *nobody* – ever, ever, *ever* was going to so much as *touch* her

–

Penance grabbed his wrist and snarled, "I know." She yanked him forward and slammed his head down with her elbow as she drove her knee up into his face, smashing his visor into sharp splinters of glass and plastic. "I'm *yours*."

Hot plasma flames wrapped around both her hands, fueled by rage and humiliation. The edges of her field crackled and roiled, contacting a metal fire escape and sending arcs sparking madly from it. The fingers of her left hand twitched as she sensed the precise frequency of Justice's protective energy field and memorized it with the unique mnemonic technique she had created as a child. With it, she could use her energy field to play back any electronic signal. Played precisely enough, she could generate feedback to scream through the Prime's brain as she attacked.

He recoiled, grimacing in pain as she dialed in on his field.

*It's only getting worse for you from here out*, she thought grimly.

She wished her left fist smashed into Tall Guy's smug, disgusting face right now, her right crashing into his unguarded ribcage.  She unleashed a furious blaze to slash across Justice's face and struck him full in the gut with a round-house kick that drove him backward into the alley across the street. Advancing on the Prime, her fists burned through the air, leaving a white-hot plasma trail in their wake. Plowing under his guard, she popped a brilliant flash of electricity right in his eyes. In the next instant, she dropped low and hooked the back of his knee with her steel-toed boot while he still blinked away the afterimage. He faltered and she put everything she had into an uppercut, launching up like a rocket from her crouch. His head cracked back and her next kick landed solid in his ribs, knocking him sideways into the opposite wall of the alley.

Instead of catching his balance and coming for her, Justice crumpled to the pavement and lay, his body bent and unmoving.

Penance froze, panting, her trembling fists clenched. After a minute she edged a little closer and popped a quick kick at his ankle. Nothing happened. She couldn't see his chest rising and falling in his armor when she crept closer again.

Her fury cooled as she stood over the Prime. Tall Guy was probably a mile away, still running, too scared to look back. Scared of Justice, when he should have been scared of *her.*

*Too late to make his sorry butt pay for that*, Penance thought. Her job wasn't over yet. She still had to remove any identification before the body could be disposed of.

She dragged Justice's body a little away from the wall, and knelt beside him to rifle through the slim outer pockets of his gray armored suit. She only found a few dollars and a cell phone in a case made from the same material as his suit, with a little slot that held a screen stylus. Made sense – that gray material was ugly, he wasn't wearing it for fashion. So if his energy field destroyed electronics like hers did, it was probably some kind of insulation.

Her fingers found the zipper to the outer layer of the armor, and she un-zipped the top half of the suit to reveal a plain blue athletic undershirt and several pockets on the inside liner of the body armor.

*Now we're getting somewhere*, she thought. Keys. Picture and thumbprint ID on a holographic badge - as Justice over District Earth, Base USA, Universal Security Clearance 12. A map of the solar system and numbers filled the back of the badge. She cocked her head, puzzled. *What kind of job is this for? Do all government Primes have a picture of planets circling the sun with "Earth" clearly labeled?*

But she didn't find a regular ID – no driver's license, no "normal job" badge, not so much as a library card. Nothing told his name or his address or even his age.

She looked at his face and peeled back the soft-shell helmet. He had close-cropped brown hair, sprinkled slightly with gray. His face looked younger than Acid's, but then, Acid looked like hell. So maybe about Acid's age, a bit older? And familiar – she recognized him as the Prime who'd come in the store yesterday. *Small world.* Unless he'd been looking for her?

A small lump beneath the undershirt attracted her attention. She hadn't noticed the silver chain before – that looked valuable. She fished it out from his shirt.

*A silver cross spun in the darkness...*

Pain twisted Penance's gut. A dim memory surfaced, the distinctive silver cross that Mama never took off, not ever – identical to this one. Just a worthless bit of twisted wire...

She rocked back, dropping the necklace to the man's chest, and closed her eyes.

Fresh fury rolled through her, this time at herself. Finally, Acid had got what he wanted out of her – she'd become just like him.

Penance clenched her fist and stared at the writhe and crackle of hot plasma energy burning around it, scorching her sleeve. *What a good little minion, doing just what I'm told*, she thought. *Didn't even think that Justice could help me, could get me away from Acid... And now he's dead and he ain't helping nobody...* She staggered to her feet and turned away.

Behind her, Justice groaned.

She stopped in her tracks.

*He's not dead?*

# Crossroads

## ALLEY, UNITED STATES, EARTH

P enance stared at Justice for a minute. He wasn't conscious, but she could hear his breath rasping in his throat now. Was it too late to fix this? Her knees buckled - whether because of what she'd just done or the idea of defying Acid, she didn't know.

She knelt down again and thought. The area was full of old warehouses and storage buildings, most of them empty. If she hurried, she could stash him out of the way and tell someone he trusted where to find him. Whether he'd be alive by the time they got him, she didn't know. And she didn't know how long she'd be alive either, once word got back to Acid she'd betrayed him. That she'd even thought about it.

But she didn't like any of the other roads, either. Should she finish off Justice, go back to Acid and wake up tomorrow to do this again to someone else? How long could she keep out of Acid's way the times he saw demons and flew into a paranoid rage? How long until his client offered a price for her too good to pass up? Or worse, how long could she stay with Acid until he died of his habit and couldn't protect her anymore? She'd never met his dealer, but she didn't doubt he'd swoop in the instant Acid was out of the way. *I'd rather not work for the man who makes switchheads out of people. That'd be some creepy evil to live with.*

Just – run? Where? Forever? No. *That* had been Mama's plan. She needed friends. But friends were yet another luxury she didn't have.

Perhaps she could make herself useful to Acid's enemies. As a kid, she'd met a couple heroes. Like Victoria. They put stock in saving people. They wouldn't want to throw Justice away; he was too good. Maybe trying to save Justice would be worth something to them? Now that she'd actually fought against him, she could hardly believe she'd managed to knock him out. But then, he hadn't tried to kill her outright, and she couldn't deny that's what she'd been after.

Penance hefted him awkwardly over her shoulder and staggered to her feet. *Good thing I'm strong for my size.* Stronger than most men. But still not big enough to carry him more comfortably – and lugging him around after she'd rearranged his insides couldn't be good for him.

It couldn't be helped. With no idea how long before Acid's cleanup team arrived, she focused on getting out of the alley. Next she crossed the road, turned down another alley, and passed a couple more warehouses before choosing one at random and kicking the door in.

She glanced in the dim interior first. Dusty, not so much as a footprint or a human smell anywhere. And stairs, leading up to a loft. Stairs were good – nobody *wants* to go upstairs.

The muscles of her thighs burned by the time she finally dumped him in the corner of the loft.

*Now what? He better still be alive.* Groaning, Penance stretched the kinks out of her back and then knelt by Justice to check his pulse. She brushed her fingers against his neck and paused.

Not just alive - awake. His eyes caught hers and she stared at him. She waited for the anger, the disgust, the hatred to show on his face, but his expression remained gentle.

"'M sorry," he whispered. A smile tugged the corner of his mouth. "Friendly now?"

"Shut up," Penance said, and glanced away, ashamed. "Save your strength," she added, a little more politely. Something prickled her senses, right at the edge of her consciousness, like the barely audible buzz from an old TV. She skimmed her hands over his belongings in her pockets and found a little cushion of static surrounding his badge.

She pulled it out. It – or the coating on it - reacted to his energy field, which had returned with his consciousness. "Is it supposed to do that?"

The Justice focused on the badge with difficulty. "Hm?"

"It's broadcasting a signal," Penance said. Weak, but distinctive. And he had a cell phone, too… it'd be pretty simple to get the phone's GPS to pinpoint his location whenever his energy field caused the badge to react. She stuffed the badge in her own pocket and grabbed his cell phone. "You're being tracked. Stay put. Try to keep your field down."

Justice coughed weakly. She didn't want to look and see if blood was on his lips.

Instead she stood. "I'll lead them off and try to find your people to come get you."

"Wait," he whispered. "I can't... leave Earth unprotected. Major event coming. You must be a Prime...Please, act for me. I can deputize..." He coughed again.

Penance shook her head. She couldn't waste time here listening to nonsense and letting his phone ping a satellite with his hiding spot. Maybe the feedback she'd blasted him with had scrambled his brain. Talking like the whole planet depended on him. That was silly. With all the Primes out there, none of them saved the whole world. Her mind simply couldn't wrap around what else he wanted from her - she wasn't powerful enough to be a Prime and no way was she 'deputy' material. "When I hit the door, cover your mouth – it's gonna get dusty."

She raced down the stairs and skidded across the floor, leaving dust in her wake. At the door, she thrust her arm out toward the middle of the room and charged the air with a quick burst of static. A great cloud of dust rose up and drifted down, obscuring her footprints.

Then she yanked the door closed again – slightly bent, but maybe nobody would notice. It wasn't like Acid hired smart thugs.

She jogged away, hitting a casual just-out-for-my-health stride, and circled around to where Tall Guy had abandoned his motorcycle. No one had shown up yet.

Penance pulled the badge from her pocket. She had Justice's energy field memorized. If she concentrated, she could copy it just strongly enough to get the badge to broadcast the same signal it had when Justice was awake. That would make them believe he was still in action somewhere.

She slid her leg over the seat of the bike – Tall Guy had run off with the key, but popping an arc of electricity off her fingertips to bridge the ignition contacts was an old, easy trick – and took off.

Penance raced the motorcycle through a maze of alleys and back streets, eventually angling toward the city proper as she worked out her next move. She had to find Justice's people.

There was no way Justice worked alone. He had to eat and sleep and go to work somewhere. He had to get equipment and his energy-insulating suit from somewhere. He had to get information from someone. Penance paused at a red light at a crossroads and touched the pocket that held the Justice's cell phone.

Someone from his team would be checking in on the rescue mission.

In the meantime, she wore a crime scene. Splattered blood covered her hoodie. Residue from Acid's skin burned her shirt. And she rode a stolen motorcycle.

She had to find some new clothes and dump these somewhere. Then she could cruise the city until she found a good spot to ditch the bike. With any luck, she could spin a good enough story that Justice's headquarters would buy it. After she told them where to find him, it would be safe to let the signal from the badge die and she could promise info for safety.

*Oh no, that won't work.* Her fingers twitched on the handlebars. *They have a leak. Acid's gonna know. I can't just tell a story and skip out when I feel like it. They got to catch whoever talked to Acid.*

She realized the light had turned green at the crossroads, picked a direction at random, and took off.

Now late in the morning, the roads started filling with traffic. Church bells pealed somberly in the distance and she remembered it was Sunday. Normal people dressed in nice clothes today to go to church, while she roared around on a motorcycle wearing dirty, bloody, torn-up clothes. Not the way to blend in.

Although she noticed lots of out-of-state plates, too. A car edged up beside her, waiting to make a turn. She glanced at the flags mounted to the windows and remembered. The big game was on tonight. Football-crazy tourists had flooded the whole city.

And that was the other reason Justice had to be done today – if he was investigating the missing girls, this is where a lot of them would be. Big events always attracted buyers and sellers. Acid probably got a lot of girls cheap for his special buyer.

Whoever it was. Someone rich, really rich, and really good at hiding a whole organization and dozens of girls that Acid sent every week for the last couple months.

So good at disappearing, they might as well be on another planet.

Penance gasped. *No.*

That was crazy. But still... Justice talked like his job covered the whole Earth. But how could Acid call up aliens and ask if they want to buy some girls?

For all she knew, that could be it.

Or maybe she'd scrambled her *own* brain somehow.

Penance gripped the handlebar tighter. She'd tried to hold back the feeling of being in over her head, but now she couldn't escape it. She squeezed her eyes shut. *So long as it ain't me getting shipped off, it ain't my business.*

She didn't believe herself. That stupid tattoo on her back proved that if the price offered for her was higher than Acid could get out of her, she'd be in the exact same mess as hundreds of girls she'd ignored.

She needed backup. Why would Justice's people help her? She'd never done anything good in her life. Whatever the qualifications for joining their hero club, she wouldn't pass their muster.

All she could do was focus on what was in front of her. Her own hands, dirty and bloody. Her own clothes, also dirty and bloody. Time to find a place to change.

Penance turned off the main road and slowed as she passed a large parking lot full of people at some kind of fair. Music blasted from a stage at the far end near a large, plain building, and were those... swimming pools? In February? Sure, it was getting to be a warm day, but why would there be a pool party and a fair and... she sniffed. Tailgaters grilling burgers and hot dogs.

*All right, they got me*, she thought. *I have to see what this is about. Maybe I can sneak some food.*

She parked between a couple of big trucks, well back from the road, and walked up toward the action. A big guy was rapping on stage, and as she came closer she could make out the words, "So afraid of dying but I was already dead, but for my sins my Savior hung and he bled, to reconcile me with God's own grace, to make it so I could again show my face..."

Penance glanced over to the pools, each of which had a man standing in them ready to help people in, one at a time. "Who is your Lord and Savior?" the man asked the young woman who'd just stepped in the pool.

"Jesus Christ!" she answered. Pure joy shone from her face.

"Because you have confessed Christ as your Lord and Savior, I now baptize you in the name of the Father, the Son, and the Holy Spirit," he said, and he dunked her backward in the water and pulled her up again.

The whole crowd cheered as she came up – a group of her friends crowded right up against the pool screaming – and someone helped her out, wrapped her in a towel, and set her on a path of carpeting that led into the building. A big outdoor heater was set up by the path, so at least she didn't freeze on her way in.

Penance smothered a laugh. *This whole fair is some kind of Jesus pool party? Why does everybody look so happy?* People moved busily around her, but they smiled and nodded at her as they went past. Like she was welcome there. Like she wasn't an outsider. A guy with a nametag tried to catch her eye, but she glanced the opposite direction and lifted her hand to wave as if she'd seen a friend in the crowd. She dodged around a few people and worked her way around to the door of the building.

The carpet path would lead to the changing room, and there would be clean clothes.

She slipped inside and glanced around, wondering if the place was a full-time church or if they'd just rented the building for the day. It didn't look very churchy on the outside.

A man emerged from the hallway and smiled at her. "Hi there! We're using the bathrooms as dressing rooms for people who were baptized today, so if you need to use the bathroom, we have portables set up outside."

Penance pulled the cell phone out of her pocket and smiled. "I just need to give my friend her phone – she got a call a second ago."

"Oh, okay then," the man said, and waved her on.

She waved back and walked down the hall. The carpet path ended at a door a little way down the hall. When it opened, Penance ducked into a nearby open doorway. It was a brightly painted classroom, with low tables and toys in bins around the walls. She slipped behind the door and watched through the gap between the door and the frame as the young woman she'd seen baptized passed, now wearing dry clothes.

As soon as the young woman turned the corner, Penance moved silently from her hiding place and hurried to the bathroom. Things were winding down outside, and she should have a couple minutes before the next person climbed into the pool and pledged allegiance to Jesus or whatever they were doing.

She opened the door and listened before ducking inside. She glanced around quickly before she shed her hoodie and shirt. Dropping them beside the nearest sink, she turned on the hot water full blast. As fast as she could, she lathered up her face, down to the neck of her tank top, and scrubbed clean with a handful of paper towels.

She started on her arms when the bathroom stall behind her opened and a pregnant lady stepped out.

Penance ignored her – until the lady gasped, "Acid?"

*Don't look. Act normal!* But she couldn't stop herself. Her eyes met the woman's in the mirror.

The lady looked like she might cry.

"Please," the lady said, her voice hitching. "Please, have you seen my sister?"

Penance couldn't speak.

The lady's voice broke. "She called me in the middle of the night. She'd been drugged, and woke up and found somebody – *Acid* - had tattooed that on her." She pointed to Penance's back, her shoulder left bare by the tank.

"And then the phone went dead. The police can't find her. Do you know anything, anything that can help?"

Penance looked down. Finished washing the suds from her arms. She shook her head. "No. I never saw any others." She glanced at the lady. "You didn't see me, either."

The lady pressed her lips together and nodded. "I understand."

Penance turned, dropped her hoodie and shirt and the pile of soggy paper towels she'd used in the trash, and turned to leave and find somewhere else to steal a change of clothes from.

"Wait," the lady said. She held out a black t-shirt with a pink cross and a few words in script on it. "Here. These are for volunteers, but it doesn't fit..." She gestured to her rounded belly. "Anyway you need it more."

Penance took the shirt and held it close to her chest. She mumbled thanks as the lady washed her hands. Waiting until she left, she read what the front of the shirt said.

"Beautiful. Psalm 45:11."

*Mama used to say I...* Penance swallowed hard and turned the shirt inside out before she slipped it on. In her hurry to get away, she didn't even think to sneak food off one of the grills in the parking lot before she left.

*Or maybe I was just scared they'd give it to me,* she thought later, as she pulled the wad of Justice's money out of her pocket and bought herself lunch at a tiny restaurant. She found a booth in a corner where she could watch the door and the space where she'd parked the motorcycle, and slowly picked at her bowl of gumbo. *What makes people like that? What made that lady give me a shirt when I wouldn't help her find her sister?*

She wanted to think of them with contempt, to believe they were just religious weirdos. But they'd looked at her – in her dirty, ugly, torn-up clothes – like they *saw* her. As if she was a person on the inside, just like they were.

*Beautiful.*

She scrubbed her face with her hands, trying to stop the sudden upswell of tears. It had been a long, hard day and it was barely half over. She still had to work out an angle to get in with Justice's team, and keep avoiding Acid and anyone who might recognize her. Mentally, she rehearsed what she'd say when they called the cell phone to check on Justice: 'I beat him pretty bad, but I had to make it convincing. Except I didn't really have any witnesses once Tall Guy lit out, so I guess I kept beating him until I thought he was dead because I didn't think of escaping sooner. I can tell you everything I know about my boss....'

Penance shuddered. *Not everything.*

She sank down and rested her head on the table. It was impossible.

The cell phone buzzed.

# Incoming Storm

## LOCATION: PLANETARY JUSTICE HEADQUARTERS, EARTH

Technical Specialist Mariposa Ramirez slammed her phone on the table. "Still not answering," she said. She glanced at her assistant. "Any change in the anomaly?"

Dr. Robert Janus checked over the screens he had open and shook his head. "Same steady gain. If the energy signature of the anomaly continues at this rate, it looks like we'll have an unscheduled event this evening."

Tech groaned. "How big of an event?"

"No way of knowing until they arrive."

"Can you identify a location?"

Janus brought up a map of the city and the local Lightning Detection Network records. Fortunately existing weather tracking installments could pick up some of the signs of impending alien contact – they weren't made for it, but by running atmospheric conditions through a filtering algorithm, he could identify abnormal conditions brought about by alien interference. He pulled the anomalous data to a mapping application and superimposed the image over the map of the city.

The woman swiveled her chair to face the large screen as Janus put the new image up, running her own algorithms extrapolated from the data it displayed.

Tech spoke first. "Of *course* it's the stadium," she said. "Why would we have a major event somewhere out of the way, without live television coverage and thousands of people sitting right in the middle of it?"

She swiveled her chair back to the phone and grabbed it off the table. "I'll send a text."

Her nails clicked rapidly on the screen. [Major event at stadium. Possible invasion. Where are you?]

She set the phone down again and drummed her elegantly manicured fingernails on the table. "Time to start warning the state government. What do you want to bet they give us the runaround and hold the game anyway?"

Janus shook his head. "I wouldn't bet against it. Do you think they'll at least add security? Call in some Primes?"

"Not a chance. They've got as much security as they can get already. Besides, nobody's trained to handle aliens. *We're* hardly trained to handle aliens. Without the Justice, all we're good for is predicting when they invite themselves over for dinner." Tech rubbed at the headache beginning in her temples. Her latest improvements had not integrated well.

The phone buzzed. Tech grabbed it and swiped the message view.

[Hurt. Sending some1]

"What on earth?" Tech said. Janus came over to see. "What is that supposed to mean?"

"He's injured? Sending a replacement?" Janus ventured.

Tech gave him an odd look. "What could have injured him? And who is he thinking of sending?" She tapped a reply. [Where are you? Need support?]

A reply came immediately. [U have info leak. Not safe]

"A leak?" Janus said. "We've already dealt with that. We're running a skeleton crew as it is now – the Justice knows that." He shook his head. "Maybe we've been hacked. I'll run an extra security program." He turned to another computer and began clicking on the keyboard.

Tech eyed the phone with suspicion. She replied, [Verify ID]

There was a long pause, and then, [Not Justice]

"It's a bogey," Tech said.

"A what?" Janus paused his clicking for an instant. Tech's passion for old war movies tended to manifest itself in obsolete slang.

"An unknown has the Justice's cell phone," Tech said, and replied to the text: [Who are you?]

[Will tell IRL. Want 2 help], the bogey answered.

[No] Tech replied.

[Need escape. Fair trade]

[No]

[Stop me then]

Tech's next message went unanswered. She called the number, but was sent straight to voice mail.

For the second time, she slammed the phone on the table. "Bogey turned off the phone."

Penance's hands shook as she held the phone. If this failed, she'd have a superhero team after her as well as Acid. The light bulbs in the restaurant flickered like mad as she gingerly tapped her texts with the stylus, trying to sound out how nice these people were without saying too much herself.

The phone had only a few contacts, and none of them were real names. Whoever answered was listed as "Tech," but "Path" and "Doctor" and "Law" were on there too.

After a pause, a new text appeared: [Verify ID].

Every light bulb in the dining area exploded at once. A loud bang followed by screams from the kitchen told her that the microwave hadn't fared too well either. Penance hunched in her seat, embarrassed. Happily, the gray case and stylus seemed to prevent her erratically spiking energy field from destroying the phone.

*Time to 'fess up.* She blew powdered lightbulb glass off the screen and tapped hints that she'd bargain with them, but Tech wasn't having it. *Can't blame them, but I need a hiding spot!*

She scowled and typed [Stop me then]. *Fine.* She'd play a variation on the hot and cot scam. If they wouldn't work *with* her to put her somewhere safe, they could *catch* her instead. A little civil disobedience would force them to put her somewhere safe enough for the night. If they didn't want to keep her longer than that, she'd wipe out any records they made of her with an EMP before they gave her the boot.

Time to move. By now, Acid was looking for her, and he'd recognize the kind of disaster she'd left in the restaurant. If she could get found by the Justice's people first, he wouldn't be able to get to her. Tech had mentioned the stadium, so she guessed Justice's backup would head there now. She'd meet up with them whether they wanted or not.

Penance dug in her pockets for the rest of her change and left it on the table.

The Justice's people weren't going to be happy about working with her, but so long as he stayed breathing and safely stashed in his hiding place, they'd have no choice. And she'd make sure to put them in her debt before she told them where he was. How, she wasn't sure. But they had to have some use for someone like her.

Probably.

Outside, electricity hung in the air in anticipation of a storm, though she could've sworn another wasn't due already. She slung her leg over the motorcycle, carefully zapped the ignition, and headed for the stadium.

The traffic was gridlocked, of course, but the motorcycle had the advantage of slipping into spaces too small for cars. So long as she didn't think too much about getting smashed by an SUV, she made decent time.

As she cruised through traffic, watching for openings, she glimpsed a familiar face. Her stomach clenched as she recognized Tall Guy standing on the side of the road – and two of Acid's regular enforcers with him.

*Switchheads.* They were too far away to tell if they'd had a dose and switched already, but they'd have it on them. It'd only be a minute before it kicked in, speeding up their reflexes and increasing their brutality as it peeled away hesitation and conscience. One would have an edge on her, and with two of them, she didn't stand a chance. Switched, they wouldn't care about anything but getting the job done. They might even shoot her in broad daylight in the middle of traffic.

She slowed down and allowed an SUV into the space she'd been about to take, putting it between them. For a tense few minutes, she kept pace with the vehicle beside her as traffic slowed again to a crawl at the exit to the stadium.

On the exit ramp, she pulled onto the side of the road and revved past the backed-up traffic. The blare of car horns followed her path as annoyed drivers honked at her. Penance ignored them, her mind focused on putting as much distance between herself and Tall Guy as possible.

*Acid knows.* Fear surged through her and she accelerated down the frontage road. *They shouldn't be looking for me here. His inside guy must have told him something.*

When the enemy knows the plan, it's time to make a new one. Her only hope was to move quickly, so maybe only one or two at a time would catch up to her. She could force them to split up, send false info to the Justice's team, counting on Acid's inside guy to relay it. With any luck, Acid would take the bait and give her some breathing room. But what else could draw his attention?

Penance pulled off the frontage road and zigzagged through the streets, slowing as she passed a police station with fenced-in impound lot. It gave her an idea.

She pulled into a shopping center parking lot and parked right up against a shop window, halfway in a handicapped space and halfway on the sidewalk, and grabbed the cell phone out of her pocket.

[Have 2 run if u wont help. Borrowed bike. Owner will talk.] She grinned.

*Maybe owner will run, too.* She hoped that pervert would have fun as a fresh new target for Acid's suspicion. [Going dark. Will leave note w bike].

She shoved the phone back into her pocket and glanced through the shop window. Somebody headed for her — the shop manager, to judge by the ticked-off look on his face. She revved the bike loudly a few times and then hopped off to casually walk away.

"Hey, kid! You can't park here!"

She didn't turn around, though she flipped him off as she left. There was a truck stop down the road — a perfect place to bum a ride out of town. For the phone, not her. It was on even though she'd turned it off and it looked like it was off. Clever, but her energy field still pinged back against the electrical pulse humming faintly inside. She guessed it was in some kind of recording and tracking mode, an official tracker rather than the more subtle combo with the badge. Inside Snitch would track the phone in the truck and relay the fake lead about Tall Guy and the bike to Acid.

Tall Guy's bike would be impounded by the time they caught up to her trail, so that would slow them down. Now they'd also be looking for the bike, a nonexistent note on the bike, *and* Tall Guy. That should be enough to distract Acid, if just for a little while.

When she really headed for the last place on Earth she ought to go if she wanted to stay out of Acid's reach... but the only place she knew that she'd find the Justice's support team.

She glanced up at the late afternoon sky. Clear and bright, it held no sign of a storm except the prickle of not-quite-existent sparks hovering in the atmosphere.

Something gathered from above, and it grew stronger the closer she got to the stadium.

# The Plunge

## SALVAGE BREAK, GREAT DESERT, HYLINEK

"Supply Officer Kail, the signal is aligned and the initial portal is prepared," Deyn said. He drummed his fingers lightly on the control panel. Beside him sat the initial makeshift rig – Kail's helmet with the receiver linked to the miniature portal focus unit. From there, he could open a portal as wide as his thumb through the relays to the alien planet. Through there, he could strengthen the signal and copy the frequency to the large portal gate they had ripped from the derelict spacecraft that had supplied the plasmic reactor. Kail would then be able to take his helmet off the rig.

Kail leaned over and inspected the control panel as well. "How much time will we have to set up the stabilizers and the containment field?"

"I'm not sure. Perhaps three, five minutes for the stabilizers. Put the best ones closest to the portal – we want it to remain open as long as possible. Containment will pull a lot of energy though, and will destabilize the portal. I'd rather tap into whatever energy source they have."

"Relying on their energy is risky," Kail said. "They could take down containment if they think to shut down power remotely."

"The portal itself is at risk if we don't," Deyn pointed out. "I'm bringing a gauge to monitor energy output, so if they have an auxiliary generator, I'll find it. If it's within the containment field, we should be safe enough... though I haven't done this before, so I have no idea what's on the other side."

Kail flashed a quick grin. "Me either. But I know what's on *this* side – *nothing*. So let's go."

Deyn nodded. "Yes sir."

Kail strode out to organize the men. He would go through with the first four as cover for the next four with two stabilizer posts each, followed by eight soldiers with containment packs. Deyn would come in with the second group to set up both of the better stabilizers and oversee the containment field. The remaining four left behind would monitor the homeworld side. If the raid was as successful as he hoped, the civilians of this half-dead town could also be mobilized to sort and pack the goods.

The troop lined up on either side of the portal and stood at attention. Deyn flicked on the miniature portal focus. Energy coalesced into a ball of plasma in the center of the tiny portal frame. Slowly, the ball flattened and stretched to the inside edges of the ring. Carefully he increased the power and the disk of plasma energy opened in the middle, rolling apart to reveal the target.

"Incredible," he breathed, gazing through the tiny opening. Only Kail allowed him to do such a thing – to create what he'd been passionately studying. Under ordinary circumstances, an *ibak* like himself would have been passed over in favor of giving someone with a name the opportunity to lead such an intricate technical project. But here he was, privileged to be the first in the troop to glimpse an alien world.

A strong signal came through. Nothing obscured the target area. He nodded at Kail, who raised his arm in preparation.

Deyn hit the switch for the large portal. The upsurge of static prickled his face as energy coursed around the rim of the portal and gathered, spinning, in the center.

With a sudden crackle, the portal snapped open and cool air rushed out.

Kail dropped his arm and charged through. After an instant, the rest followed.

The attention of the entire world seemed to be converging on the stadium. At least three helicopters circled overhead, and even more news vans arrived by the minute, only to be blocked and turned back by the police. Back in Serenity City, a massive energy bomb getting this kind of media coverage would be swarmed by heroes and wannabes, but out here, so far only Penance and the newshounds cared to head *toward* the thing.

*You'd think the looky-loos would know better*, Penance thought. *Imagine thinking a pulsing dome of energy, big enough to cover an entire stadium like it's a cake on a stand, would be safe enough to share a county with.* She shook her head slowly. *I keep expecting one of those choppers to fly right into it like a moth to a bug zapper.*

The dome rippled with enough power to vaporize the stadium it covered and leave a crater a mile deep. The helicopters had to stay well back – the static from a field like that would fuzz electronics for a quarter mile. Police had blocked off the stadium and the roads leading to it for a few miles, and they worked on evacuating the area.

*The police need to think bigger. If I'm right, that's the same energy in the dome as when I get spells, and I know how destructive my small energy field can be. This monster? The whole city's in danger.*

But, not her problem. Her problem lay in the vast parking lot across the road, hidden somewhere among the vans and buses.

Acid *knew* her.

He could always find her.

And he could always take her out.

Penance squeezed her eyes shut and tried to forget all the times he'd proved he was bigger, stronger, smarter and more vicious than her. It was no good. There was no way he'd shared all her secret weaknesses with the ordinary thugs waiting for her to walk past, but they'd know how to subdue her long enough for Acid to arrive. He might already be somewhere in that parking lot. Waiting for her.

She should leave. Someone else could handle the missing girls and their rich, well-hidden buyer and the plasma energy covering the dome, and she should just get out while she still could.

But she could never tell where Acid waited for her until it was too late. And then she'd be dead. Or worse: sold.

Penance looked up at the dome again. He wasn't in *there*, though.

*I might just be able to get through the parking lot and reach the dome. If I'm lucky enough to make that, I'll be lucky enough to get through the energy.* She snickered with black humor. *Lucky.*

If she read the energy right and pushed just a bit - just enough to get through – she could hide inside the dome. Acid could do a lot of things, but walking through a curtain of plasma energy wasn't one of them. She might not be able to either, but she had a chance.

Too bad she couldn't just make her field into a personal shield like that all the time, but she just didn't have that kind of control. Her bubble of energy had more in common with a cat's whiskers than it did with a force field. It told her what kind of energy was close, and she could *shape* it a little. She didn't have the real words to describe what she could do, but she thought of it like tuning up or down frequencies. Copying a frequency pulled that energy closer. Flipping them repelled. She could get a loop going that way, and gen up heat to melt anything she punched, but she had to see what she was doing so that trick was limited to flaming fists. Taming lightning would be less scary than trying to push past what she felt safe doing without knowing how she did it.

*Take a deep breath, Pen. And another. Just tune out all the crazy and focus on getting there. Cross the street, get past the cars, hit the stadium and try not to fry. And* where *is that buzzing coming from?*

She checked the parking lot again, focusing on the noise. There. Between those two buses. And there, two rows over. And there... evenly spaced, coordinated little spots of static. They could be regular cell phones, same buzz as everybody's pocket – but it didn't feel the same. Penance's nerves had her field spiking so that the energy washing up and down the dome pinged her and *then* each of those little specks responded. Not to see demons where there weren't any, but why were those specks tuned to *her?*

Outside the parking lot where she hid in a ditch, she wasn't close enough for one of those specks to detect her directly, but that dome amplified everything. It bounced back echoes of her energy as she put out feelers on it, and the specks reacted and the dome bounced that too.

A perimeter, just for her. Acid knew she was coming, and had given out handy little trackers to at least a couple dozen people down there so they could tell when she was in range and stop her.

If that big plasma dome hadn't been so similar already to her energy field, she wouldn't have noticed them at all, but the feedback was hard to miss. So now she knew where they were, and they knew she was around somewhere. She hoped they hadn't pinned down her exact location yet.

Penance hadn't tried to tune to a field from so far away before. Maybe... if she could match it, she could make a little bubble around herself and get through. It did a good job of keeping things out. She stretched out a hand toward it and concentrated.

Nope, just fuzz.

Creeping closer to the parking lot, she broke cover and dashed to a low wall. Still fuzz.

The buzzing specks - the people carrying the trackers - broke the perimeter formation to converge on her.

They would only get closer the longer she stayed put.

Her time had run out.

Penance gathered herself and vaulted over the wall. She landed lightly on her feet and sprinted for the stadium. Gunshots popped around her, peppering the ground where she'd just been. She dove into a roll under a tour bus. Now Acid wanted her *dead?*

More shots popped, but she didn't see anything hit. Peeking out from under the bus, she glimpsed a thug emerging from his cover a few rows down to take aim at a new target – a man who had leaped over the low wall into the parking lot as well, plowing through cars and thugs alike. *Big guy. Strong. Fast. Must be a Prime – an old hand at heroing, to judge by his white hair and ease under fire.* She squinted at him, wondering if he'd come charging in just to help her out. *Nah, nobody knows you and nobody likes you, girl. Maybe he's retired and pissed about his plans to watch the game getting interrupted.*

Whoever he was, he'd come in at the perfect time to distract Acid's thugs so she could break cover and get a read on that energy field. Her fingers twitched as she noted its resonances with her own field. Nothing could get in or out – except maybe her.

Impulsively, she thrust an arm out to the stadium and *pulled.*

Her mind stepped back in disbelief at herself pulling such a stupid stunt. But, the rest of her was caught up in getting some of that shield for herself. She scrambled out from under the bus to meet it. She didn't hear many gunshots as she stumbled forward and looked up, but somebody screamed.

Possibly her.

The massive, roiling beam of energy she had just aimed at herself barreled from the stadium. It blasted through unlucky vehicles, shearing them in half, melting them where they stood. Gas tanks exploded and the thugs ran out from hiding to get out of its path. The white-haired old Prime had disappeared already, gone as quickly as he'd arrived.

The beam writhed and crackled as it flipped back toward the stadium, creating an arc. Like a soap bubble, it wanted to pull back into the dome, but like lightning, she'd attracted it. Like a fool, she ran toward it.

*Oh dear lord this is the stupidest...*

She leaped into the beam and the plasma washed around her — hot and dangerous but running smooth and slick over the insulating oils in her skin and hair that kept her safe from her own energy. Now that it had her, it was free to snap back to its dome, taking her with it. Like the most deadly soap bubble in the universe.

The parking lot zipped past and she slammed to a halt, suspended in the plasma dome, swimming in it. Not having any air to breathe added to the underwater feeling.

She shoved against it with her hands, but only bobbled in place. She closed her eyes and concentrated on her energy field, finding a rhythm with the ripple of power and breaking free to fall inside the dome.

Gasping for air, she staggered up and glanced back.

The thugs in the parking lot didn't even bother to hide anymore, emptying clips at her as fast as they could. But the bullets splattered helplessly into slag across the dome's surface, and sparked retaliatory lashes of energy.

"This thing is awesome," Penance remarked, stroking the plasma dome with her fingertips. "I'm going to have to learn to copy this. I can be bulletproof!"

She winked at the thugs and sauntered off along the exterior, looking for a door.

---

Kail's temporary conquest of the stadium was, fortunately, bloodless. He didn't want to cause an interplanetary incident — at least not on *that* scale. He noted with relief that aside from their clothing, Earthers didn't look alien. The aliens seemed to be the same species as his own, which meant the raid should garner useful goods.

Deyn had done his work well. He'd dropped them in a perfect place to maximize the advantage of surprise, and Kail had his bearings within an instant of his boots hitting alien ground. He sprinted toward a small room built to overhang the ordinary crowd in open-air seats. Obviously designed to provide a superior view of the championship game on the field below, it must have communications equipment and important people. He vaulted the barrier, knocked down the guards outside the door, and barreled in before any alarm sounded. One guard, three other men, and a woman wearing a rich-looking red garment turned to stare at him, comical in their matching shock. Their unpreparedness made it easy to secure the room. With the occupants safely disarmed and facing the back wall, Kail was free to supervise his men as they leapt through the portal and dashed to their positions. To their credit, the men had performed smoothly as a well-coordinated unit should. Nobody seemed to be armed, aside from security guards who his men quickly identified, stunned and restrained.

All the native people simply cowered, stunned, in their seats. Half of them seemed to be drunk or convinced that the invasion wasn't possible and therefore wasn't real.  A few potential troublemakers had a disciplined, military awareness of the situation, but they were scattered and leaderless. The stadium was a perfect size and shape for encapsulating in a plasma energy containment dome, and his unit had no difficulty placing the stabilizing posts and rigging the packs. From his place in the box, he could issue orders over the announcement system, in his own language for his soldiers, and in English for his new hostages.

"So long as you cooperate," he assured the Earthers, "You will be released soon. Delaying my men will only delay your own freedom. We will only be here until the Justice for this planet arrives to negotiate. Please remain in your seats."

"However," he continued, "if any person chooses to fight one of my men, that person will have his fingers broken. And if any person uses a weapon against my men, you will *all* die." The audible gasp that went around the stadium assured him that he did indeed have a basic grasp of communicating in English.

One of his men came up then with a good report – food, water, and supplies were available in the stadium. They wouldn't have to wait on negotiations with the Justice to start transferring goods after all. Deyn would be happy about that – he'd tapped into the stadium's main power supply for the containment dome and now busily rigged a backup line to the stadium's own alternate generators, but he'd already said that he was uneasy about leaving the portal open for as long as he'd expected the raid to take.

They ran a hose from the water supply along the aisle and through the portal, where civilians on his own planet filled and loaded the large canisters for the military. He gave permission for them to fill their own canisters once his unit's quota had been met, and ordered them conscripted for temporary duty identifying and sorting confiscated foods. As Earth humans were a similar species as the people of Hylinek, it would be safe enough to delegate the task of determining the basic food types. They would get the open containers to test, and label and group the closed containers according to their findings.

In other words, a feast.

He grinned at the thought. This raid had turned the disaster in Salvage Break to his own advantage. He'd learned from Caretaker-General Baos that goodwill made a more valuable currency than credits. The governor had only gratitude to repay him with – which reminded him to corner one of the Earth officials and get the locations of not only the food, but the medical supplies as well.

Bandages and equipment were easy enough to decipher and label, but he personally translated and labeled medications before sending them through the portal. He gave strict orders that anything over quota belonged to the townspeople. Once he finished all the announcements, he left the box to assist with the heaviest plunder.

In the midst of stripping the stadium clean of everything of use, the only break in the men's discipline came from Vorak. Kail caught him dragging a dark-haired woman through the aisle to the portal. Casually, he reached out with one arm and blocked the soldier's path. "You wanted to see me, Vorak?" he asked.

Vorak scowled. "Yes, sir." He couldn't very well admit that he did not, in fact, want to see Supply Officer Kail.

Kail cocked his head, putting on a show of patience. "What concerns you, soldier?"

Vorak yanked the woman forward. "I'd like to claim my conquest bonus for this raid."

The giant officer raised one eyebrow, looking over the frightened woman. "An interesting prize. But I gave orders that we would not be taking captives today." Detaining civilians on their own planet was not an urgent matter for the Interplanetary Council, but taking them off-planet or killing them could be.

"It is my right!" Vorak insisted. "We have cleared and conquered this area. I was one of the first through the portal, and I saw her first!"

Kail rubbed his chin soberly. He chose not to remind the man of who had been the very first to cross. "Ah. She is quite beautiful. Her clothing and ornaments look costly and attract the eye. I see why you want this one... though I don't think she likes you." The woman couldn't break free of the soldier's grasp, but she leaned as far from him as possible, revulsion plain on her face.

She turned pleading eyes up at Kail as he spoke, and Vorak yanked her arm again for attention. "She will learn," he snapped.

"Have you calculated the taxes?" Kail asked innocently. "Those will be due as soon as she sets foot in Hylinek. I hope you've been saving up." Out of politeness, Kail pretended not to know everyone's financial situation, but Vorak had not been subtle about his spending habits on leave. Of course such a young *inek* soldier had not hoarded his pay for such an extravagant prize. "You wouldn't want to owe. If you can't pay, you're declared *ibak* and it'd be years before you earned the privilege of breeding."

Color drained from the soldier's face as he belatedly ran some mental calculations.

A tiny, furious defender launched past Kail, jumping from somewhere beneath their feet. A small Earther boy leaped onto the soldier's arm, biting and kicking. "Leave my mommy 'lone!" the child howled.

Kail scooped the boy up and set him on his shoulder before the soldier could hit him. The boy shrieked at being so high up and grabbed on tight to Kail's helmet.

"I'll clear up this mistake," Kail said in English to the woman. "Tell your child."

The mother smiled bravely up at her son and nodded. "Mommy's fine. It's going to be okay. Just... wait right there."

The soldier scowled. "I'll sell the boy to pay the taxes," he declared.

"I admit I don't know much about women, as I'm an *ibak* myself from birth and it's none of my concern," Kail drawled, finally showing contempt, "but I've always heard selling a conquest wife's child is a sure way to wake up some morning missing the ability to make more children. You seem a bit stressed, Vorak. Go swap out with Chintu."

Vorak spluttered but obeyed, realizing too late he'd been given enough rope to hang himself. The boy on Kail's shoulder made a disrespectful noise as Vorak disappeared through the portal. Kail covered a smile. Little boys might well be the same across the universe.

"Sir!" a soldier shouted from his watch over the field. "There's a hostile. Do I shoot?"

Kail strode over to the soldier, the boy still on his shoulder and his mother following anxiously behind.

A lone man, wearing the uniform of the game's players, ran across the field toward them.

"Andy!" the woman shouted.

Kail glanced over at her. "You belong to him?" he asked.

She glared back. "We *belong* to each *other*," she said, holding up her left hand so he could see the rings that ornamented it.

"Then tell him to stop before he is shot," Kail said, nonchalantly.

Her alarmed gasp and prompt obedience led him to believe she genuinely cared for this man's life. She leaned over the wall separating them from the field and waved her hands in an exaggerated cross, screaming, "Andy! Stop! We're okay!"

Fortunately for the player, he heard her and slowed to a jog, coming to a halt before he crossed the midway point.

"Tell him we're coming to him," Kail said. "Then you will all wait with the rest of the players until we're done."

The woman relayed the instructions and Kail vaulted the wall down to the field, landing lightly on his feet with the boy still secure. The child squealed, "Again! Again!" and pounded his helmet, making Kail laugh. His little barracks-brothers had all loved to try to weigh him down during obstacle runs.

His mother wasn't as pleased, though, and tried frantically to climb over the wall after them. Kail reached up and steadied her – per regulations with the outside of his wrist, of course. He wasn't sure of her caste, but he knew his own, and he had even less of a right to grasp her than Vorak had. She wobbled but accepted his help, and he set her down smoothly while pretending he had not seen so much as she leaned toward him. Her clothes clung to her figure and left her cleavage bare.

Perhaps the garment would have covered more from a vantage point that wasn't essentially looking straight down on her. He couldn't help his height, so all he could do was not to let his eyes be captured as Vorak's had been. Even with a successful raid here, he had years of hard work before he could afford a name to give to sons of his own.

"Daddy!" the little boy squealed from his shoulder, breaking into Kail's thoughts as they walked toward the lone man waiting tensely at the center of the field. "Hi Daddy! Look at me!"

Jealousy struck Kail as he set the child down and watched him and the woman run to embrace the man. Vorak had tried to obtain his desires in as stupid a way as possible, but Kail couldn't fault him for wanting this. A fiercely loyal, eye-pleasing woman and a sturdy child to protect and lead, who both clearly, openly loved him. The family embraced in the middle of a stadium full of thousands of witnesses.

The player scooped his son behind him and nudged his wife back as well, to shield them with his body. The woman, almost as if they had drilled on this situation, nudged the boy between them.

Deliberately, Kail straightened and clasped his hands behind his back, staring straight ahead with outward composure. He waited for the sudden hot blush to leave his neck before he strode to the midpoint where the family waited.

The player spoke to him first. "Who are you? What is it you want?"

"I am Supply Officer Kail *ip ibak* of Hylinek. I'm here to negotiate with the Justice for this planet," Kail answered directly, if not entirely honestly. "You need to take this woman back to wait with you and the other players until the Justice arrives and negotiations are complete."

"What are you going to do with us?"

Kail grinned. "Nothing, I hope."

As he turned to leave, the woman asked abruptly, "Do you have children?"

He stiffened. "No," he said, and walked quickly back the way he'd come.

# The Big Game

## STADIUM, UNITED STATES, EARTH

"Well, that was interesting," Penance said as the player and his family entered the locker area. She flashed Justice's badge, her thumb covering his picture on the ID. Since she was here, she needed as much information as she could get to bargain with later... assuming there'd be a later. She tried to act official, like a cop taking a statement. "I think I saw most of it, but I want to hear it from you. So what went down out there?"

"Who are you? I thought Justice was a man?" the wife asked.

Penance shrugged. "He is. But I'm the one who can get in the stadium past that force field. Congrats, you're stuck with me." She sat down on a bench and tilted her head up at the couple. "I need to know everything you can tell me. Who's the big guy?" The alien soldiers all had armor and helmets that covered their faces, but they looked like nothing special. Except that one who dwarfed everybody. The other hostages she'd talked to while skulking around had compared him to Achilles, the famous giant of the frst wave of Primes, but she hadn't yet gotten a good enough look at him to see for herself.

The football player – *not a big guy, must be the kicker* - stepped forward. "He says his name is Kail... something. He's some kind of officer..."

"Supply officer," his wife added. "They're raiding the entire stadium for food, and there's a hose leading through that..." she waved her hand in the direction of the portal, "opening... for water."

"They take any people through?" Penance asked, wondering if these guys were Acid's clients, and if they'd gotten impatient. But that would mean Acid could contact aliens, and her brain still stuttered around allowing the fact aliens even existed. *Just roll with it, girl. Sort it out later.*

The woman shook her head. "The leader didn't let that one take me through."

*A different bunch, then.* As far as Penance knew, Acid didn't deal in legal contraband. This raid might be completely unrelated to the missing girls. She needed to know more to continue the Justice's investigation and get protection from his support team. Pretending to be his sidekick practically guaranteed her a safe spot with them, and it wasn't a total lie. Or at least not the most brazen one she'd ever gotten away with.

"He didn't let the soldiers shoot Andy, either," the woman added.

"He was nice," the little boy piped up. "He was giant!"

Penance grinned at him. "I saw! I saw you being so brave too." She looked up at the player and his wife. "Anything else?"

"He's waiting for Justice to arrive to negotiate," Andy said.

Penance flinched. "He'll be waiting a long time," she mumbled. Andy and his wife looked at each other in alarm.

She put on an upbeat tone. "Okay, the good news is, the goal isn't terror. They aren't interested in kidnapping people and they're trying to avoid anybody getting hurt. As long as they don't get bored. Once they finish with the priorities, they could start in on..." she glanced at the little boy and broke off. "Not nice stuff."

"Since Justice himself can't be here, can you go out and negotiate with him?" Andy asked.

Penance looked away. *Dang it. Sidekick duty sucks.*

She was there to hide, not get involved. Buying a few more hours of life didn't mix with playing bouncer to alien looters. She stood up to leave.

"Since you said yourself just now, you're the only one who can get in?" the player added.

*He's right. I just said it. No one else* can *get in. There's no help coming for any of us in here. But still, it doesn't have to be me.*

Andy looked at his wife and son, brows drawn together thoughtfully. "It's okay," he said. "I'll do it." He grabbed his helmet off the bench. "I never understood why heroes put kids in danger like this anyway."

*What?* Penance turned to stare at the football player. "I'm not a kid."

The man pressed his lips together, eyebrows raised with doubt. "Teen, then. Look, you're a nice girl and I appreciate what you're here to do, but it isn't fair to pit you against a trained soldier five times your size."

*Like an ordinary kicker is tougher than I am. Besides, his family is right here. They don't need to watch him die. God knows, I know what that's like.* The little boy was even younger than she'd been. Penance's face warmed. "Well, you're a nice man and all, but it's my gig and he already talked to you once. Don't you worry about *me*. Besides," a happier thought occurred to her, "backup is coming and they'll figure something out. All I gotta do is distract him awhile."

She peered out the door at the enormous soldier across the stadium. Massive in his dusty gray and reddish-tan armor, he easily hefted a stack of kegs through the portal. At this rate, they'd clean the place out and start looking for more trouble in no time.

She'd have to talk to them. Possibly with her fists.

Penance buried her face in her hands and groaned. "God hates me. I swear, this is the day I'm gonna run out of free passes on stupid stunts."

The woman came up beside her and patted her back. "Oh, honey, God loves you. You said yourself they aren't here to terrorize us. I think... I think the leader is a reasonable person. He'd talk to you."

"I... I don't think you understand," Penance said. "I don't...I'm not good at... I'm just as likely to piss him off."

"Moses couldn't talk either," the little boy said, balancing on one foot.

Penance lifted her head. "Who?"

"In the Bible. But God gave him the words, and he said, 'Let my people go!'"

Penance nodded, a little dazed. "Oh yeah, that guy. Sounds about right." After spending years not thinking one way or another about God, suddenly religious stuff was showing up everywhere.

Maybe God was telling her something.

*Better make it obvious, God*, she thought with bitter humor. *I'd hate to miss the moment you finally decide to rescue me.*

Deyn returned from the generators, frowning as his hands worried at a scrap of cable. "Something outside containment produced an anomaly a little while ago," he said. "It looked like a competing stabilizer was set up to try to draw the field off the stadium, but it wasn't strong enough to do more than produce a brief flare."

"Is containment compromised?" Kail asked.

Deyn shook his head. "No, not for now. But I didn't think that our technology was available on this planet. With more power, they could take down the dome." He glanced at the stabilizer posts. "It might not even take more power. Repeated strikes might be enough, if they don't care about the safety of the hostages."

"No, these are good hostages," Kail assured him. "This game is broadcast all over the nation. There's no way for the government to destroy the stadium in secret."

Deyn scowled. "That's something else that worries me." He pulled an unfamiliar rectangular device from his pocket, likely confiscated from a too-bold civilian. Whether on Hylinek or Earth, Deyn tended to acquire bits of technology wherever he went. "Did you realize that everything here is recorded? Containment is disrupting the live video feed and outside communications, but recording is still going on. And it seems that everyone here has a recording device in their pocket. Should I trigger an EMP before we leave, to erase the data?"

Kail thought it over. "No... It's tempting, but it will make us look guiltier than we are. Allow the recording. Let it show that we have killed no one and only taken necessities. Our infraction here will remain low on the list of priorities for the Interplanetary Council."

One of his men, overlooking the field, called out. Someone else crossed the field instead of waiting patiently. And apparently, there was something funny.

Kail caught the end of the joke between two men as he approached: "No wonder the *ibak* are isolated from women, they get more in a single day..." They shut up when they realized he was close enough to hear.

Kail scowled. His men were getting too comfortable and losing discipline. The joke was, of course, that he couldn't afford a woman.

He looked over the field at the new problem approaching the midway point. And looked again. "What is that?" he said aloud.

"It appears to be a female," Deyn said, not having caught wind of the joke a moment ago. One soldier choked back a laugh.

*Another one to plague me. First the governor's wife and daughters, and now again on Earth, thanks to Vorak's idiotic idea of stealing a conquest wife. Everywhere underfoot, just to put me off balance.*

Today's sudden onslaught of interactions with women had left him uneasy. He found their demeanor toward him shocking and weird. They put him on edge with their mixture of terror and keen observation, looking to him for mercy and wary of potential sudden violence. The deference disturbed him. No one not under his direct command should defer to an *ibak* like him – not even a woman. The men they belonged to would see him as a threat, and he wanted to avoid trouble.

This new one approaching, however... after a moment he pinned the difference. "She moves like a fighter," he said. A decent one, at that. Aware, balanced, unafraid. She looked up around the perimeter and nodded slightly to acknowledge each of the soldiers monitoring the field, unconcerned about the sidearms aimed at her.

The female sauntered up to the midway point and stopped. Singling him out in the stands, her gaze locked with his. One eyebrow quirked up and a corner of her mouth lifted. She cocked her head and gave a little shrug, hands open and loose at her sides – *Well? Come on and meet me.*

All she'd done was look at him. Directly, as an equal. Without testing or measuring or need of any sort of proof that he was worthy of speaking to. Without dread or supplication.

Just a desire to meet with him and the expectation that he would come.

It hit him like a punch to the gut.

He straightened a bit further, squaring his shoulders. Deyn gave him an odd look.

"I'll see what she wants," he said, and vaulted the wall to the field.

Her awareness of him intensified as he strode closer. She may not have been measuring him before, but she did now. Her expression changed subtly. It was a different sort of appraisal than he usually got. She didn't seem dismayed or challenged by his evident size and strength at all. If anything, she liked what she saw of him. He suppressed the urge to swagger.

As for her, she seemed neither bulky or frail, with an easy, casual stance and nice balance. Doubtless she could change to a fighting stance in an instant. A bit spare, as if she didn't get all the regular meals she ought. Not tall. She had to tilt her head up to meet his eyes, but she wasn't uneasy about that. Her eyes seemed large in her pale face, vividly green under black brows, her nose a bit pointed, her chin more so. Her mouth drew his attention for a heartbeat more than strictly necessary, rounded blush-pink lips with a mischievous quirk that seemed at odds with her combat-ready poise.

She raised her right hand, flashing a badge between her fingers. "Penance Copper, Deputy Justice, Earth," she said. Her voice sounded pleasant, almost musical, to his ears.

He squared up again to his full height. "Kail *ip ibak*, Supply Officer, Hylinek."

"Hylinek," she repeated. She glanced around the stadium. "You're a long way from home, Kayel."

He was unprepared for that. His entire body betrayed him in a flooding, all-encompassing blush. He could win exemplary service for fifty years and never afford the 'El' honorific. That was reserved for favorites of the Emperor himself, those elevated to near-god status.

She'd somehow found the one unguarded sore on his soul, and stabbed into it without mercy. No one had ever called him that.

"You are mistaken," he said, fighting to keep his tone and expression impassive. "My designated name is Kail." *Not Kayel*, he thought, furious.

She blinked, her expression pure innocence. "Isn't that what I said?" Except her "I" softened to "Ah" and there was an extra half-syllable to "said," and "isn't" had come out more like "it'n't." Was this drawl regional, or sarcasm? And why did he want to hear it again, whether she mocked him or not? He couldn't tell if she flattered him or insulted him.

"Anyway, I heard you wanted to negotiate. You're way outside your bailiwick, Officer," she said.

His ears perked with interest. Bailiwick was a new word. He memorized it to analyze later.

"You and your boys get off my planet before I kick you off. There, I've negotiated."

*What?* True, he didn't really have a right to be there, but slinking away now wouldn't be good for morale. Besides, he needed to buy more time to finish making quota – over quota if he could.

He crossed his arms and grinned down at this upstart girl. "No," he said. In spite of himself, Kail wanted her to keep talking in her rhythmic drawl. Maybe she'd accidentally flatter him again.

She crossed her arms too, cocking her head back to look at him through slitted eyes. "No?" she queried, her voice skeptical and dangerous.

"I have control of this entire stadium," he said, gesturing to indicate the stands. "I conquered it myself. If you want it back, you'll have to give me something. I have a list of demands..."

She barked a laugh. "You can shove your list of demands up your -"

"I'm not leaving until -"

"Until what? You get your butt whupped by a little girl? Because I swear I'll -"

"If you'd like to try. Hand combat is also an acceptable means of negotiation."

She spread her hands and offered her face for a punch like an arrogant challenger. As if he was as without honor as she was without armor. "What you waiting on then?"

"Prepare yourself for combat and meet me here in five minutes." Once she put on her armor, he'd defeat her and then depart of his own accord, leaving her in shame. That would be payment enough for insulting him.

An insult to an *ibak* wasn't worth that much, after all.

"Fine. You just tell your boys to leave it between us." She spun on her heel and marched back to the players' quarters.

Penance kept it together until she was back in the locker room. "Of all the arrogant, entitled, self-centered bas..." she glimpsed the little boy staring at her and backed off her first choice of words. "Big. Big dude is a first-class jerk."

"But we prayed for you!" the little boy said. "Is it going to be okay?"

"Yeah, it'll be fine. Right after I kick his butt."

"But he told us..."

"What? Fighting gets your fingers broken?" Penance held up a fist and let energy flare around it for a moment. "Let him try. He told me hand combat counts as negotiation and that's something I can do." She put her boot up on the bench and tightened her laces, then tightened the other one, then shook the loose braid out of her hair and combed it back with her fingers to redo.

The boy's mom came over to help braid it back tightly – she flicked her fingers in and out of Penance's hair, making a French braid. Penance had never learned how to do one. "You're just going to fight him? Just like that?" the woman asked.

"I forgot to ask him some questions, too," Penance admitted. Something about him had put her off balance and she hadn't been nearly as prepared as she'd thought when she was out there facing him down in real life. She tugged guiltily at her shirt. It was nice of that other lady to give it to her. "Here, can you hold on to this?" she asked. "I don't want it to get torn up." She shucked out of the t-shirt and handed it to the woman, who folded it as she took it.

"Acid?" the woman asked, staring at the back of her shoulder.

Penance clutched at her shoulder, stifling a swear. Her face heated up as she whispered, "I don't belong to him anymore." More to remind herself than anything else. But this was how Acid marked the girls he sold so he'd get paid. If these aliens *did* turn out to be the same ones buying up girls, that big entitled jerk out there would think he was entitled to her, too.

She groaned. "I can't go out like this."

The mom patted her shoulder. "It's okay. We'll cover it up." She went to a locker and grabbed a tube of eye black. She drew a thick line over the tattoo. "I'd use makeup but I left my purse in my seat. This will stay on better anyway." She found a mirror for Penance to see it.

"What if he wonders what got crossed out?"

They considered the black line in the mirror for a moment.

"I could make it like a design. Maybe add another line down the middle and make a cross," the mom said.

Penance snorted. "That would kinda be the same as saying..." She stopped, eyes widening.

*Holy sh... sorry God.*

No way. It was a coincidence. The lady was holding her t-shirt, turned right side out now, probably thinking, 'Oh, this girl has a Christian t-shirt with a cross on it. She'd be cool with a Christian cross to cover this tat.' It doesn't mean anything.

But she had just told God to make it obvious.

She'd done everything she could on her own, and it just got her in deeper and deeper.

Outside the dome, Acid waited. Her jaw clenched. He'd had those thugs *shoot* at her. If she didn't do something to get some protection, he'd have her. Every nightmare he'd always sworn would happen if she even thought about leaving would come true. She'd beg to die by the time he got done.

Inside the dome... well. It was like being inside a bomb with a whole stadium full of hostages. How it was going to turn out for everybody depended on her.

No doubt about it. This was a crossroads. She'd better slow down and figure out what the question really was before she made a decision.

*I'm so sick of being alone*, she thought. Her eyes slid to the player, to his little boy, and met his wife's gaze in the mirror, waiting on her.

She'd met some good people today. She blinked as tears stung her eyes. Some *moms*. They just stepped up and did things to take care of her without her even asking. Why? What did they have in common?

*A silver cross spun in the darkness...*

*Jesus, save my baby...*

"I got a question for you," she said to the woman. Maybe, if God was there, and He wasn't mad at her, maybe He had some hope for her.

Kail stared in disbelief as the girl returned, uncertain of whether he ought to be fascinated or appalled. She did not wear armor. Her hair was freshly braided back, in a tighter, more intricate style, presumably to keep it out of the way and less likely to give an opponent a handhold. That was the only indication that she had prepared at all for combat.

She wore even less clothing than earlier. Her loose black shirt was gone, and she wore a tight, sleeveless undergarment that stretched across her torso, that rode up and exposed a sliver of her abdomen. He could see the definition of her shoulders and the lean, trim muscles of her upper arms, her delicate collarbone, her...

He forced his gaze to meet hers, but her attention seemed far away, as if she listened to something he couldn't hear.

She jogged up to the midway point and opened her hands, holding them up for him to see. "Full disclosure," she said – for an instant his brain turned stupid while translating and parsed that into something completely inappropriate – and her hands flared bright with energy like white-blue flames.

Interesting. This looked like an organic ability, and to be honest he'd expected the Justice to have some ability beyond the ordinary. It still counted as hand combat to him, so he waved a signal to his men to stand down.

He could deal with that. What bothered him was the lack of armor or any sort of bulk to begin to match his. Flaming hands or not, this was not remotely an equal fight. He was acutely aware that most of the hostages recorded him, and that negotiating during combat was already a gray area in interstellar law. Just by being his size, he pushed the acceptable boundaries – large males beating small females never looked good. He guessed that she deliberately accentuated this factor.

"Where is your armor?" he demanded, as if she was a disorganized recruit.

She rolled her eyes. "At the cleaners. I'm ready when you are."

He turned away and headed back to the stands, stripping off his helmet and unbuckling the sleeves of his armor as he went. He tossed the helmet to Deyn and finished unbuckling the upper half of the armored vest.

"Leave the lower half," Deyn advised. "Small fighters tend to make up for their size with madness."

"I know," Kail said, tossing the upper armor to him. He left the spine protection on as well, as it was part of the undergarment that supported the lower armor. He wouldn't let her goad him into fighting with less.

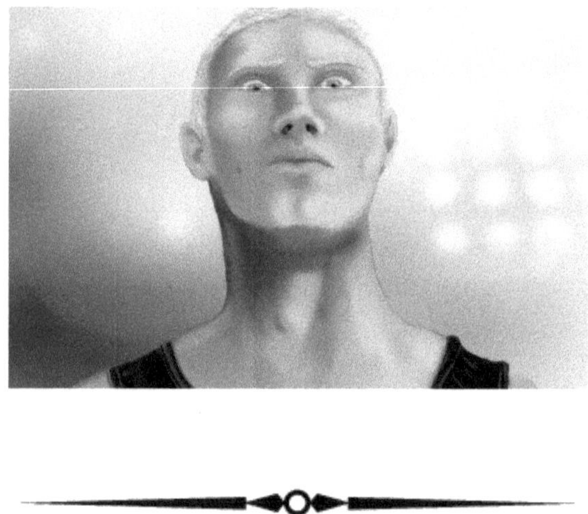

*He's young,* Penance realized as Kail returned. Without his helmet and visor, she could see his face clearly. *Other than being freaking enormous, he looks human. A good-looking one.* Sure, his nose had been broken a couple times, and she considered his sun-bleached, near-white hair clipped a little too short for her tastes. But she'd never seen such vivid violet-blue eyes. His bronze tan hadn't cracked his skin at all, not even around the eyes. The dusting of stubble on his square jaw and dimpled chin didn't mark out a full beard, yet.

Hugeness didn't make him bulky. Not like one of those 'roided up guys with huge necks and popping veins and that mad rage just behind the eyes. His arms were lean, hard muscle that saw work, not weight machines, covered with an interesting collection of scars. Incredibly, he might even have a little room left on his frame to finish filling out, adding to her impression of his youth.

In any other circumstance, she could have mistaken him for a hero.

Her gaze traveled down his massive chest and back up again. Comparing him to Achilles had been an understatement.

"Dang," she said. "How are you bigger without your armor?"

"How are you prepared to fight naked?" he retorted.

She snickered. "I'm showing the same skin as you." She hooked her thumbs in the straps of her tank top and snapped them.

*Whoa. That's a reaction.* Emotions flickered briefly across his face, too quick to measure, until he settled on annoyed. *He isn't* attracted *to me, is he?* she wondered. *Nah, couldn't be.* She trained too hard to get much of a figure. She wore baggy jeans, steel-toed work boots, and a dirty tank top with a built in sports bra that bound what figure she did have. He was probably just ticked about fighting a girl. Some guys had a hang-up about it. That didn't happen much, but it was a lot more often than the other thing.

Good. She'd have an easier time if he had any doubts to make him hesitate. He moved pretty smoothly, even in armor. His size might slow him, but she didn't want to count on that. And she really didn't want to let him get close in. She eyed his arms again. If it turned to a grapple, she was toast.

"Since we will be negotiating, I won't hit your face," he said. "I want you able to talk."

Penance snorted. "That's real thoughtful, but I don't care either way."

Assessment and banter done, the atmosphere between them shifted.

Penance dropped her arrogant pose and skipped back, on her guard. "Ever been here before?"

Kail shifted easily to defense and sidestepped, preparing to circle. "I've been in many arenas."

"Real cute. I mean do you particular aliens make a habit of invading Earth?"

He shrugged. "I don't know. First time for any of us here." He threw a punch – a big, lazy, slow punch that she easily avoided. "This is a supply raid. We want water, food, and medical supplies."

Penance blocked his sudden attack. He pulled back in time to avoid more than a singe from her fists.

She pressed an attack, faking left, coming up for a nice strike to his gut - *goodness knows his head's too high to hit* - but he was too fast and nearly grabbed her. Diving into a quick roll, she bounced up to resume circling out of reach.

Southpaw, she suspected. Also, it looked like he'd figured out the same thing she had – if he could grab her, it was over. The big alien kept moving in close and she kept having to spring back.

"Anybody from Earth go to your planet?" she asked, taking a different tack.

She landed a kick to his knee – it only bounced off the armor. Kail returned with a swift jab that kept her moving to avoid it. The girl suspected he'd allowed that kick to gauge how hard she could strike.

"Never met one," he said. He wasn't even breathing hard. "Why so far away? I thought you wanted to talk?"

Penance glared at him. *This is nothing but an exhibition match for him!*

She blazed up hot and charged, intending to make the massive soldier strike so she could sear his hands and arms. Then the big bully would be in too much pain to grab her. "Then why come here to pick on us!"

He rolled – how could a target that big get out of the way that fast? - and lunged to grab at her from behind.

*Nononono no!* Panicked for an instant, Penance dove forward to a hand-spring, half-twisting in midair to land facing him. Fists up to meet his attack – and he wasn't attacking.

The huge alien was all the way back where she'd left him, half the field away. With exaggerated slowness, he straightened up from his crouch. His head tilted incredulously as he measured the distance between them with his eyes, and then he topped off the whole performance with a big show of dusting off. The alien soldiers in the stands laughed.

*Oh, terrific*, Penance thought, her face warming. *I got a joker.*

So what if she'd panicked just a little bit and overshot her getaway a lit tle... a lot, actually. She glanced up at the plasma field overhead, casting its ever-washing pulses of bluish light over the arena. Had she accidentally pulled on it? She hadn't launched into the stands, at least. But now she looked scared and skittish, and he refused to waste energy chasing her. Fights – especially an exhibition match like this had turned out to be - were a mental game, won in the stands as much as between opponents. Penance couldn't afford to look weak or scared.

*'Always keep the next fight in mind,' like Acid said.*

She spread her hands and beckoned him over. "Where're you at, slowpoke? I thought you wanted to negotiate?"

Kail crossed his arms and shook his head no. He jerked his chin to beckon her back. "Over where the fight is, *lapik*," he called, taunting her right back.

His men snickered from the stands.

*Ugh. The least he could do is take me seriously before he takes me apart.*

Penance circled wide of the alien soldier, buying a little more time to consider the problem. Combat got her nowhere, so she needed to dial up the mind game. *Which angle needs solving first?* She needed to get to the beginning. If she understood why these guys picked Earth, she might pull off an effective bluff to get them gone. But her thoughts kept gnawing on the giant soldier's insufferable attitude instead.

As he waited on her to come back in range, the big soldier yawned and stretched, taking the opportunity to flex a bit for the crowd. The alien soldiers scattered throughout the stadium whooped for their champion. Even the humans in the seats murmured, impressed.

Penance rolled her eyes. *What next, pushups? Massive showoff... what did a huge, tough – and damn him, handsome - guy like that have to prove?*

She blinked, seeing it all come together. *Everything.*

*Young leader, first time on Earth, showing off... Being superior did not help that boy one whit. All it did was attract jealous challengers.*

Her steps slowed and stopped. She forgot all about drawing him out to wear him down. Understanding welled up, and with it, uncomfortable sympathy.

Looking at him, Penance could see less of an unknown alien threat and much more of a young man trying to excel so far above the rest that nobody would dare suggest he didn't deserve what he gained. This young soldier needed to ride high on a wave of popularity, because the competition would drown him otherwise. *I guess when you're that big, all you* can *do is own it. There's no hiding anywhere.* She took a deep breath against the sudden tightening in her chest. *I shouldn't feel bad for him! He came here picking a fight for no good reason!*

Glancing again at the portal beyond him and the soldiers still busy loading goods through, Penance reconsidered. Maybe he *had* a good reason on the other side of that door. On her way to the locker room, she'd spied as they robbed concessions booths – of food and drinks, not cash. Everyone in the stands still had their jewelry and phones. That one soldier who'd tried to kidnap a lady had his field trip to Earth canceled early.

"So all you want is food and supplies, huh?" she asked, resuming her pacing. *If so, I'm in no place to judge*, she thought ruefully.

Supply Officer Kail of Hylinek nodded slowly, his eyes narrowing. Her pause must have made him suspicious.

"Any special reason to come to Earth in particular?"

He shrugged. "You were in range."

"Care to take down that force field so we can ship in the rest of your list?" Penance smiled sweetly. *Might as well throw everything I've got at him.*

He smiled slightly but didn't answer. Penance's impression that the whole fight was just stalling for time only grew more certain. *What do you know - against all reason, the girly approach shows promise.*

"Gonna make a habit of this?"

"I'm not likely to," he allowed.

"Aww, has your visit not been nice?"

He broke into a big, genuine grin at that and turned his palms up, finally relaxed. "On the contrary, it's been far beyond my expectations," he said, his voice purring deeply from his chest.

*Oh God that ain't fair. I'm gonna end up flirting for real and I can't do it when I mean it!*

She tucked a loose strand of hair behind her ear, ducking her head shyly. "So you ain't here for the cute girls?"

Penance expected a laugh but instead, the big soldier stilled. He shook his head slightly, staring at her. He didn't look like he wanted to flirt back, so he must have cottoned on to the act. Though she had an uncomfortable suspicion that she hadn't entirely been acting.

*Maybe he's an alien Prime*, she thought. *Super charisma? Or I'm making excuses for my idiot self. Either way, his guard's back up, dangit.*

She toned down the girlish teasing and met his eyes with sympathy. "You're gonna show 'em all, huh?" she asked quietly.

He shifted back, rebalancing at the change of subject. "What do you mean?"

She stepped toward him, forgetting to be cautious. "I know how it is," she whispered, "but it won't turn out like you think. The harder you try, the better you are, the worse they'll hurt you. You think you'll be a big hero back home but I guarantee you, this big raid you're doing for them is just upstaging somebody else."

Unusually for Penance, every word was true. It'd also serve her purpose if he believed her, but that didn't make it less sincere. Tears filled her eyes. "Please. I like you, Kail. Go back home and lay low, before you attract too much attention."

He gave the barest shake of his head again, still staring seriously at her. For a minute she thought he was as worried about her as the kicker had been in the locker room.

"I'm an officer of the Emperor of Hylinek, and only the Emperor himself may find me unworthy," he replied at last. "I've broken none of our laws and in his infinite wisdom, the Emperor will not permit me to be unjustly accused. But you, however," he broke off his rote recitation, "have no such protection. I... Who is your owner?"

Penance's jaw dropped. "What?"

"The mark on your back. Whose is it – the Justice? I have some savings. I'll pay a fair price for you – or if you don't like him, I'll fight him for your contract. It's up to you."

He offered a boyish grin. The smile was almost shy and completely sincere. Like he had just asked her to prom instead of offering to *buy* her.

Penance shut her mouth. *Well, that's a turn.* She gathered up her wits again before he could make another grab for her. "No," she said. Almost unconsciously, her arms rose to shield her body.

His eyes dropped for a fraction of a second and his mouth tightened, almost a flinch, before the cool mockery returned and she wondered if she had imagined it.

After that initial scandal about her showing up under-dressed, nothing got him out of his amused, laid-back attitude. She didn't know how else to deal with him. Fighting, talking, flirting and even outright begging didn't make him budge, and all she'd learned was that he thought his Emperor made him invincible and that she'd make a nice... what? Housekeeper? Harem girl?

What did she have left after using up all her tricks?

A strange little shift moved somewhere deep in her heart. She tilted her head, listening, though it wasn't something she could hear. She'd go with that, then.

She dropped her guard.

"Listen, let's start over. I don't have any armor. I just started this gig today. I didn't come out wearing this to put you off or make you uncomfortable. The shirt I had on was a gift and I didn't want it to get messed up, so I left it with that lady – the little boy's mom." Penance touched her hair shyly. "She braided my hair. And that's as ready as I could get. So here I am. I wasn't kidding about the girls - Do you know anything about the girls we're missing? Or a man named Acid?"

Kail dropped his guard as well, and walked up to her normally – much more normally than anyone else ever did once they'd seen what she could do. His amused expression disappeared, replaced by something complex, serious, intent. She tilted her head back to maintain eye contact, wondering what he could possibly be thinking. Though her stomach dropped suddenly and the temperature seemed to increase a couple degrees in the stadium.

Mesmerized by his unreadable, intense gaze, she didn't stand a chance when he made his move.

# A Hero's Welcome

## ENORMOUS PLASMA BOMB FILLED WITH HOSTAGES, EARTH

Quick as a snake, Kail grabbed her right arm and spun her, shoved her down to the turf, and pinned her arm behind her back.

Penance spun a blaze around her left hand and swung back over her head, hoping to connect with his face, but he slammed his forearm over her wrist to pin it to the ground. She flexed her fingers, trying to gen up more heat, but only melted the artificial turf. Even if she could see her right hand, she didn't dare blaze it right against her own back. Twisting beneath him, she tried to writhe free or at least get enough room to swing a kick. No luck. The big alien covered her completely.

Getting desperate, she bucked under him, but he only shifted his weight to maintain control. He kept a tight grip on her right wrist when he leaned to balance his elbow on the ground.

Her right shoulder dislocated and she screamed. It hurt like hell – but it also felt like betrayal, and for the first time she was well and truly afraid.

*He's huge and unreadable and I thought I had him pegged but now I'm gonna die -*

He whispered urgently in her ear. "Please," he said.

*Why would he beg when he's winning?*

"The Emperor conquers all planets," Kail continued, speaking rapidly just above a whisper. "Now that Earth is in range, it won't be long until he comes and lays waste to everything here. I haven't seen your missing girls, but he steals females to distribute among his favored officials before he conquers a planet. That is one of the first signs. Please, surrender now, or if you can't surrender the entire planet, surrender yourself and I will keep you safe." His lips brushed her ear and he drew back. "Sorry."

"Piss off," she mumbled, her face grinding into the synthetic turf.

Kail shifted again, letting her turn her head but still keeping her pinned. It almost seemed like he was attempting to be delicate about this. As far as she could tell, he held a somewhat awkwardly-balanced one-armed push-up, touching as little of her as possible.

*How nice. But he still weighs a freaking ton!* His weight pressed the breath from her lungs. Spots gathered in drifts at the edges of her vision.

"Just pass out. I'll set your shoulder and pay for you – I don't care how much. I'm already in debt, more won't matter."

"Not gonna buy me," she said. "Been owned. Didn't like it." Her vision slid rapidly toward darkness, but if she gave in, he would *own* her. *I've only been free from Acid a couple hours! I don't need a new owner!* She sucked air rapidly through her gritted teeth, trying not to give him the satisfaction of seeing her cry.

"It's a good offer," he insisted. "If our positions were reversed, I'd take it."

The shouts and jeers of his soldiers in the stands gave her a good enough idea of what he wanted with her. Some things sound the same in any language.

Except one of them started to sound almost as panicked as she felt.

Kail put his face near her and sniffed deeply. "Deyn is saying... A bomb?" he asked. "You don't smell like explosives."

He lifted his head and shouted back to the men in the stands. The one guy with the edge in his voice – Deyn - called back, and then all of a sudden Kail couldn't get off of her fast enough.

Pen gulped in a breath of air and scrambled up, grabbed her arm and wrenched it back in place. She wanted to scream every profanity she knew at him but she didn't have the breath to do more than gasp and glare at his retreating back through her tears.

Unbearable brightness filled the stadium.

People in the stands shrieked and that *coward* Kail herded his men through the portal as the light from the plasma field brightened and pulsed, throwing stark shadows throughout the stadium.

She shaded her eyes and looked straight up.

*Oh no.*

The plasma field fluctuated wildly, rippling up from the edges, tearing free of the ground around the stadium. It coalesced overhead, pulsing out in arcs in time to her own rapid heartbeat, faster and faster, zeroing in - on *her*. Terror clawed up from the bottom of her soul and forced its way out in a desperate scream. She threw her hands up against the massive beam as the plasma energy of the entire dome hammered down on her.

"Don't look back! Just come on!" Deyn yelled, tugging Kail through the portal. "There's nothing you can do!"

Numb, Kail followed. He let the stabilizer rod drop from his hand and strike the dirt of Hylinek, as Deyn shut down the portal.

The frame powered down, leaving darkness. After the brilliant white of the stadium, lit by the implosion of the plasma containment dome, his eyes took a few moments to adjust to the few scattered torches set up around Salvage Break.

The entire town erupted in cheers, breaking the silence. They shouted his name.

The governor came up and clasped his right hand in both of his. "Supply Officer Kail, we offer you our gratitude. You will be forever remembered as the savior of our district, the merciful provider of all you have given." He led Kail to the head of one of the tables set up outside, covered in stolen food and drink from the stadium.

"I'd rather you didn't," Kail said, but the governor's wife pressed a drinking vessel in his hand and the older daughter poured water for him. Carefully chosen metal ornaments adorned her hair and throat. Even with her injured arm, she had arranged her hair and scarf to cover as many bruises as possible and come to serve him, in a blatant display of favor. She and her young sister both smiled shyly at him, hiding their faces quickly if he turned in their direction.

*An* ibak *should not be getting this kind of attention*, he thought uneasily. And the stadium behind him – he had no idea how much damage had been done.

He caught Deyn's eye. "Did... do you think... they could have survived?" he asked.

Deyn turned his palm up, but Kail didn't miss the slight shake of his head as well. It was possible that Kail's raid had been completely free of civilian deaths, but not likely that the one he really asked about had lived.

So, a success. A resounding, perfect success of a raid, that had brought in well over quota and given him the adoration of an entire town on his first commissioned task. On schedule and with no casualties, and nothing that would cause the Interplanetary Council to prioritize an investigation. The way it had ended might even be blamed on the girl herself for destabilizing the field.

He should have been proud, but instead bitterness and shame filled him. He had reached too far and opened his hands for more than he could grasp. Penance Copper had refused him – outright preferred death that she brought down on herself, that she may have intended to bring down on them both.

Belonging to Death was more desirable than belonging to him. *Of course it is. I am only an* ibak, *after all.*

He didn't know why he wanted her. He could resist a merely pretty girl. But she had impressed him with her quick strikes and quicker wit, and when she leaped away from him, he'd lost his breath at the graceful beauty of her arc. She had treated the negotiation more honestly than he had. When she had stopped fighting and held out humble truth as a peace offering, his will to fight had vanished, replaced by a desire to reciprocate and even protect her. Not just for that day, but for all the rest of the days as well, through the war that would inevitably come to her world. The Justice and everyone connected to him would die. He didn't know yet if it would be an overt war or if those tasked with protecting the Earth from alien threats would be quietly replaced with the Emperor's chosen ones, but Penance was not the Emperor's choice.

Her only chance was to surrender to him and live the rest of her life in obscurity, the eccentric prize of an *ibak* soldier still fighting the endless war, striving to earn his way out of his life-debt and buy an honorable name. The vague thought of sons someday had been replaced by the inexplicable desire for this real, existing person.

He had handled it clumsily.

Not just by dislocating her shoulder. Though that had been an accident, he doubted she would have believed him even if he'd had a chance to explain. She'd been so much lighter than anyone else he'd ever fought. His lack of control embarrassed him, but that wasn't the worst of it.

No, he'd given in to his impulse to claim her and had been unprepared to give her an actual offer, aside from the consequences of not accepting. He couldn't think of anything he had that was any good. No private dwelling. Few excess supplies set aside. Nothing that could have made her believe that she really would be safe with him. Nothing that could have led her to forgive him even if she had surrendered. She had given him all the time he needed to complete his mission, spoken to him with the honor of truth, and in return, he had pinned her to the ground, in a way that must have suggested shame to come.

The worshipful glances of the governor's daughters and his name cheered by soldiers and civilians alike meant nothing when he and Penance Copper knew the truth of what he'd done. He'd repaid her honors with humiliation. After she had -

*"I like you, Kayel."*

He was dishonorable filth. Of course she'd rather die.

"Make them stop," he said quietly.

The governor, his wife, and daughters all stared at him, questioning. Deyn sat up from brooding over his own overfull plate.

He slammed his fist on the table and there was finally silence. "Stop saying my name," he said, just loud enough to carry through the still air of the desert night. "I want no credit for this." He rose from the table, leaving his plate untouched, and went to his quarters.

Someone had thought to gift him a large jug of precious water during the raid. He poured a measured amount into the bowl of his washstand and paused as he noticed a strange mark on his left forearm. Some kind of black grease, in the shape of a slightly smudged cross with one bar a little longer than the others. Where had it come from?

This mark had been on the back of her right shoulder. Her owner's mark, he'd thought, since it was where the Emperor's bought girls usually bore the name of their previous owner. It must have transferred to his arm when he'd pinned her down.

Now it was all that was left of her. He didn't want to get rid of it.

The military, and by extension, the Emperor himself, already owned Kail. He couldn't have some other mark on him. But perhaps he could preserve it. He walked to his bed and hooked his foot under it to drag out his uniform kit. Inside was what was left of his old sand camouflage, before he'd outgrown it – again – half a year ago and had to take it apart to enlarge his newly-issued uniform with. Kail chose a scrap that had been washed nearly white, so thin it was almost transparent now.

Pressing the cloth to the mark, he breathed on it, then rubbed it in until the warmth of his fingers transferred the cross to the material. Letting the cloth fall to his open palm, he considered the faint mark. It wasn't unheard of to keep a memorial of a fallen friend. But this – keeping an enemy's mark in memory of… of… something he wasn't allowed to have with someone he couldn't have afforded anyway? Forbidden.

Two or three times over, it was a forbidden thing. The owner's mark of a woman who wasn't his, a memorial of an enemy who stood in defiance of the Emperor, a symbol of uncertain meaning – an *ibak* had no business holding onto it.

*I should get rid of it*, he thought as he carefully folded it and tucked it between the joints of his bedframe, near his pillow. There was a persistent squeak there every time he laid his head down. A grease-stained scrap, no good for patching anything with, served to muffle it.

That done, he returned to the washstand and obliterated every trace that was left of the mark on his arm before he lay down on his newly-silent bed for the night.

# First Impressions

## TROUBLE, USA

Penance lay on a field of melted plastic grass. The stars overhead looked blurry and bright, and eventually her brain nudged together a few pieces of what had happened. Sirens came closer and she didn't care at all.

Heavy booted feet stomped across the field, deep voices asked questions, hands grabbed under her and lifted her to a stretcher. A van – maybe an ambulance? - backed up close and the men picked up the stretcher and slid her in. She was too wrung out to worry about who these people were or who they worked for, or to listen much to the female voice ordering them around.

Out of nowhere, cold water splashed her face.

Spluttering, Penance lurched upright and wiped her eyes to see an elegant lady, her angelic, expressionless face framed by a mane of dark curls. She wore a cream-colored suit and held an empty plastic cup in one hand, and a phone in the other.

Seeing her awake, the lady launched her verbal barrage. "Who are you? Who are you working for? Why did you come here? What is your connection with the aliens? How did you pass the force field?" There was more, but Penance tuned her out and curled into a ball to sleep.

Someone smoothed her hair back. "Dr. Janus? Is Path online? I'd like to get her opinion on this girl." a woman's voice asked over Penance's head.

"Not just yet," a man answered. A sharp pain stabbed the back of her hand. "Such tiny veins," he remarked. "They collapse as soon as I find them."

*Veins?* Penance jerked awake. She yanked her hand away from the strange man. When she jumped up to stand on the cot she'd been lying on, her energy field flared anxiously. Something sparked near her face. Hot metal melted and spattered like solder on the sheets. Blood spurted from her hand to join the coppery splatters. The cot rolled beneath her and she fell off, landing with a solid thud on her butt. She hadn't realized how off balance she was. Energy roiled away from her in time to her convulsive shudders.

There were things in her hair, taped to her forehead... she ripped them off as she backed into the corner. Electrodes. She dropped them to the floor as if they'd bitten her.

Penance looked around the room wildly, trying to focus on her surroundings through her panic. White room, rolling cot, cold tile floor beneath her bare feet, electronic medical equipment that was probably toast now, an older gentleman in a white lab coat – he must be Dr. Janus - and the elegant lady in the cream-colored suit.

The lady raised an eyebrow at Dr. Janus. "Maybe she doesn't need an IV after all." She rolled up what was left of the electrode wires and unplugged them from a port in her cell phone. She held the phone to her ear. "Path? You'll have to wait to evaluate her. The girl is too upset at the moment."

Penance nodded vigorously in agreement, intensely relieved that the lady called off the white-coated man. Immediately, she wished she hadn't when the room went from slightly wonky to full-on spinning. She braced her hands against the walls to steady herself.

*Ugh, what has he done to me?* The insides of both her elbows and the backs of both her hands sported ugly bruises, covered with taped-on cotton balls. Her jeans were shredded into long strips on her legs. "Who are you people?" Penance whispered, her voice more hoarse than she expected. "What do you want?"

The elegant lady fixed an unsettling stare on her. "I am Mariposa Ramirez, Technical Specialist of Planetary Justice Headquarters. This is my assistant, Dr. Robert Janus. You were the last person to have contact with the Justice. You were found with his identification. Where is he?"

Penance heaved a breath of relief and slid to the floor. These were the people. They would straighten this mess out. "I... I put him upstairs in a warehouse on the south side, near where he was watching the route. No more than five blocks away. He was in pretty bad shape and I couldn't carry him far."

"How did he become injured?" Dr. Janus asked.

Penance hung her head. "I did it. I'm sorry. I... didn't really think I even could."

The lady's expression didn't change. "Since you have managed to destroy the Psychometric Assessment device just by thinking about it, I am unable to verify the sincerity of your apology. What did you intend by taking the Justice's place at the stadium?"

Penance shrugged, feeling miserable. "Damage control?" she offered, her voice very small.

The lady turned to Dr. Janus. "The Justice has been in need of medical attention for approximately the past sixteen hours. I'm going to retrieve him. You can acquaint Miss..." she paused and glanced at Penance.

"Penance Copper," Penance whispered.

"Miss Penance Copper with her quarters as she completes her recovery and finish the interrogation," she said, and left the room.

Penance looked at Dr. Janus, alarmed. "You don't have to interrogate me. I want to cooperate," she said. "Just ask me. I'll tell you everything I can."

The doctor gave her an amused look over his glasses. "The word 'interrogate' means to ask questions, Miss Copper," he said.

"Oh. Well, that's good. I hurt plenty already," she said. "I'm ready when you are."

"Very well," he replied. "You may dress in the scrubs from the closet there, and then I'll run some tests. After that I will show you to your room, and then we shall write a complete account of your activities starting with what you were doing when you encountered the Justice and ending with the robbery of the stadium."

It sounded exhausting, but Penance nodded, eager to start getting on somebody's good side. "Okay, I can do that." The doctor left the room and waited in the hallway while she dressed. When she peeked outside the room, he beckoned and she followed obediently, determined to be on her best behavior for as long as it took. She was desperate for sleep, but she thought she could keep it together long enough to do a few tests.

He led her to a large white room with a high ceiling and a few large pieces of equipment. She recognized a generator, but no power ran from it.

Dr. Janus checked a monitor and frowned, noticing the erratic readings caused by her field as it reached out and explored the equipment. "Miss Copper. Would you disengage your electromagnetic field so that I may get a baseline reading?"

"Sure," Penance said. "You want me to stop my brain or put out my eyes while I'm at it?"

He didn't appreciate the sarcasm.

Hours later, after all the tests were done and she'd done her writing, she was finally allowed to fall into bed. Tired as she was, she couldn't sleep. She was exhausted and alone and nobody liked her. Just like at Hangman House. Impatiently, she scrubbed her eyes. What was she crying for? There was nothing to cry about. There was nothing new about being alone.

The following day, Dr. Janus entered Tech's private lab, holding a slim folder.

Tech looked up from her monitors, each one playing a short loop of the lab footage of the girl, wearing loose scrubs and attempting to follow Dr. Janus' instructions as he evaluated her abilities. Beside her, a box of confiscated cell phones from the stadium awaited sorting and processing, but the girl was more interesting at the moment. Penance Copper brought to mind a certain project that the Justice had been working on for as long as Tech had known him, and she owed it to him to check out this possible lead.

"Well?" Tech asked as she muted the videos.

"I didn't have an opportunity to test the suppression device on the girl. On the other hand, she seemed quite eager to cooperate," Janus said. "She has a... limited understanding of her own capabilities." He flipped through the papers in the folder, selecting one.

Tech clicked her nails on the desk. That much had been obvious from the recordings. As Dr. Janus had tested the girl's control of her plasmic energy field, Penance had to stop many times to ask him to repeat his instructions. Her heavy accent contributed to the impression of ignorance. "And? Any additional information from the raid on the stadium?"

Janus shook his head grimly. "She seems to mean well, but I don't hold much hope for her ability to tell us anything. She asked for a job application."

Tech raised an eyebrow. "A job application."

Janus spread his hands. "I supposed it was a good way to learn about who she is and what she wants, so I printed off an information sheet for her to fill out. She didn't notice anything amiss with it." He pressed his lips together and handed Tech the paper.

Tech scowled at the sheet, filled with oversized, crooked letters strung together in badly-spelled words and incomplete sentences. "This looks like a six-year-old wrote it."

Janus blew out the breath he was holding. "I didn't want to say what my opinion was before you saw it."

"And your opinion is?"

"She isn't very... ah well, she simply isn't that intelligent. She certainly didn't mastermind a plot against the Justice, though she confessed to being an accomplice in the assassination attempt."

"And her next thought is that we should hire her?" Tech asked.

"In her defense, she did claim that she was coerced. I have several pages of her, ah, understanding of what attacking the Justice was supposed to accomplish. Though she seems quite far down in the organization and has never seen the side of the operation that we are concerned with."

Tech looked down again at the "job application." Under "Goals," the girl had scrawled "the opsit of killing people." Tech's slight smile at that disappeared as she read the scribble beside "Skills:" "MMA, tracking, plazma energy feld & blasts, melting stuff, static, EMP, cell phone charging."

She did not look forward to reviewing more of the same disjointed nonsense in lopsided stick-and-ball scribble. Her visual center had too much difficulty processing it as written language, for one.

Tech sighed. "Leave it on my desk. What do you have on the alien invasion?"

"I haven't finished reviewing the evidence, but from what I've seen so far, we were lucky. It appears to be an isolated case of a rogue agent, finding himself with the technology to reach Earth and motivated to plunder it of whatever could be of use to a small tribe. You'll notice the priority was to obtain clean water, followed by food and rudimentary medical supplies." Janus mopped his forehead with his handkerchief. "Fortunately, their leader maintained discipline and prevented his men from harming any civilians."

"I suppose he was aware that the Interplanetary Council would launch an investigation of their own if he violated more than a few minor statutes regarding Earth," Tech said dryly.

"It does seem likely. Do you think the general population will guess that this was an extraterrestrial invasion, or should we take steps to place blame on a technologically gifted villain?"

"All the better if people do decide it was just another homegrown threat, but I'm not sure if we ought to run an op. They'll have to find out about aliens sometime – though preferably *after* we are well able to deal with unscheduled events like that. Let me know if your investigation uncovers anything else. I'm leaving for Washington later today. While I'm there, I'll run Miss Copper's prints and check with my contacts in Serenity City to see if they know anything about her. Perhaps Adrian..." She drummed her fingers on the desk thoughtfully. "On second thought, I'll set Path on that. I won't have time to track the gentleman down, with all the coddling and flattery those bureaucrats will need."

Janus gave her a tight smile. "At least they can't say we didn't warn them."

"They're politicians, Janus. They say whatever will cover their butts." She paused, appraising the video again. Without sound, the girl did exhibit a certain smooth confidence in some abilities. She attacked the tasks as she understood them wholeheartedly, if not with the level of precision and polish the Justice had. And she evidently had more raw power at her disposal than he did.

Tech added the drive containing the video to the folder she was bringing to Washington. They would need some sort of explanation for why the Justice had not taken care of the stadium incident, and the girl's initial subterfuge of claiming to be deputized into service could be plausible with the right evidence. Planetary Justice Headquarters needed to strike a balance between competent handling of interplanetary matters and pushing to acquire decent equipment and personnel, and the recent necessity of clearing out potential leaks from the department had not gone over well with officials already uneasy about the threat of hostile aliens.

Earth's application to remain a sovereign planet depended upon these officials. They needed assurance that cooperating with the Planetary Justice was the right course of action.

She'd think of something to tell them.

# Lab Animal

## UNDISCLOSED

Nobody ever told her anything.

Penance lolled off the edge of the cot and planted her hands on the floor, using her core muscles to pull herself off the cot slowly to a handstand. If nobody would show up and give her something to do, she could go through stretches again, then pushups, then crunches, some shadowboxing... But that wouldn't stop her from being bored out of her mind.

There were a lot of rules. She had to stay locked in her room during regular working hours because she was top secret and couldn't go bumping into anybody. She'd been told not to damage the room and furniture – not that she wanted to, and there wasn't much in there to damage, but the room was small enough that what little there was didn't leave much room to work out. She couldn't spark or gen a field unless she was told to during a lab test, and even then she had to do it in a very specific, unnatural way so Dr. Janus could get his readings. At least in the process of working around all the restrictions, she'd figured out interesting new uses for her field. She had an idea of how she might gen up heat at the outside edge of her field, without having to cycle energy around her wrists for plasma flames. More distance between herself and the heat she generated meant she wouldn't risk burning herself as much.

If she could've done that before, she'd have toasted that alien jerk instead of letting him pin her down.

Some of what Dr. Janus tested her on was just too far over her head. What were weak and strong bonds even supposed to be? Nothing that she sensed could really be described like that. If he'd just explain a little more, she wouldn't have to waste so much time staring at him asking him what he'd just said.

Instead of explaining more, though, he'd gotten tired of her questions. The doctor left her alone for longer and longer each day, telling her that he'd get back when he had some news for her. Except there wasn't much news beyond getting packages of food and clean scrubs delivered through a chute to her room. A couple times, she'd been left alone so long in the plain white room that her mind edged toward an old, familiar path, desperate to feel something, to run somewhere. Happily, she found the strength to avoid that abyss and carry on another day. No point in working so hard to stay safe if she did herself in, after all.

She just hadn't realized safety would be so boring.

She shouldn't complain. She was safe, she got three hot meals and a cot, and nobody asked her to do anything difficult.

Except this wait and see business. Penance had never had much patience.

A knock at the door startled her.

"Come in!" Penance called, before turning upright again and plopping on the bed.

Dr. Janus entered the small room and smiled at her. "Feeling a little bored today, Miss Copper?"

Penance rolled her eyes at him. "Yes! There's nothing to do. I was wondering if I could maybe get a book?"

"A book? What sort of book?" Dr. Janus asked, his tone amused as he checked her eyes and ears with a small flashlight.

"A... a Bible, maybe?"

Dr. Janus sat back in surprise for a moment, then set his stethoscope in his ears and checked her breathing and blood pressure. "All normal!" he announced. "Quite incredible that you survived that surge with no lasting damage."

"I'm fine. I've been fine. Every day I've been fine, other than bored out of my mind."

Dr. Janus spread his hands. "It really couldn't be helped. But today things will be different."

"Are you gonna tell me yet if you guys found the Justice? If he's even still alive?"

"Now, Miss Copper, that information is classified far above your level."

Penance perked up. "I have a level now? What'd I get?"

Dr. Janus gave her a small, dry smile. "One. But today you are to come and assist me in my lab. In the less-sensitive lab, to be precise."

"Sensitive classified or sensitive electronics?"

"Ah... both."

Penance bounced off the bed. "I'm good with just getting out of this room!" She paused and shot Dr. Janus an anxious glance. "It... It's a nice room. I appreciate it. I really do. Just kinda blank in here, is all."

Dr. Janus chuckled. "Of course, of course. Now follow me and ah... don't get too excited. Wouldn't want to blow any light fixtures, now would we?"

Penance ducked her head, embarrassed. She'd been trying to do better about controlling her energy over the last few days, now that she had time to concentrate on it. She had precious little else to do, and a sinking feeling that even one slip-up could put her good standing in jeopardy. "Yessir."

He led her through a maze of white corridors to an elevator lobby and pressed the up button. In a moment, the doors slid open. The beautiful lady with the dark hair was inside.

"Ah, Acting Commander Tech," Dr. Janus said, pulling his handkerchief from his pocket and dabbing his forehead with it. "May we join you? I was just taking Miss Copper for some tests."

She inclined her head to him and they stepped inside. The doors shut and the elevator rose.

Penance clasped her hands together and leaned forward to look around Dr. Janus at the lady.

Acting Commander Tech. The boss of the operation. More importantly, the boss who let Penance stay. Even after Penance failed every attempt to wear the electrodes for the psych evaluation with the as-yet-unmet Path – and accidentally fried several expensive pieces of equipment. Most incredible of all, Tech never, ever got mad. Her voice stayed calm and even, she made no sudden moves, and after Penance's failures, she simply rescheduled for a new day. Penance never saw any approval from her either, but Acting Commander Tech embodied fairness. *Someday*, Penance thought, *I'll finally do right, and she'll like me. When I deserve it.*

Tech would know whether the Justice was alive or dead... but nothing in her expression betrayed any emotion at all. She was probably really good at poker, too.

It wouldn't do any good to ask after him, but if she could just show Tech that she was ready to do whatever it took to make up for what she'd done, then maybe she could have a real shot at getting out of wait-and-see not-quite-prison and getting a life she could be proud of. Maybe some of Tech's class would rub off on her and she wouldn't seem so stupid and unimportant to everybody anymore.

The elevator stopped and Dr. Janus beckoned her to follow him out. She stopped with one foot out of the elevator and turned to the lady, her heart in her throat.

"Ma'am," she blurted, "I'm real sorry. I know you can't say whether he's even alive or not but I hope he is. I wish I could take back what I did. Just, give me anything to do, anything, I don't care what."

"Miss Copper!" Dr. Janus hissed behind her, plucking at her elbow.

Tech raised one eyebrow. "Very well. If you want to make up for actions that cost lives, you can start by learning how to save them. Janus, you're qualified to teach basic first aid, aren't you?" She pulled a book out of her bag and handed it to Penance.

Janus mumbled something that was probably a yes.

Penance bounced on her toes and backed out of the elevator, hugging the book. Through her excitement, she remembered to be extra careful to damp down her energy before it could spark. "Thank you, ma'am, I'll learn, I swear I'll be the best you ever saw, just wait!"

"See that you do," Tech said. The elevator doors closed.

Penance stroked the cover of the brand new, thick hardcover book as she read the title. "Basic First Aid. I've never had..." She turned to Dr. Janus, brimming with excitement, but one look at his sour expression killed her joy. She dropped her eyes and wondered what she'd done wrong, weighing whether it might be safe to ask or not.

"Come along," he said, and she followed him down more sterile white corridors until they came to a door set in a glass walled room. He unlocked the door and waved her inside before following her in. He locked the door again behind them.

At the click of the lock, Penance instinctively moved forward and scanned the room for threats, but no one else was there. Just desks and shelves and a gigantic fish tank against the wall. Something moved along the bottom of it.

"Wow, what's that?" She jogged up to the tank, still alert and aware but not nearly as nervous. "You have a pet in there?"

"That is not a pet," Dr. Janus said. "That is *sepia officinals*, a common cuttlefish. I am studying its chromatophore cell structure and nervous system to develop practical applications as camouflage."

"It's like a lil' baby squidlet! What's his name?" Penance pressed her face to the glass to see the creature as it slid bonelessly across the craggy floor of the tank.

"It's a female. And it doesn't have a name."

Penance gasped as the cuttlefish changed color and texture to blend in precisely with the rocks around it. "That *is* some good camouflage. Can I ... never mind."

"What is it?"

"Nothing. It doesn't matter."

Dr. Janus sighed. "Penance. Don't keep secrets from me. Your position here relies entirely on our level of trust. How can I help you if you don't trust me?"

She hung her head. He was right. She was here at their mercy, and even if they decided not to prosecute her for going after the Justice, they could kick her out as quick as they'd taken her in. This was her big chance to learn how to do some good and make up for the stuff she'd done in her former life. Not to mention, no more comfy bed, no more reliable meals, no more clean clothes – even if all they gave her were pajama-like scrubs, they always smelled nice. No more safe hiding spot from Acid. And she'd probably have to give the book back. She couldn't throw all that away just because sometimes she felt uncomfortable letting Dr. Janus in on what was going on in her head.

"I thought for just a second that maybe I could give her a name, but then I realized that if you're studying its nervous system, then... Well. You don't name critters headed to the butcher shed."

"Quite. If it's any consolation, they have a rather short lifespan in any case. It will serve its purpose in allowing me to engineer an artificial means of replicating its organic ability, which is infinitely more useful than a cuttlefish."

"Oh." At least he didn't take it like she was questioning what he planned to do.

"Say," he said then, in a tone that sounded like forced cheer, "How would you like to feed it? We'll see how you do and it might become a regular duty for you."

"Sure!" Penance said. She still hadn't pegged what had bothered him, but as long as he had a use for her, he'd keep her around. If that use was feeding the lab squid-creature and cleaning the tanks, that was good enough for her.

"Ugh! Dead again!" Penance sat back from the dummy and grabbed the first aid book to page through it again. "Clear airway, open mouth, pinch nose, three breaths, chest compressions... what am I doing wrong?"

Janus glanced up at the monitor screen with a bored sigh. "You've crushed the ribcage. Again." He turned back to testing the latest prototype of his camouflage suit. "Too much ambient static tripping the sensors," he muttered. "Perhaps I should copy the external neural interface from the Psychometric Assessment Device for greater control..."

"It says 'press firmly,' though."

"Miss Copper, 'firmly' from you will bend steel."

Penance groaned. "I've tried to be gentler but that does nothing at all! How do I tell what's enough with a lump of rubber?" She rubbed her mouth with the back of her hand. "Blech."

"That is a very finely calibrated and sensitive lump of rubber. Why don't you look at the monitor?"

"Because if I try to make the monitor look right, I gen a field and accidentally cheat. Besides, real life won't give me a monitor."

"I highly doubt you'll ever have the opportunity in real life," Janus said.

"Because you won't pass me!"

"I won't give you a grade you haven't earned."

"But Tech is going to think I haven't done anything at all! I need to show some kind of progress." Tech had tasked her with two things – to do the psych assessment with Path, and to learn the book. So far all Penance had to show for the first was a smoking pile of junked electrodes. She simply could not use them. Tech's inhuman patience with her had to run out sometime.

"That's your problem."

"When is she coming back?"

"Oh, tomorrow or the day after, I expect. These things take time." Janus stood and stretched. "Come along. It's past your bedtime."

Penance rolled her eyes but got up anyway. It wasn't that late — he just wanted to be done with her for the day.

While Janus saved his notes on his laptop and tidied up his desk for the night, Penance jogged over to the aquarium. "Got some fresh crabs in for you today, Squishy," she cooed. "Here, you can have a snack before bed."

"It isn't feeding time," Janus said, but Penance had already dropped a crab into the cuttlefish's tank.

Squishy slipped out from hiding and flattened into a saucer to glide above the crab, dots and dabs of color glimmering along her tentacles like lights from an alien craft. Sensing danger, the crab paused in its scuttling.

As quick as lightning, Squishy snatched up the crab and fled.

Penance giggled. "She's like an alien spaceship abducting crabs."

Dr. Janus sniffed. "Actually, that scenario only exists in movies. The Interstellar Charter prevents alien abductions from taking place."

Penance made a face, careful not to let Janus see. *Killjoy.* She hadn't learned much about it yet, but still, all the Interstellar Charter had was a rule. That didn't mean it *prevented* abductions. People broke rules all the time and got away with it — Penance herself was an expert at that, even if she didn't currently use that expertise. *Stuffy Janus* would *think rules were always followed just because they existed.*

Dr. Janus led her back to her room, even though she didn't need help remembering how to get there. Blank as all the hallways and doors were, she had the place memorized... at least, as far as she was allowed to go.

There was another floor below hers that wasn't marked on the elevator, but it had to exist. Tech had been on her way up that day last week, when she'd given Penance the book before leaving.

The book.

She'd left it in the lab.

Penance sat on her bed and looked around her small, plain room. Tomorrow was a weekday, so she'd be left alone until six o'clock the next day, maybe later if Janus forgot to come get her. He had, a couple times.

Tech would come back any day now. If Penance couldn't actually do everything that was in the book, the least she could do was have the thing memorized.

She had to go get it.

Penance jumped up and grabbed the doorknob. It was locked.

*Well.* She drummed her fingers impatiently against the wall. *I guess I can just go to bed then.*

She smirked and swiped her palm down the electronic lock, generating the precise magnetic field from Janus' badge. The lock clicked open, and she was out.

She needed that book. Tech herself had given it to her. She couldn't let the Acting Commander down.

Penance reached out with her senses and checked the locations of the security cameras. There were a ton of them, but the ones in the corridors weren't on all the time, just when the motion sensors were tripped. She eased out of her room, building a soft field of static to blur the edges of her figure and fool the infrared beams. They were easy enough to get by. She'd worried all her skills had been rusting away in that room, but she still had the knack for making the right sort of echo back at the right intervals. She made it down the corridor in record time.

Now, the lab room cameras were on all the time. But she knew right where they were aimed and there were desks and chairs for cover. She swiped the lock open and fuzzed the entryway camera for a second while she dove in and rolled under a desk. It'd be best not to fuzz any cameras again for a good long while, so she tucked up into a little ball and waited a minute as she visualized the lab.

She grinned into the crook of her arm. This was the most interesting thing she'd done all week.

Penance started to change position when she sensed the magnetic field from a high-clearance card outside the door and froze. The lock clicked open and Tech and Janus walked in, continuing what sounded like a long argument. Tech's heels clicked right past Penance's hiding spot as they went on to the cubicle where the suit was.

"This suit will revolutionize warfare," Dr. Janus said. "But if I'm unable to complete my research on the mechanism by which the nervous system achieves instantaneous communication with the chromatophores, I won't be able to have an efficient prototype. I did acquire the specimen for the express purpose of dissecting it, after all."

"But the girl has demonstrated an attachment to the specimen," Tech pointed out. Her clicking heels paused by Squishy's tank. "I understand you've had to put off your preferred projects in order to accommodate her needs, but it's been healthy for her to care for the creature. If I'd realized at the time what a positive influence that would have on her, I'd have introduced a more appropriate pet than your specimen. A puppy, or a kitten."

"It is critical that this facility remain clean at all times," Dr. Janus sniffed. "Think of the shedding. Where would a dog go to do its business? And cats are notorious for getting into trouble and breaking things."

"Rather like Penance herself," Tech remarked, with more humor than Penance had ever heard from her. "Getting that neural interface to work with her is proving to be quite a challenge. Perhaps the new surge protector will prevent another critical failure on her next evaluation appointment with Path. If not, Path will have to evaluate her in person, and I'd rather she didn't leave the Justice yet. I haven't been able to ask Adrian yet if we could impose a second patient upon his safe house or I'd simply bring her with me on my next trip."

Penance flinched. She knew she'd failed at that. A lot. Making all those appointments and never succeeding at keeping them had to be aggravating for Ms. Path, too. Getting on the bad side of this professional evaluator lady was the absolute last thing she needed if she wanted a good report to get back to Tech. *But... did she say the Justice was alive? That's good news, right?*

"It's so nice that there's progress on this personal project," Dr. Janus said. Penance could hear the sneer in his voice. "However, I highly doubt anything useful will come of your efforts. The girl is much too damaged to form meaningful relationships with anyone. Including my cuttlefish. Which I will be dissecting. I promise you, she will hardly notice its absence."

Tech walked past again as they continued the conversation and left the lab.

Quickly, Penance executed the rest of her planned maneuvers and grabbed the book she'd come for. She retreated to the suit cubicle to wait a reasonable interval before fuzzing the camera again. But standing and waiting gave her time to think about what Dr. Janus said.

Was she damaged? Well, probably. A screwed-up life makes screwed-up people. She squeezed her eyes tight shut but hot stinging tears leaked through anyway.

What else did they say about her? Did he want to convince Tech to give up on her and kick her out? She wished she hadn't heard any of it.

*Damaged.* The word throbbed in her head, relentlessly pounding away at the foundation of who she was and what she was doing. What if, when she finally did the evaluation, Ms. Path said so, too? That in addition to being stupid and dangerous and destructive, she couldn't ever belong anywhere, with anybody? Where would she go then? Penance hugged the book tightly, bending the hard cover. Loneliness ached in her chest. *Stupid girl. Nobody on Earth would want me.*

It was too soon to leave the cubicle. But she couldn't stay. She had to follow them and find out more. Her eyes slid over to the invisibility suit. It would be stealing.

*No. Borrowing.* It wouldn't be permanent. She could just use it for a little while. It wouldn't hurt anything.

On the other hand, dissecting Squishy would be a permanent thing, and Dr. Janus was a-okay with that.

Dr. Janus would be mad if he caught her even touching the suit. Penance smirked. Even better. He wasn't going to catch her, and she'd get one back on him without him ever knowing.

He had an alarm attached to the power supply for the suit, but she didn't need that. She could gen a low-level electrical field to make it work without the stupid battery thing. She slipped the suit on over her scrubs and activated it.

She disappeared. In the quiet, empty lab at night without being able to see her own body, she could almost believe she was a ghost. Looking at where her hand ought to be, she could barely detect the blurry outline of the edge of the suit. She waved her arm and noticed a tiny bit of lag in the projected image. In these identical white corridors, now dimmed for the night, the suit shouldn't have any trouble keeping up with the surroundings at all. She grabbed her book and held it close to her chest. It disappeared too. Penance was impressed. The suit was smart enough to hide carried objects and not just show them on the other side. *Time to go haunting.*

"Goodnight, Squishy," she whispered as she passed the tank. "I can't see any way to save you, but I figured you'd appreciate getting one up on him before he kills you."

She opened the door the barest possible bit and squeezed out. Were her hips getting wider? All these regular meals and not enough room to really work out might be putting weight on her. Kind of hard to tell what size she was when all she wore was elastic waist jammie pants and loose smock shirts. She supposed she could have paid more attention when she bathed, but that was the one activity that she didn't stretch out to take the most time possible. Bathing made her feel vulnerable.

The elevator had been used recently. Elevators were easy, even ones that needed key cards to get to specific top secret floors. She didn't even have to press a button – just copied Tech's own key and introduced a little blip right when it was supposed to chime, so that the doors slid open on the secret level without warning Tech and Dr. Janus.

She crept along more white corridors, ears and field wide open, and was rewarded with the faint sound of voices down the hallway. She found the door to the room Tech and Dr. Janus were talking in and leaned against it, listening.

She was disappointed that she was no longer the subject of the conversation, but as she listened, she grew puzzled. Tech was harder to hear, but it seemed like she didn't know anything that Penance had written in her report.

"... It's only a temporary solution. As soon as whoever opened that portal realizes that we've hacked their focus device, they'll shut down the compromised unit and resume porting without interference. We have no means of determining where the hostiles are coming from, and without knowing for certain which planet is the threat, it will be harder to get the Interplanetary Council to investigate. Nothing ties this group with the missing girls, and I'm still uncertain that they've been trafficked off-planet. It's all just suspicion – we've had no more events since I implemented the rig so I assume all the events originated from the same planet."

"There's no proof of anything at all yet," Dr. Janus agreed. "Certainly nothing here indicates that invasion will be a regular occurrence."

Penance blinked. She knew which planet. Hylinek. Was her spelling that far off? Didn't Tech think that the warning she had gotten from the big soldier was even worth mentioning to the Interplanetary Council? Did they not care that some Emperor was going around stealing girls to pay his thugs, right before he conquered planets?

The only thing Penance could imagine was that Tech didn't think her word was good enough to go on. Didn't they trust her yet? Then she thought about what she was doing right at that moment and stifled a groan.

Janus asked a question, but Penance couldn't quite make out what he asked.

Tech answered, her voice carrying more clearly, "All the Council will do is offer to supply us with a force field to filter out all unwanted alien interference, but it would come at the expense of Earth's sovereignty. Once I develop our own technology that will allow us to do that..."

They moved out of earshot again, but in a moment Dr. Janus' familiar, lecturing whine returned.

"I understand the appeal of sending a team through to determine what planet we've set the interference signal to, but it's too dangerous to jump in blind. Besides, we don't have access to the amount of power that would require." Dr. Janus left off lecturing and yawned.

"Thank you for helping me with this," Tech said, "But now we really should close up for the night."

"I'll see you out," Dr. Janus offered.

Penance heard heels clicking on the tile floor in the lab, headed her way.

# Out Past Curfew

## UNAUTHORIZED

Penance backed away from the lower level office before Tech and Janus emerged. She had to hide somewhere – the camouflage suit was good, but not so good that she thought they'd overlook her right in front of them in the hallway. There was nothing nearby at all, though. No doors to duck into – wait. She sensed a slight electrical field through the wall to her left. Someone had left a TV on in a room across the hall. If there was a room, then there was a door.

A tiny seam in the wall caught her eye, and two small indentations along one side of that at shoulder height. She pressed her fingertips into the indentations and the wall slid open.

Penance slipped inside and the wall closed behind her.

After weeks of living among glossy white walls, dull gray carpets, and plate glass cubicles, this room looked interesting. Old brick walls, some maintenance stuff, massive pipes run across the low ceiling, a massive braid of wires plugged into an equally massive power distribution box and leading across the damp concrete floor. And that wasn't quite a TV she sensed. Something else vibrated the edges of her field and put her curiosity up.

*Might as well follow that braid and see what's plugged in,* Penance thought. *Whatever it is, it needs a lot of power.*

The braided cords led to a cavernous room, the ceiling supported by concrete pillars. It seemed familiar, or it would have been if the ceiling had been lower... Penance spotted a black van in the shadows by the far wall. A concrete ramp led to a huge steel door, big enough for a car to get through.

"Parking garage," Penance said out loud. Her voice echoed and she winced. That must have been how she'd been brought in. That van looked like what they'd tossed her into after the stadium battle. She walked past it, following the cords around a partition.

There, she found the source of the static she'd been sensing – several monitors set up, casting faint blue light on an odd collection of metal parts and pieces arranged on a workbench by the wall. The wall itself had a loop of thick cable, ten or twelve feet in diameter, stapled into the concrete. The cable led to  the workbench and branched off, to the power supply, to a set of monitors, to something round and familiar on a stand on the workbench.

"Alien helmet..." Penance whispered. "Kail took it off when we fought. Must've left it behind... there's his upper armor, too."

Penance touched the helmet with one finger and the monitors flickered on. "Oops. Closed a circuit there." She forced a laugh at her own jangling nerves and rubbed her hands together, trying to dampen down her energy field.

The monitors made no sense to her. Endless scrolling lines of code and numbers didn't interest her much, though she did wonder how they got all that from the helmet. It must be a more complicated piece of equipment than it looked. The other monitors that had been left on played video on loop. She set her book down and crossed her arms, tucking her hands under her elbows to keep from accidentally turning on anything else.

Kail's face flickered across one screen and she gasped. This was from the stadium. She'd thought they'd have the stadium surveillance to review some-where, but she had expected that to all be grainy overhead shots. Not up-close views of the alien soldiers and the portal they had come through... A box of neatly labeled and bagged cell phones on the floor caught her eye.

*Oh yeah.* Never having had a phone herself, she hadn't really considered that.

She sat in the chair facing the monitors, fascinated by the various viewpoints that she hadn't seen while  fighting. This bit happened just before the force field came down and hammered her. The monitors in the array were arranged in columns to play their loops in the order they had occurred, according to the timestamps in the corners of each.

The force field dominated this one, pulsing bright ripples toward its apex. Occasionally a bolt came streaking down to hit one of those long black posts the aliens had spaced around the stadium. Alien soldiers and spectators alike cast anxious glances upward. The next monitor held a close view of one of the soldiers, who had what looked like a pink phone sticking out of his upper front pocket. He held a gadget Penance didn't recognize, and whatever he read from it worried him. He stepped out of frame and the girl found him again on the next monitor, trying frantically to flag down Kail.

Penance nodded. "Yeah, that's when Kail had me pinned and said something about explosives. Next should be the big coward running away..."

*Yep, right there.* Running for his life, one arm signaling to the soldiers to fall back toward the portal. Another screen showed an alarming wobble in the force field as a soldier picked up one of those tall black posts and headed back to the portal with it. Kail at the portal waving the rest of the soldiers through. And there... wait. What was going on?

Penance shook her head. What was he waiting for? For all he knew, the stadium was about to go nuclear. Why was he standing there holding one of the black posts and arguing with the gadget guy soldier instead of getting out?

She grabbed a pencil off the workbench and carefully bumped the volume control for that monitor.

Lots of static and panicky crowd noise in the background, and Kail was speaking alien anyway, but then he said her name.

Penance watched the video loop again, fascinated. "Penance Copper," Kail said, in the middle of a whole lot of rapid-fire alien words and gestures, and finished by grabbing the last black post from his soldier and turning to go back.

For her.

Penance shook her head violently. *No, that can't be it. He just left something else.* She stole a glance at his helmet and armored vest on the table beside her. *Something left on the field, important enough to make him forget his helmet and armor right next to him.* She shifted uneasily in her seat. *Though the only thing left on the field right then was... me.*

The loop ended again and Penance stood up from her seat to find the next monitor at the top of the next column. That just showed the force field – she knew that bit. She'd never forget how it gathered up and pooled above her, like a fierce, brilliant eye aimed directly on her.

The next monitor down, though, featured Kail again. He stared toward the field in horror as everything brightened. Kail's lips moved, ever so slightly.

Even though the sound from that monitor was off, she could hear him in her mind.

"Penance."

Penance's whole world tilted and rearranged again. She sat in the flickering blue glow of the screens, hands over her mouth, tears streaming down her face as she watched Kail pulled through the portal.

She shook her head again, angry sparks glimmering around her, and shoved back away from the monitors. *He did* not *care. He did not! That gigantic jerk with his mocking eyes and dimpled grin and... and... completely naked grief and shock written all over him.*

*Damn him, he* was *a hero. Hellbent on saving everybody.*

*Even me.*

A hot blush rose in her cheeks. What if he had wanted to save her, and he had to own her to do it? What if she'd completely misread his actions at the end of the fight? Pinning her down *had* put him close enough to whisper in her ear about the Emperor's habit of stealing girls, instead of shouting across the field making sure everybody could hear him. He'd given her the best lead she had. Maybe he had to keep up appearances to stay out of trouble.

Penance rubbed the tears from her face and turned away from the monitors, facing the circle of cables and equipment on the wall. Squinting at them, she realized what exactly was familiar about it. She'd only seen one like it from the other side, but the energy she sensed from it rippled to a frequency just like the portal at the stadium.

What was that Kail had said, about if their positions were reversed?

Had he meant it?

Right in front of her, she had a way to find out. There wasn't enough power going through it to actually open the portal, but she could fix that.

Having to be so careful during her sessions with Dr. Janus had improved her control. She ought to be able to gen a field and channel the energy right in. Nobody would miss her for hours and hours. She had a nifty stealth suit.

Penance squared up in front of the portal rig, pressing her palms together and squeezing her eyes shut as she concentrated on feeding power into the cable. Waves of energy pulsed from her and echoed back from the portal, and she looped them back in, amplifying the signal.

It needed more.

She couldn't gen enough with a spinning magnetic field — not unless she wanted to wreck the rig and throw it out of tune with its destination. Pushing her field out, she tapped into the power grid and gently arced more power directly from the main conduit, while still managing the portal. Still it needed more. She pulled harder and the pulses she managed became stronger, starting to resemble the plasma force field. Eyes still shut, she held out her palms to shove the energy back to the beginning of the portal. She needed more power!

Something shifted in her mind, in the way she thought about the problem and getting the energy. The experiments Dr. Janus tried to do with her field came to mind. If she understood correctly, everything was made of energy. There was plenty if she could just unlock it... like starting a stolen motorcycle, or swiping an imaginary card key... or... no, the idea wasn't to close a circuit, but to uncouple the inside...

She reached blindly with her field, feeling for something to work with to try out the abstract concept that hovered just barely in reach of her comprehension. Something solid, heavy, to crack open and turn into energy.

Suddenly she had it. Power poured through her, overflowing, as the portal ripped open from the middle and blasted her with cold, dusty air.

With difficulty, Penance shut off the outflow of energy, stopping the chain reaction she had drawn upon for the surge. The last thing she wanted to do was leave the lights on while she was out, and keeping it going made the room spin.

Penance opened her eyes and grinned with satisfaction at the window – no, the doorway to another world that she'd created. Stars glimmered in the dark sky on the other side, and dust blew gently in. What if she learned to do this all the time? She'd always have a place to run.

Before she could have second thoughts, she leaped through.

# Far From Home

## THE DUNES, GREAT DESERT, HYLINEK


Deyn collapsed on his knees in the frigid desert night. Despite the ever-changing dunes in the otherwise featureless wasteland, he knew exactly where he was. Though now, he had nowhere to go, and in the desert, that meant Death owned the only door that would be open to him now.

Everything, everyone was gone from him. After the Secret Enforcers had come for Kail, Vorak took charge of the unit, leaving Deyn as the lone *ibak* and Kail's known friend. Deyn knew it was only a matter of time before he was dead, and the means were only limited by Vorak's cleverness and imagination. The desert held a thousand ways to die. Accidents, venomous creatures, land mines... Vorak had little imagination, and so would have him scheduled for ritual humiliation, followed by some needless skirmish with rebels or a rival unit, where his unit would abandon him as he was conveniently killed in action.

So before Vorak could come for him, he left. First he stole the rest of the water Kail had received as a gift before he was taken, and then he packed his kit with odds and ends that wouldn't be missed. He'd have a good head start on his way to start finding out how to join the rebels.

After what had happened to Kail, the Emperor could not be the just and worthy ruler he'd been portrayed as. There was no justice in Kail's arrest and sentencing. There was no justice anywhere on Hylinek, nor any of the other worlds the Emperor ruled.

Surely he would not be the first disillusioned *ibak* to join the rebels.

But it hadn't taken him even a full day to see those bitter hopes crushed. All the talk in the towns was how Jael, the leader of the rebels, had been captured at last by the Secret Enforcers and delivered to a secure outpost. There she had been picked up by a prison convoy unit, which paraded the prisoners through the towns on chains. Jael must be made an example of... along with a giant of a man, some stranger who must have committed an unspeakable crime to be sentenced to the prison mines. The convoy that held the prisoners moved quickly. On foot, Deyn couldn't catch up to them, and now they had been at their destination for weeks as he lagged behind.

Without Jael, there were no rebels to join. Now, Deyn truly had nothing.

Unless he walked up to the prison and turned himself in. He was under no illusion that he'd be allowed contact with Kail, but at least then he could join his friend and commander in death, somewhere in the same structure.

Deyn sighed and stood, facing the black outline of the prison in the distance. There was simply nowhere else to go, and he was getting close.

He shrugged out of his knapsack, abandoning his kit in case some other despairing traveler needed it, and began methodically emptying his pockets as he walked to the place of his death. Touching the pink phone in his upper pocket, he hesitated. He'd found no one to assume responsibility for the device and the evidence it contained, yet he didn't want to drop it.

Unable to decide what to do with it, he left the phone in his pocket and chose another pocket to empty.

Something burned his fingers, bringing him out of his suicidal reverie.

Panicked, he jerked the thing out of his pocket and threw it on the ground, wondering who had managed to tamper with his uniform before he'd escaped camp. It bounced with a metallic ring and he recognized it as his portal focus unit, the tiny version he'd used to aim the portal to Earth for the raid.

Suddenly an arc of intense light shot from it and ripped open from the middle – a new portal. Blinded momentarily, Deyn staggered back. He heard something – someone – land on the ground near him, and he backed away from it, stumbling. He scrambled to a crouch and threw his arms up defensively.

Nothing attacked.

He blinked, eyes adjusting slowly again to the darkness. Starlight revealed nothing near him, and for a moment he wondered if he'd been hallucinating.

"Hey."

He jumped back. The voice came from directly in front of him. But he could see nothing.

"Oh. Lemme just..."

Deyn's eyes tracked the rustle of fabric. A face appeared and floated in the air inches from his own.

He swallowed a gasp, and then swallowed a couple more times to get his heart back down in his chest where it belonged.

The face snickered. "Boo."

Now that he concentrated, he could see the warp in the air outlining the edges of the person in front of him – just a girl, in very sophisticated camouflage. But not just any girl. Now that he recognized her, he realized that the situation was much worse than a hallucination or a ghost.  Though she might still be a ghost. "Pence C'per!" he choked.

"Penance... Call me Pen... Never mind," she said. She peered closer at him and spied the pink phone, still poking out of his pocket. "Hey, I know you! From the video. You were talking to Kail."

Deyn flinched at the sound of Kail's name – the only word he'd understood. He rocked forward onto his knees and waited for the walking, talking, alien plasmic reactor to kill him.

She wasn't interested in him, though. She stood up and dusted off her knees, looking around the emptiness of the desert night. "Where's Kail? I wanna talk to him." She poked Deyn's shoulder. "Hey. Kail?"

Deyn shook his head, staring at the ground. If Penance had any interest in taking apart his molecules or dragging him to eternal torment in the underworld, he didn't think she'd begin by talking and poking his shoulder. His racing heart calmed. At least now he knew what she wanted, but he couldn't help her.

She poked him again, then knelt down in front of him and grabbed both his shoulders to shake him. "Where's Kail?"

How could he make her understand? Just then he remembered his alien recording device. Turning his palms up first to show he wasn't reaching for a weapon, he slowly removed it from his pocket, but she refused to touch it. He turned it on and accessed the correct file, and set it down between them on the ground.

Deyn glanced around to make certain that the empty desert hid no witnesses, ignoring the alien girl's snicker at his expense. If she had seen the things he had, she wouldn't be so quick to laugh.

He tapped the triangular symbol to start the recorded images. Kail's lips moved silently and Deyn clicked the volume up, even though the alien girl wouldn't be able to understand the words.

"... if this is what you want to spend your bonus to keep, it's fine with me," Kail told him. "But you need to do something about the color. Paint it, or make a cover or something."

"The color?" Deyn had flipped over the device then to look at the back of it. He hadn't seen that it was drastically different than his uniform. It looked the same shade to him. The device began recording from the camera on the back instead of the screen side.

Kail laughed. "You really can't see that color?"

"Kail *ip ibak!* You are under arrest!" Many voices thundered, combined with the rhythmic stomping of boots. The Secret Storm.

Deyn had jammed his device back in his pocket and backed away, the camera lens still above his shallow front pocket. The recording captured Kail as he immediately fell to his knees, wrists above his bowed head. The Storm rushed in, surrounded him, clapped a collar around his neck and chained him to cuffs. Once he was safely restrained, the leader took Kail's own sidearm and struck him with the butt of it. As if on cue, the rest of the Secret Enforcers holstered their sidearms and drew new weapons, short rods with fist-sized metal balls chained to the ends. Compact and fairly lightweight, the police-issue flails were weapons that relied upon velocity rather than weight.

Deyn watched, frozen in horror, as the Secret Enforcers rained blows upon their prisoner. Kail grunted as the first struck him in the back, but held his position on his knees, cuffed hands still above his head. If he could stay upright through one hundred strikes, the ordeal would be only a test from the Emperor, and he would be pardoned and released.

Kail closed his eyes to count each blow as it struck him, and Deyn, also *ibak* and raised to track debts carefully, silently counted as well.

The next caught Kail's ribs, and then another struck his face, and more, so rapidly that Deyn could hardly track them all. Flails whistled through the air and landed with sickening thuds against his friend, the initial chaotic pounding resolving into rhythm.

The Secret Storm laughed as the number of strikes exceeded one hundred and Kail, bloodied and bruised, swayed, struggling to stay upright.

Abruptly, the beating stopped.

The Enforcers stepped back, and Kail raised his head to take a shuddering breath. His still-raised arms trembled. Dark splotches of sweat showed through his uniform.

The leader cracked a whip of metal cables.

Kail gritted his teeth and dropped his head again, steeling himself. The whip lashed against his back, shredding the thin material of his uniform. Flecks of blood and skin sprayed as the captain of the Secret Storm flicked the whip back for another strike.

On the third lash, Kail screamed, his voice hoarse and strangled as he fought and failed to hold it back.

The Enforcers laughed.

One took his attention from their prey long enough to turn to Deyn, a cruel smile stretching his face. "Soldier! What do you see?"

Deyn's core filled again with shame as he heard his own voice in the recording say, "Nothing, sir. I see nothing."

Satisfied, the Enforcer turned to Kail and delivered a savage kick to his ribs. Kail crumpled and curled on the ground, finally broken, as the rest of the Enforcers closed in to kick and stomp on him.

Deyn had known it was the last time he would ever see his commander. His friend.

This strangely colored little device was all the evidence that the Secret Enforcers even existed, outside rumor. And now it was all that was left of Kail's existence, as well.

Two drops of water fell on the ground beside the phone. Deyn glanced up to Penance. Her hand came up slowly to cover her mouth as more tears spilled down her cheeks. Her eyes widened with the same sort of horror and grief he'd seen in Kail's, when they had witnessed – they thought – Penance's death. He wondered if Kail had attempted to include the girl herself in the negotiations at the stadium. As commander of the mission and the first through the portal, Kail would have been within his rights to claim a woman from the conquest, though it wasn't like him to splurge on something so expensive. But she had returned for him, and now she grieved him.

The alien girl's breath hitched and she shuddered, precious water pouring from her eyes. Deyn grew more certain that Kail had wanted her. Didn't every soldier wish to be remembered, after Death took him to oblivion? His commander would have spent his credit wisely, then.

Perhaps she'd had to finish a prior commitment, or maybe she had to be negotiated separately. For all he knew, she was here to fetch Kail so he could go bargain with her owner.

In any case, it was too late.

On the tiny screen, the Secret Storm prodded and lashed Kail until he staggered to his feet, and forced him to trudge into the waiting vehicle.

The recording ended.

The soldier and the alien girl knelt together in silence, each lost in thought.
Penance spoke first. "So. They took him off to jail?"

Deyn jerked his head up, startled. Did she just say Jael? How could she have
heard of Jael's capture on her backwater planet?

Penance stood up again, dusting her stealth suit off impatiently. The dust
looked like it might clog up the camouflage effect. "Where is he now, then?"
she whispered. She felt sick, knowing what had happened to him once he'd
come back. Had he done a bad job of the raid? Or... had he done too good and
shown somebody up? She rather suspected the latter. Nobody got that vicious
over a simple screwup. But stealing glory from your boss? That'd do it. This
Emperor ran a big ring, with whole planets of territory, and there could be a
million higher-ups Kail could've ticked off by going out of turn. And here, those
guys were the law.

She turned back the way she'd come. She'd dropped the portal, and while
where it had been still hung warm in the air, she couldn't quite get a handle on
how to get it going again.

"Oh, shh... shoot," she hissed. She was stranded. At least for right this second.
No need to panic. She did it once, she could do it again... But she had nothing
to pin it on but thin air.

Worse, when she even thought about digging down for more power like she'd
done in the garage lab, she started feeling lightheaded again and lost the whole
thread.

Deyn looked at her strangely. He rose to his feet, still staring at her.

She stared right back. "What? I don't speak alien. If you wanna tell me something, we need Kail first."

Deyn nodded slowly, his expression turning hopeful. "*Eyh*, Kail." He pointed to a black structure on the horizon, shaped like two halves of a pyramid. "Jael." He pointed to Penance and mimicked her fighting stance, raising his hands and flexing his fingers like flames, then gestured to himself, then broke off and picked up some things from the ground. He showed her one small alien gadget, but she had no idea what it was.

She did, however, have an idea what he wanted now. "Let me guess. My sparks, your brain? You want to go bust Kail out?" She expressed her guess with her hands as best she could.

He nodded.

Penance burst out laughing.

Deyn looked a little hurt. Then his expression changed. He glanced from her to the empty air where the portal had been and smirked. He stepped back and waved for her to leave.

She blew out a breath. It was going to be a little harder to figure out with an expectant, skeptical audience at her back. Still, she gave it a shot.

Deyn edged away as the girl built up field after field, trying to loop it back in neatly like she had done back in the parking garage lab on Earth, but it was like sorting a sack full of cats by color in the dark.

About eight tries in, she took a break and Deyn approached to show her the little gadget again.

This time, he pointed to the portal she'd tried to create and back to the little device while speaking rapidly. He gestured to indicate a small circle to a large one. Meanwhile the little gadget buzzed silently, with a frequency that reminded her of... the helmet back in the lab.

She smacked her forehead. "Of course! This is the thing Tech said! The focus thingy. This and the transmitter in Kail's helmet are from the first portal. They're still linked up! I just came to where *it* was. And I can use this to make it line up right and get back?"

Deyn grinned... and switched it off.

Penance sucked in a long, horrified breath – and let it out with a sigh. "A'ight," she shrugged. "I got twenty hours before anyone's going to miss me. Let's go jailbreaking."

# Free For All

## PRISON MINE, GREAT DESERT, HYLINEK

"Maybe I'm tired," Penance continued as they approached the prison. "Even if I could get aimed right without the frame for the portal, I couldn't dig up the power I had before. I don't know if I can do it again or not. You might be stuck with me."

She glanced over at Deyn, who ignored her. She might as well be talking to herself. "I can tell when somebody thinks I'm just a weapon, you know. I'm not stupid." She tossed her head back the way they'd come. "And I can tell when somebody's just come off a death wish, too. Suddenly they care a lot about things they dropped over the last mile and have to go back and get them." Zero reaction from Deyn. She felt a little bad about bringing it up anyway.

"I guess even if you understood English, you wouldn't want to talk about that. No judgment from me, though – I been there. Just last year." Absently she rubbed the scars on the inside of her wrist. "The only thing that stopped me then was that I couldn't be sure that I'd get to see my mama again. Stuff was going on and I really needed her, you know?  At least now I know my mama's in heaven and I prayed the prayer with the nice people at the stadium, so I guess I'm signed on and right with Jesus now. Hope so, anyhow. But only a couple nights ago I was wondering, why shouldn't I go on and die? And then I wondered, why doesn't everybody? The world is misery... I guess the universe is too. Why not just die as soon as you know you're safe enough after that?"

"So I started praying, I think, trying to talk to God about it all. And I think I got an answer." She paused. It had been a strange feeling, at the end of the loneliness and the quiet, isolated from everyone and knowing there were still another ten or twelve hours before anyone other than God remembered she existed. But God, out of everyone and everything, hadn't left. And when she'd unloaded every question and hurt and doubt in her mind on Him, something had risen up and quietly, so quietly, answered.

"I was so ready to die. So sick of being alone again. If I didn't know better, I'd think Dr. Janus was trying to break me, leaving me in solitary like that. But once I'd prayed it over, I could stand it again. And now at least I got you to talk to, even if you don't have a clue what I'm saying and we're on our way to probably die like dogs." Penance laughed. Deyn gave her a sidelong glance. That tickled her even more – the guy on the suicide mission giving her the side-eye.

"At least there's a reason. There's something for me to do. I'll be sorry if I don't get that Bible I asked for, so I can see what it's got to say about what to do if I live much longer. I like readin', but I'm bad at it."

She skipped happily a few steps. "I got one book for my shelf already, about first aid. About got the thing memorized now, too." She smiled to herself. "It's good to know there's ways to undo harm done to a body, you know?"

They crested another dune and the prison came back into sight just below them.

The black pyramid structure was much larger than Penance had originally thought. It wasn't just two halves of a pyramid, either. Dozens, maybe a couple hundred smaller half-pyramids surrounded the larger structure, poking up from the ground like shards of wreckage.

"Dang. That ain't just a jail, that's a city," Penance whispered. She rubbed her arms, wrinkling her nose. Radiation pinged the edge of her field, in a pattern that suggested massive drifts of particles. It wasn't a huge problem, though she preferred to work with straight electromagnetic fields. She cast a glance at Deyn. He probably didn't have a natural ability to catch radiation at the boundary of his personal space before it could catch him.

A high wall topped with sharp-looking wire surrounded the prison. Square towers marked the corners. A track rose high in the air above the wall, leading from the split in the core of the prison building to a sorting depot outside, like a slow rollercoaster for the massive, swaying containers that hung from it. Aliens in bulky suits operated machines with long-armed scoops to load vehicles from platforms along the rail's path.

They edged closer to get a better look as a container the size of a train car slid down the rail and jolted to a stop above a platform. The bottom opened and glowing yellowish ore poured out. Penance flinched and strengthened her shield.

The container jerked and jolted again, shaking out the last of the ore, and a limp body fell out and rolled down the glowing mound.

Penance sucked a breath through her teeth. "Radiation poisoning," she whispered. She shook her head in pity. "Bad way to go."

They watched the empty container continue around the loop of track, behind some outbuildings and past another platform before it rose again over the wall and descended into the prison.

Deyn's eyes met Penance's. She shrugged. "Worth a look, ain't it?" she said, and got up to follow him. As they skirted the sorting area, they were able to get close enough that the rail passed directly overhead, since the outbuildings were deserted. Either the mines weren't producing enough for all the platforms to be in use or it was still too early for most of the workers to be out.

Another box rattled along the rail and clanged to a stop above the empty platform. Across the depot, a full container stopped on the first platform to be emptied.

Penance climbed up the platform and looked up inside the empty container, wondering if they could ride it in. It was pretty big up close, about half the size of a shipping container. There were some reinforcing ribs on the inside to brace against, and it wasn't airtight. It had a huge square hole in the ceiling that she could see the rails through. It didn't look comfortable, but it was doable.

Deyn scrambled up with her and dug in his pockets. He brought out a new little gadget and switched it on. It pinged. A lot.

He blanched, but Penance pushed her shield around him until the gadget – some kind of Geiger counter – shut up.

The container rattled, about to start moving again. Penance hopped up, grabbing hold of a rib in the interior and bracing one foot against the hinge of the trapdoor. She reached down, offering a dusty hand up to Deyn. He hesitated just long enough to stuff his gadget back in his pocket and fasten it shut.

He grabbed her hand and she hauled him up. They braced themselves for the long, bone-shaking ride over the wall and down into the prison.

As they swung over the split in the main building of the prison, Penance saw that the split went deeper, into a massive pit surrounded by thick walls, spiraling down to an ominous red glow. Heat rose from it, scorching her skin as they passed over its center and began the descent. The container jerked to a stop and then slowly scraped along a bar that shut the trapdoor underneath them. A mechanism latched the trapdoor together with a solid thud.

Deyn said something that might have been a swear.

"Don't worry about it," Penance whispered. The prickling radiation reminded her of something she'd done before. They clanged to the ground and heard a loud clacking overhead as the container was decoupled from the rail. The container tilted and rushed downhill, banging suddenly to a stop, and Penance let go at last and dropped to the bottom, staggering. Deyn followed.

Deyn looked up at the ceiling of the container, about five feet out of their reach. Penance ignored him and reached for the side of the container, placing both hands against the wall between the ribs.

She searched back in her mind, thinking how to move the energy just beyond her hands, at the outside edge of her electromagnetic field. A little warp and wobble and she could gen up enough heat to melt straight through the side — without burning her own hands off.

Metal melted off the container from the outside, sheering off into slag until she could punch through what was left like tinfoil.

She hopped out and Deyn followed cautiously, avoiding the still-smoking pile of slag. He pointed to it, then inside the container.

"You want me to hide it? Sorry, can't pick up hot metal any more than you can," Penance whispered. "Or do you mean why didn't I melt it inside in the first place? That would've cooked us."

Deyn just stared at her, frustrated.

"Get Kail to ask me," she grinned.

He nodded and gave her a tight smile. "Kail."

They stood amid a cluster of containers, all decoupled from the overhead rails and waiting to be sent for a payload.

Penance dusted off her suit again and pulled the mask back on. The camouflage had just about quit working. She'd have to tell Dr. Janus that his suit he was so proud of had a stupid weakness. His camouflage suit worked perfectly in super clean lab conditions, but it couldn't handle the real world test — it attracted dirt like nobody's business. The dirt covered up all those perfect little receptors and made the whole thing black. Not the worst color for camo in a dark mine, but if she'd wanted a black suit, cheaper ones existed.

Deyn peered around the collection of containers. He must've got his bearings, because he came back and tugged her down so she could watch him draw a map in the dust. It didn't really make sense to her, though.

"I'll just follow you, okay? We stick together."

His hastily sketched plan in the dust didn't make much sense to Deyn, either. He rubbed it out and stood, and the alien girl made it plain that she would stay right by him, like a dusty shadow. He could see why Kail had liked her so much, but she still made him nervous. She was an extremely dangerous plasmic reactor who controlled her emissions by a means he didn't understand. But at least she was friendly and competent. Even though she could destroy them both in an instant, she held a sort of disarming charm and dogged resolve that slowly eased his fear. So long as she coupled that resolve with an awareness of the overarching mission and the flexibility to change the plan to achieve the goal, she'd be an asset rather than a liability.

He glanced back at the pile of melted metal by the container, heat still warping the air around it, and suppressed a shudder. She shielded him from radiation, but she had so much more power than just that at her disposal.

He hoped he'd be able to help send her back to her world. He'd hate to have her angry with him if he couldn't.

The floor rumbled. A container slid toward them and they dodged it. It passed and bumped onto another rail. This one locked onto the bottom of the box, and carried it away downhill through an archway. For lack of a better direction, they followed it and stationed themselves by the opening to peer out.

On the opposite wall, a line of prisoners trudged up from the mines, chained together at the wrists and necks, headed for the barred cells that lined the walls. The container rattled down the rail, gaining speed as it disappeared, deep down into the mining complex.

They had two choices – to continue to follow the rail into the mines and hope to encounter someone who knew of Kail there, or to take a chance on the shift of prisoners that was now trudging up to their cells for their meager rest.

A scuffle near the back of the line drew Deyn's attention. A guard struck a prisoner, sending her to her knees, and grabbed her hair to hold her in place as he waved to the guards further up. They laughed and waved back, leaving him and the prisoner behind as they herded the rest into their cells.

The back of Deyn's neck grew hot as he watched the guard haul his prize up by her hair and drag her to a deep crevice in the wall. He looked down at his clenched fists and straightened his fingers deliberately. Glancing to Penance at his side, he gave the signal to move out.

They crossed the rail and hurried to the secluded crevice while the guards were occupied with the prisoners. Penance pressed against the wall outside as Deyn entered first. He blinked as his eyes adjusted to the dark interior. It went further back than it had first appeared, narrowing and then widening to a closet-sized area, where the prisoner and the guard scuffled. But she moved as though exhaustion weighed on her limbs, and the guard overpowered her easily. The prisoner hit the floor hard, yelping in pain. Neither of them had noticed him yet.

Rage boiled up in Deyn. He didn't bother to issue a challenge to the guard before tackling him. He kneed the other man hard in the groin and punched him on the side of the head before he escaped the sudden attack. The prisoner rolled away as the guard got up and faced Deyn.

The two men circled each other in the small space.

Deyn dodged the guard's first punch and slammed his fist deep into the man's gut, driving him back into the wall. Quickly, before his opponent could catch his breath, Deyn punched him twice more in the head and grabbed his shirt to throw him into the opposite wall.

The guard struck the wall on his neck and fell limp to the floor.

Deyn straightened and turned to the prisoner.

She stood, her hair loosened from its braids to fall heavy around her shoulders, her strong arms and legs left bare by the tattered gray shift she wore. Heavy chains linked the cuffs around her wrists to a metal collar. Her lean, intense face and her dark eyes, endless in their regard, reminded Deyn of a desert feline. An acid scar, two fingers wide, marred her skin from cheek to jaw.

He recognized her by the official description given to all soldiers of the Empire before her capture.

"Jael," he breathed.

Her mouth lifted in a slight smile.

Fresh sweat beaded his forehead as dread swept down his spine. Belatedly, he realized that the leader of the rebels that had persisted for seven years against the Emperor would be a wary and formidable foe, should she deem him unworthy.

A blade appeared in Jael's hand as she shrugged off the appearance of exhaustion.

Deyn dropped to his knees and bowed his head... like an *ibak* awaiting the decision of death or pardon from his superior. Which he was. He had already given the rebel leader his loyalty and life when he left camp weeks ago. The fact that it had taken this long to actually meet her made little difference.

Light flared suddenly and he heard the alien girl speak behind him.

She sounded annoyed.

Jael laughed softly and relaxed, friendly now. "I don't believe we've met, soldier."

Her hand came into view, offering to draw him to his feet.

Deyn froze for a moment before he accepted, raising his wrist. But instead of placing her wrist under his to steady him as an *ibak* would, she grasped his wrist and pulled him up. Her palm crossed his briefly as he stood and looked down at her, surprised that he was taller than she was. She tilted her head up to look at him, warmth and approval in her eyes. He didn't understand. He'd given himself away as *ibak* just a moment ago. He'd broken so many regulations that everywhere he turned, shards of guilt stabbed his heart, and this... incredibly beautiful woman saw worth in him.

Penance poked his shoulder, hard. He glanced over and she jerked her head back the way they'd come.

"Hey, Deyn. Kail?" she said, impatient.

He could see now that the light was from a ring of plasma energy she had wreathed around one hand. Jael looked at the girl with interest, and Penance returned the same.

Concern flitted across Penance's expression, and she opened her free hand to send a gentle wave of static in Jael's direction, which lifted the dust and trapped it at the outside edge of the energy field that now encased the three of them. The cloud of dust hovered, glimmers of radioactive glow apparent within it.

"Thank you," Jael told the girl. "Though I am of the Laevii and the radiation has less effect on me, it is good to be clean of it." She turned to Deyn. "You've broken into this prison in search of the giant who was sentenced for treason?"

"And in search of you," Deyn said. "Supply Officer Kail was my commander. When he was taken, I saw that my loyalty to the Emperor was based on lies. I left my unit to join the rebels, but you had been captured..."

Jael nodded, considering. "And as it happens, both your old loyalty and the loyalty you chose are here." She cocked her head at Penance. "And this alien?"

Deyn shrugged. "She has some business with Kail. We've... made a deal that I will help her return to her planet once he is recovered."

Penance ignored them as she busily dug through the guard's pockets with one hand while holding up the other as a torch. As she didn't look up, even though she was the topic of conversation, Jael looked up at Deyn again. "She has no idea what we're saying."

"Kail will be able to interpret when we find him," Deyn said. "Do you know where he is?"

Jael broke into a feral grin. "I do. The Emperor may own the dirt here, but I now hold the loyalty of the prisoners. I know everything that happens here."

Nonchalantly she braided her hair back. "But as these are now my people, I must take care of them. If you want my help to free one, you will have to help me free them all."

Deyn tensed. "How many?"

"Four hundred and eighty-six." Her eyes unfocused for a moment, and her expression saddened. "Four eighty-five," she corrected. "Not counting your Kail. I could not speak with him on the prison convoy, and we were separated immediately when we arrived. Still, I have heard of him from the others. The guards moved him down through the levels over the past few days, and he became known among us as a great help to the sick. He used his great strength and endurance to take on their burdens in secret, and added a portion of his mining to help fill their quotas, so that they might rest while he worked in their section."

"Nearly five hundred. That's a town."

"Yes."

Deyn thought of how deep the mines must extend to contain so many and despaired.

Penance jumped up from the guard's body, waving a device.

"The key," Jael said. "I hoped to knock him out and get it from him." She looked around at Penance and Deyn, smiling. "Though I wasn't sure I could do it on my own. I'm glad you arrived so I didn't have to." She held out her wrists and Deyn scanned the key against the lock. The cuff fell open and Penance caught it to examine it. She closed her eyes and a moment later, the locks on the other cuff and the collar fell open as well.

Deyn stared at Penance. Suddenly freeing nearly five hundred people didn't seem quite as impossible. "How much range do you have?" he asked, forgetting she couldn't understand. Even if she could, the scope of the mission went well beyond what either of them could have expected. Perhaps she wouldn't want to free everyone when the deal had been to free Kail.

Jael's calm gaze swept over Penance and she nodded once. "She understands. She will help."

Deyn's spine prickled once again. "How do you know?" he whispered.

The rebel leader turned to him. Mischief glimmered in the depths of her eyes and the small smile returned to the corner of her lips. "The God of Truth has gifted me."

It wasn't possible to communicate the finer points of a plan, but Jael seemed satisfied that Penance would gladly unlock everything they came across on the way to get Kail. Beyond that, the prisoners would have to fight to free themselves.

The alien girl had one question for Jael before they set off. She indicated the back of her right shoulder and repeated an alien word, then gestured toward the opening of the crevice. The back of the shoulder was where slave girls were marked for sale.

"I don't know that word," Jael said. "I'll have to see the mark. Is it yours as well?"

Penance tugged at the neck of her suit, and then turned to stare pointedly at Deyn.

"Deyn, you should guard the entrance," Jael said, and he turned immediately to the opening of the crevice, inexplicably happy to serve.

A rustle of fabric, and then Jael answered. "I am not certain if any with this mark are here, but if I find any, I will protect them. What planet are they from?"

The alien girl didn't understand, so Deyn answered for her. "They call it Earth."

"Earth," Penance affirmed. Fabric rustled as she covered herself again.

Penance concealed her face and crept outside while Deyn and Jael peered from the entry of the crevice. The guards locked the prisoners from Jael's shift into cells carved into the rock above them, and below, another line of prisoners and guards approached. "This next shift will have one of my generals," Jael whispered. "They thought that by separating us, they would weaken us. But they have instead caused our reach to be greater throughout the mine."

"We will have to move quickly once Penance releases the prisoners," Deyn said. "The further we get before the alarm is sounded, the better off we'll be."

"Don't worry," Jael said with a confident nod. "My people will know what to do."

As the prisoners marched down the path near the crevice, Penance's grip tightened on the key. Her fingers twitched in a pattern as though she counted something complex, and her head listed dreamily to the side. Abruptly, she snapped to attention and flung out one hand.

Simultaneously, collars and cuffs sprang open down the line of prisoners and fell, heavy chains thudding to the ground. In the space of a heartbeat, chains turned to weapons as the strongest turned on the guards and wrestled keys from them as well.

Jael emerged from the crevice and pointed to the cells containing her shift. Former prisoners grabbed keys and ran back uphill to the cells. Bullets spattered the ground at their feet. Penance swept up a massive cloud of glimmering radioactive dust from the rebels and set it spinning overhead, collecting more dust as it went. The dust gave them cover, blinding and choking the sentries atop the cells.

"Jael!" A grim-faced older man tossed her a weapon taken from the guard. She caught the heavy-looking firearm one-handed and sheathed her shiv at her side.

She flashed the man a smile. "Thank you, General. These are Deyn and Penance, allies gifted us from the God."

A container rattled down the rail toward them and Jael leaped to grab hold of the side to ride it down. "Come, we will open the path! The rest of you, delay the alarm!"

Deyn and Penance followed her lead, along with the general and a few others. The rest of the prisoners joined those broken out of the cells, who now struggled to overpower the rest of the guards on the top level.

The cart raced down the track, slowing as it reached the curve to the next level down. Jael leveled her weapon at the first guard and fired one-handed, taking him down. On the other side, Penance leaped off and tackled a guard. She disarmed him expertly, tossing his weapon to Deyn. He grabbed it out of the air, looping one arm through the handhold to steady the gun.

The cart picked up speed and Penance sprinted to catch up. More guards appeared behind her, but Deyn fired rapidly on them, taking them down with precision. The cart picked up speed and barreled ahead. Penance caught up and Jael's general grabbed her hand, pulling her back on.

As they raced down the rail, they passed a group of chained women, who had stopped sorting ore to stare at the outbreak of the revolt. Penance released a burst of energy, matching the new key she had taken. Chains dropped from the women, and they left their work and rushed to the bodies of the guards to get keys for the other prisoners.

Deyn realized that the keys must have different frequencies for each level to prevent a mass breakout. They'd have to take out guards and retrieve keys on every level. That would slow them down.

"How many levels?" he shouted to Jael.

"Six more! Your friend is on the seventh!"

The general looked from Jael to Deyn in disbelief. "You're rescuing someone from the execution level?"

Deyn turned to Jael, shock and betrayal in his eyes. She shook her head at him. "Don't hope! But have faith that you did not come for nothing!"

The alarm sounded while they dispatched soldiers on the third level. The prisoners – Jael's people – had done well in delaying the alarm as long as they had. Deyn gritted his teeth and shot another guard, and jumped off to retrieve his key. He tossed it to Penance, who quickly analyzed and copied the energy to blast a wave to the electronic locks.

By the fifth level, Penance seemed ill. Her labored breath and wide staring eyes worried Deyn, and so did the way the cloud of radioactive dust wobbled and drifted behind them. He hoped her protective shield against the radiation wasn't faltering. Her hand trembled as she reached to catch the next key and she dropped it.

She lunged to grab the key and fell off the cart. She rolled to absorb the shock of the fall, her blackened suit ripping against the sharp gravel. A guard took aim at her, and Jael shot him before Deyn could level his own weapon. Behind them, the metal gate clanged shut. Deyn and Jael jumped off the cart and ran to her. Prisoners shuffled, staring in awe.

Penance crawled to the key, and chains began falling. Deyn reached her first and helped her stand. She wobbled and fell against him. Tears streamed from her eyes. She rubbed them away with the back of her hand and stood, lifting her chin proudly though she still trembled.

"Penance *ip* Earth!" Jael called. "Only two more!" She held up two fingers and pointed down the rail before cupping her hands around Penance's face, wiping the tears more gently than the alien girl had done. "You are doing very well." She turned to the prisoners who had gathered around, unable to get through the gate. "Penance sacrifices much for you, my people!" she shouted. "Her mercy for my people will lead us to freedom!"

The prisoners responded, cheering until the roar of the crowd echoed back from the ceiling.

Penance sniffled and grinned, but whatever she said was drowned out.

They parted as Jael steered her through them, following the rail. Deyn brought up the rear.

Ahead, the mechanism to shut the gate had been released, but the general and a couple of his men had jammed the cart in the gateway and the gate was held open. They exchanged shots with the guards through the gaps.

Deyn joined the men, taking out guard after guard with steady, precise aim. Penance returned with a fury to sling a cloud of radioactive dust to choke the guards. And everywhere Jael went, rebels and prisoners alike gained strength, while the guards faltered in confusion.

The small team of rebels and the prisoners of the fifth floor broke in to free the sixth. But now a battle raged behind them at the closed fifth gate. The prisoners fought to barricade the area against the guards, who rallied and struggled to recapture what was left of the prison population.

They had nowhere to go but the completion of their mission.

The entry to the final level was not a gate. Instead, a large metal door set into a sheer stone wall blocked their way, with a keypad in easy reach on the face of the door. Deyn's fingers danced over the screen as he worked his way through the security protocols. The immense door swung out, and Jael and Penance descended the stairs into darkness as Deyn brought up the rear.

After the noise of battle, this level held an eerie silence – and no guards.

# Death's Door

## SEVENTH LEVEL, PRISON MINES, HYLINEK

Complete darkness greeted them inside the seventh level. The light from the doorway faded after a few steps in. The silence pressed thickly on all sides, uninterrupted except for the echo of their own footsteps. The three of them drew together, facing out to peer into the nothingness. Penance shook her head and motioned Deyn and Jael behind her. The alien girl stepped forward and held her arms to either side, generating bright, blueish plasma flames to circle her wrists. The eerie light didn't reach to the walls, and Penance pushed more energy to wreathe her body in flame.

"She offers herself as a target to enemies," Jael said.

"How do you know what she does?" Deyn whispered.

The rebel leader grinned. "We have the weapons, and she has the light. She will strip the cover of darkness from our enemies, and we will shoot them."

Now, crackling plasma enveloped Penance so that she looked like a pillar of flame herself, too bright to look at directly. She lit the cavernous room from wall to wall, bathing it in light as Deyn and Jael followed at a little distance.

They found no enemies.

Suddenly, Penance's light dimmed as she cried out and pointed - Kail's limp body, hung from cuffs stapled into the wall.

Deyn stumbled to a halt beside Jael, stricken. Kail – his commander, his friend – was dead? "No," he whispered. He fumbled for his recording device. This would be the last he saw of his friend. He couldn't forget to document the savagery of the Emperor's rule.

Penance dashed up to the dead body and tried to climb up to it, swiping at the cuffs. She fell, unable to reach. Her fingers twitched as they had when she had unlocked the prisoners' chains earlier. When she failed to unlock them using any of the key frequencies she had learned, she screamed in frustration and punched the wall with both hands, on either side of Kail's feet.

Deyn watched in shock as heat warped under the wall and Penance ripped out two thick cables, electrical lines that powered the cuffs. The alien girl yelped in pain and dropped the cables, her torn gloves exposing bloody knuckles. She blew impatiently on her palms before grabbing the hot cables again. Hauling back, she ripped them out of the wall, section by section, leading up to the cuffs and snapping them free. Static crackled and popped frantically as the giant's body fell and landed on top of her, knocking her breathless on the floor.

She shoved him off and rolled him onto his back. Her bloodied fingers pressed his wrists and throat, finding no pulse.

"It is good that she took his body down," Jael said slowly. "He should be interred properly. But what is she doing?"

Penance straightened the dead man's head and neck and pinched the nose shut. Now she took a deep breath and covered Kail's mouth with her own.

"Hrk!" Sudden bile rose in Deyn's throat and he swallowed with difficulty. The alien girl had broken the taboo against touching a dead body - disgusting enough but necessary — but what she did now revolted him.

Jael approached her, hands held out. "He's dead, little sister. Let him go." But Penance ignored the sympathetic warmth of her voice and continued, only straightening to place her hands on Kail's chest and press rhythmically. As if she could will Kail's heart to beat again.

Other prisoners, women and the injured on makeshift stretchers, filtered into the room as news spread that there were no guards inside. They stopped and stared as the alien girl tried to wake the dead giant.

"Penance *ip* Earth," Jael said firmly. "Let him go. We must leave, we have no time to spend on the dead." She looked around at the other people who had come seeking refuge enough to tend their wounded. Her gaze traveled to the grates in the floor. "This place is not safe."

Penance waved Jael back, staring intensely at Kail's inert body. She stripped off the gloves of her camouflage suit and rubbed her hands together, generating sparks.

The alien girl bowed her head and whispered something in her language, as though she spoke to someone no one else could see. With a sudden shout, she slammed her hands down on Kail's chest.

His body lurched with electricity.

Jael backed away, her eyes wide.

Kail coughed.

"Death defeated," Jael whispered, awestruck.

Deyn rushed to Kail and dropped to his knees. It was true – his friend was breathing. His heart beat again! He threw his arms around Penance, forgetting that she was female and he was *ibak*. She laughed, out of breath, and he released her to let her breathe. He didn't even have words to express how incredible it was. There had been no hope, only emptiness and failure, and now – Death's ruling had been overturned!

Jael spoke, her voice low with awe. "I am seeing prophecy fulfilled. I thought I would not see it in my lifetime." She smiled radiantly. "Our freedom is at hand!"

Shouts at the entrance of the execution level drew their attention. The prison guards rallied and beat back the army of prisoners, and now the battle raged just outside the immense door. Slowly, the guards forced a retreat inside the execution level.

A wave of prisoners crowded into the room, bringing fresh injured. Jael gasped, her hope extinguished as quickly as it had come. "No! Get out! They mean to gas us!"

But there was nowhere to go.

High on the wall where Kail had hung, a series of large vents squealed shut. Deyn hadn't realized that fresh air had been blowing on them from it until it ceased.

But it hadn't shut off entirely. Clean, cool air blew through the holes that Penance had punched through the metal wall.

His commander still lay unconscious. Jael was at a loss. The people panicked as the large door at the entrance inexorably closed. Once it shut, poison would rise from the grates. Deyn stood, tugging Penance up with him, and pointed her to the wall. He pulled his portal focus from his pocket and began setting it up. "Jael!" he shouted. "There is an air shaft on the other side of the wall. We will climb it."

Jael turned to him, then held her hands to feel the slight breeze coming from the small holes in the wall. "How can we get through the wall?"

Deyn jabbed a finger in Penance's direction. "That girl is a plasmic reactor. She needs fuel for opening portals. She can dissolve the metal at the nuclear level and use the energy to return to her planet. Even so, she will not be able to hold the portal for more than a few moments."

Jael's brow furrowed as she looked from Penance, to the wall, and back to Deyn again. After a moment she nodded. "I trust you. I will organize the people."

Deyn switched on the portal focus and Penance whipped around, sensing it immediately. He set it to project in the air a few feet in front of her. Tentatively she pushed electricity to feed it, but that did nothing. She didn't understand.

Deyn grabbed her left hand and aimed it to the wall, miming a pulling motion, and then took her right hand and thrust it toward the portal.

Penance bowed her head and closed her eyes, becoming still. Deyn backed away and knelt again by Kail. Behind him, Jael had organized the prisoners into groups. The people knelt on the floor, arranging their chains in a line in front of them. They linked the chains together by the cuffs, forming lengths to assist in the climb.

The door clanged shut.

The room fell into complete darkness.

Then... light.

Penance stood wreathed in pale blue plasma energy.

Wind rushed from where the wall had stood.

A ball of plasma emerged from the air where Deyn had aimed the focus device. It expanded rapidly, becoming a spinning loop of brilliant light that left afterimages in their light-starved eyes. A second rush of clean air and light poured through the portal.

Kail was too heavy to carry any distance, much less attempt to haul up an air shaft.

Penance opened her eyes and gasped, her expression completely shocked. Deyn smiled slightly, amused at her surprise. He had known that she could do it. He also knew that with no frame or stabilizers, it would disappear soon.

He tapped her elbow. "Take Kail!" he shouted. He threw one of Kail's arms across his shoulders and staggered up. Penance ducked under the other arm and bore the weight – she was a great deal stronger than she looked. Deyn shoved them through the portal and they disappeared.

The portal faded, and he could feel the vibrations of rusty gears grinding in the floor beneath his feet, to open the vents that contained the deadly gas.

Jael caught his arm and tugged him to join the rest of the people, who were already climbing the air shaft.

"They will be fine," she said. "And when they return, we shall have our victory and our freedom."

# Busted

## SERIOUS TROUBLE, PLANETARY JUSTICE HEADQUARTERS, EARTH

Penance fell, weightless through an infinity of space between one heartbeat and the next. She clutched Kail's unconscious body, terrified that he'd drift from her.

Not after she'd gone through so much to get to him.

Much more than she'd bargained for, when she'd thought she could just pop back to Earth before anyone noticed she'd gone missing.

A moment later she lurched through the portal and his weight returned, all at once on top of her. She collapsed.

"Oof!" How many times was her breath going to get knocked out today? She'd thought she had it tough before but she'd never worked so hard in her life as she had in the past... how long had it been?

She crawled out from under Kail's limp body and lifted her head.

A sleek pair of cream-colored stiletto heels tapped in front of her face.

Long enough to be missed.

As her eyes rose, her heart sank. Penance took in the impeccable cream-colored suit, the perfectly manicured nails, and the precise cascades of dark curls. And finally, Tech's lovely, expressionless face, as cold as if it was carved out of marble.

Dr. Janus stood behind Tech, and he had all the expression she did not. His face turned purple with rage.

"You're filthy," Tech said. "Dr. Janus, take Penance to decontamination."

Janus turned and stalked away as Penance staggered up from the floor. "But Kail needs..."

Tech gestured sharply. "Go. I will assess and treat his injuries."

Penance nodded and hurried to catch up to Janus. He waited by the hidden door to the corridor.

"Don't touch anything," he snapped.

Stung, Penance drew back. Tears pricked her eyes. She lifted her chin and marched through, trying to make her face as still and dispassionate as Tech's. She failed.

Janus strode down a corridor Penance hadn't been down before. Forcing her unsteady legs to a jog, she followed as he led her to a small locker room. She hung back at the door, instinctively afraid to be in a small space with him. "Dr. Janus?" she whispered.

Impatiently, he grabbed her arm and yanked her inside. Penance dropped her gaze to the floor and shuffled over to flatten herself against the wall as unobtrusively as possible.

The doctor wrenched open a locker and threw a pile of baggy gray clothes from it on the counter before he pointed her to the end of the room. There, a clear glass door opened to a stall with jets on the walls and ceiling. To Penance's eyes, it looked like a sleek, upscale version of a prison delousing station.

Penance hung her head. "But what about..." Her voice came out as a whisper.

"The decontamination unit is on a timer," Janus interrupted, anger coloring his tone. "Go through the full cycle, get dressed and report back to me. Your clothes – *my* experimental camouflage – are now not only garbage, but potentially radioactive garbage. Dispose of them in this container." He pointed to a trash can with a hazmat symbol on it.

The doctor opened a cabinet beside the glass door and decoupled a large container of liquid soap from a tube inside, and then hauled out a heavy jug of solution from a lower locker to replace it. He grabbed a pair of rubber gloves and put them on before unscrewing the lid of the jug, releasing a sharp chemical smell. After he coupled the jug to the tube and turned a red dial as far as it would go, he turned to scowl at Penance. "Well?" He waved impatiently at her.

Reflexively, she clutched her clothes.

He made a disgusted sound and slammed out of the locker room.

Penance flinched as the door banged shut.

*Better not keep him waiting*, she thought. She stripped and stepped in the shower.

Shivering as she stood, she wondered how to turn it on, and then a sensor switched on somewhere. The jets blasted on a split second later.

"Ugh!" She staggered and nearly fell. The stuff Janus had put in the water was brutal. It seared and stung her fresh scrapes and cuts from battling through the alien prison, and stank of chemicals she didn't even have a name for. Clapping one hand over her mouth, she held in a scream – she couldn't risk breathing the fumes. A boiling hot stream struck near her eye and she stumbled back. Her nails scrabbled against the wall as she tried to get her face out of it to breathe. Her lungs and throat burned.

It was far, far worse than delousing.

This couldn't be meant for humans. It was punishment, not decontamination. She was no stranger to this sort of thing, but that it would happen to her here shocked her. She had really stepped in it with Janus, and probably Tech, too.

It had been a mistake to believe that she was safe here.

Blindly, she ran her free hand along the wall where the door ought to be and discovered too late that there was no handle on the inside. She banged on the door but trying to punch through made her slip. She couldn't sense any electrical means of opening it, either. Whether it was a mechanical lock or if she was too disoriented by the jets and burning chemicals to think, she couldn't tell. There was no way out but to grit her teeth and wait until the solution ran out.

At last, the jets stopped and the latch clicked open.

She fell into the locker room, gagging and coughing until tears streamed from her eyes. Too battered to stand, she crawled away from the steam that poured out the door. She huddled in a corner and shuddered convulsively.

At least she was in private.

Penance coughed and spat on the floor. "Freaking napalm car wash." Her throat rasped.

A minute later, her shudders quieted to shivering and she remembered the clothes on the counter. She dressed, glad that the baggy gray shorts had a drawstring. Even tied as tightly as the drawstring would go, they still hung loose around her hips. The shirt was big enough that she could blot her face and soak up some of the solution from her hair with the hem. She tied the wet edge out of the way on her hip and hurried out to the corridor. She had to get to Kail and do something to fix this so they wouldn't take her mistakes out on him. He was half-dead already – there was no way he'd survive any more than what he'd already been through.

Penance lost her balance and fell against the wall. She could have sworn she was going straight, but the floor seemed to have pitched under her. She couldn't remember the last time she'd been so tired. Shaking her head, she squared up her stance to rock solid, and set off at a jog. She crashed into the wall again. "Oh, for crying out loud," she muttered. This time, she braced one hand against the wall as she ran. That worked pretty well, except that her hands were still bleeding and streaked the wall a bit. Tech's office ought to be close, and then across from it would be the hidden door and the damp little hall leading to the parking garage.

Penance rounded the last corner and stopped short.

Three burly masked men suited up for combat and carrying boxes of files came out of Tech's office. "That's her!" one shouted, his voice muffled by the mask. They dropped the boxes and reached for their guns.

Even disoriented and tired, Penance knew exactly which trick to pull out of her repertoire. She generated her own personal version of the plasma shield that had been used in the stadium raid and encased herself.

All three of the men opened fire on her.

The bullets struck the shield and splattered harmlessly. At every impact, the shield generated a bolt of electricity that shot back to Penance, the stabilizing center. Usually, energy like this slipped around the insulating oils on her skin and grounded harmlessly – but not this time.

Penance screamed in pain as the bolts struck her raw exposed skin. She couldn't hold the field for more than a couple seconds before she collapsed. The thugs kept firing, but the bullets whistled over her since the thugs aimed where her center mass used to be. From the floor, she slung a heavy magnetic field at them to throw off their aim as she made her escape, back around the corridor she came from and into the first doorway she found.

It was a supply closet. She braced her feet and hands on opposite walls and climbed up, around the top shelf and kicked through the ceiling. Finding the floor joists, she squeezed between them to crawl in the space between the ceiling and floor. Below, the thugs shouted, and one opened the closet door and emptied a clip. As she crushed through the insulation between the floor joists, she followed the soft hum of the wiring. Minuscule threads of fiberglass flayed her skin as she snake-wriggled her way to the next crossbeam and punched down, hoping she was right.

She fell through the drop ceiling of the secret hallway, crashing to the floor right beside the huge power supply. *Oh, good*, she thought. They'd have a time following her through there. She looked over at the secret doorway. Maybe it'd be good to block that off, too.

Penance couldn't stand yet – the shakes had returned, and her balance had not. It was all she could do to crawl to the maintenance junk in the hall and drag back an aluminum ladder to brace across the doorway. It would have to do. At least it'd clatter and give some warning if the thugs came through there. She staggered upright and stumbled toward the partitioned area where Kail and Tech were.

"Tech?" she called, and had to stop and cough. "Tech, we have to get out of here. There's guys with guns, came out of your office across the hall…"

"Your friend here is too heavy to carry anywhere," Tech replied as Penance came around the partition. She stopped in her tracks, shocked at the mess.

Broken monitors and equipment littered the floor with shards of glass and plastic. The portal frame had come loose from the wall and dangled by a cord. Strangest of all, half of the black van was missing. It was cut wide open, the edges melted and warped weirdly away from the rest.

Had she done that? When she left through the portal? Or when she'd come back?

Barefoot, she picked her way through the debris to where Tech knelt with Kail. The impassive woman had taken good care of him while Penance was gone, covering him with a dust sheet taken from some equipment. A ransacked first aid kit lay open beside him. Tech had already bandaged the worst of the giant alien's cuts and had even started a drip to rehydrate him, but now she prepared to attach electrodes to his head from a cord on her cell phone.

"Hey, what are you doing?" Penance asked, alarmed. "We don't have time! Those guys could bust in and shoot us any minute!"

Tech gave her a level look. "Shall we leave him here while we escape?"

"No!" Penance dashed over, not caring what she stepped on anymore, and skidded down to pull Kail's head protectively in her lap.

"Why not?" Tech asked, winding the cord of electrodes back into the pocket on her phone. "Just a few weeks ago he was an enemy invader."

"He's not anymore. They… they threw him away."

Tech stared at her for a long moment, her face blank. Then her nose wrinkled. "You stink. What did you wash in?"

"I dunno. Decontamination soap? Dr. Janus swapped out the regular soap for this stuff." Penance shuddered. "I feel kinda sick." Her senses blurred strangely. Janus had gotten her, all right. She never would have suspected that he could punish her so harshly. Somewhere in the back of her mind, another suspicion formed. It was terribly convenient of her to be beaten half to death before the hitmen arrived.

Tech blinked, her face blanking entirely again. *That's weird to watch*, Penance thought. *Is she... taking a break inside her skull to put things away?* "Um, Tech? Why are you so calm about the thugs with guns rampaging through your secret office?"

Tech held up a hand, listening. "The men you saw are not following you here. They're leaving."

*Leaving? Why would they leave?* Penace wondered. *They have us on the ropes. It's so hard to* think *right now... I just want to sleep.*

"Why did you go through the portal?" Tech was back.

Penance cocked her head. Why had she?

At the time, she'd been angry at Tech for not seeing what was in front of her face. For not believing her. For leaving her alone in her room and not caring about her at all. And then she'd seen those videos of Kail trying to go back for her. She blushed scarlet. She couldn't admit that she'd run off, at least partly, because she'd *wanted* to be missed.

"I... I needed proof," she said. The excuses sounded flimsy in her ears but she kept going. "You've been running around trying to figure out who the buyer is and if they're coming back and I already found all that out and wrote it in the report. I spent hours writing that thing. But my word wasn't good enough so I brought you the guy who can tell you himself." She looked down at Kail, his head and shoulders propped up on her lap. He still breathed. The raspy spongy noise in his lungs had mostly cleared up. "He's not in great shape right now but when he wakes up, he can tell you what he told me."

Tech looked at Penance as though it was the first time she really saw her. "I... I read the job application you asked Dr. Janus to let you fill out."

It was Penance's turn to stare. "That ain't how that went down at all. He said I had to write that. Then you were too busy, so I wrote everything I found out from talking to the hostages, and everything Kail told me about the Emperor and the invasion coming." She gestured to Kail. "I reckon they didn't like him acting uppity. They threw him in jail and nearly killed him." She shrugged. "I didn't kidnap him. They threw him away first."

Penance stroked Kail's close-cropped hair absently, bitterly recalling how she'd followed Dr. Janus and simply done what he said, ever since she'd arrived. "The only thing I've ever asked Dr. Janus for was more paper to write my report on. And a Bible."

"A... Bible?" Behind her eyes, Tech busily put that information away, too. Then she shook her head. "I was already acting on the possibility of another invasion. The portal I constructed scrambled transmissions from the planet that sent the first raid." She pointed to the partially melted wreck of the old portal. "This array blocked them from sending more and recorded their attempts as evidence for the Interplanetary Council. I never intended it to withstand the amount of power necessary for a functioning portal for any length of time."

Tech fixed her unsettling stare on Penance again. "Incidentally, you accessed nuclear energy to create sufficient power to do it at all. You are not permitted to do that again."

She stood and briskly dusted off her skirt. "Your hypothesis is consistent with the pattern of attacks. A larger, more organized force attempted to land shortly after his raid, but I had already installed the interference mechanism." Glancing up, a slight scowl passed over her face, and she tapped twice behind her ear. "We will need to move soon."

Sleepily, Penance let the meaning of Tech's words filter slowly in as she cradled Kail on her lap. Sudden sick horror filled her. The ruined portal, nothing but garbage tacked on the wall now, was her fault. Nothing stopped a new alien invasion. "I... I'm sorry. I didn't know..."

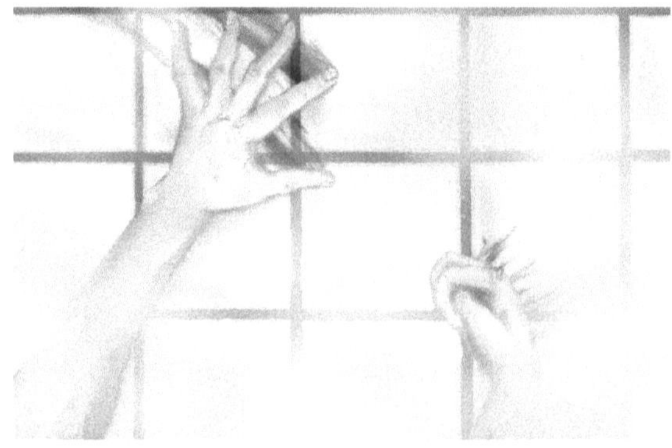

# Salvage Operation

## PLANETARY JUSTICE HEADQUARTERS, UNITED STATES OF AMERICA, EARTH

Kail ached all over, inside and out. His lungs, his ribs, his throat - all filled with jagged edges. The slightest motion of his head set it throbbing. And he was cold, though it seemed like there was at least a sheet over him. A burial sheet?

*No, traitors don't get burials.*

There were voices, feminine, softly speaking over him. He drifted sleepily, recognizing one. The alien girl. If Death wanted to take him by to meet his enemies again, he was glad she was the first. He'd liked her. She was so little and fiery.

And surprisingly gentle in this dream. He didn't want to open his eyes and confirm it, because that might wake him up to the torture chamber again, but he was fairly certain that he rested partially on her lap. Or her ghost's lap. Occasionally her fingertips stroked the stubble on his jaw or brushed lightly through his hair.

He began to awaken and struggled to hold on to the dream. It was the most pleasant hallucination he'd had since being arrested, beaten, questioned, beaten again. Whatever horror his mind shielded him from now, he didn't want to find out.

The alien girl... Penance, that was her name... spoke, distressed. Her hands cradled his head protectively. He thought back over her words, gathering them in his mind to translate.

"I didn't kidnap him. They threw him away first." Connotation of garbage. Defensive tone. She meant him. They had treated him like trash, and this upset her.

It was nice that she cared, though he didn't understand what it had to do with her. She stroked his face again and he relaxed, amused that his mind had chosen such an odd dream.

They continued talking, and though he preferred to drift along with the sweet, warming hallucination of being petted, he picked up a few words.

Portal.

Interplanetary Council.

What if he wasn't hallucinating?

*That* thought was humiliating.

The idea that the alien girl who'd rejected him looked on him with pity – worse, *touched* him out of pity....

Kail abruptly found a scrap of pride that hadn't been eradicated by his conditioning. *Pity is for the dead, but if I'm alive...*

The cold solid floor under him, the soft warmth of the alien girl's body behind him, and the smell of a frightening mixture of harsh chemicals - and something else that he ought to be able to place - convinced him.

He couldn't suppress a groan as he woke.

This was not the torture chamber. The gray and white room looked like nowhere he'd seen on Hylinek. The alien woman in front of him appeared slightly older than Penance. Her voice had spoken of the Interplanetary Council with such a calm, authoritative tone. Her expression did not, at least, betray pity. Or anything else. He shifted, and something sharp embedded in the skin of his arm moved. A metal needle directed a tube of clear liquid from a nearly empty bag into his veins. The woman pulled the needle out smoothly and taped a small ball of fluff on the wound it left.

Penance's voice whispered behind him, hesitant.

Kail struggled to sit up off her lap and away from her pity.  He sorted and translated her words: "Um, hi. How you feeling?"

He blinked her face into focus as the room settled from whirling around him. After a moment, he dredged up the words he wanted.

"Kill me."

She huffed. "You're welcome? I just went through probably literal actual hell to go fetch you and save your life and now you don't want to live? What is wrong with you?"

"Many things," he said wryly, thinking of his injuries. "I did not ask you to... anything. If you want to do me a favor, you can give me a merciful and quick death."

She folded her arms. "Not happening. I stuck my neck way out for you. You ain't gonna die and dodge out of it."

He shook his head in disgust. The motion was not a good idea, as it set the room spinning and his head throbbing again. He stopped and took several deep breaths before he could move again.

Penance edged away from him, looking miserable. The chemical smell went with her, and he noticed her red and raw skin, beginning to blister. And without the chemical smell confusing him, he finally identified the other smell. "Do you store explosives here?" he asked, his voice low and cautious. He caught sight of his own upper body armor and helmet that had been left behind in the stadium, and moved to reclaim them. The vest fitted loosely – he had lost a lot of condition in the mines. He readjusted the straps, his fingers clumsier than they ought to be.

The other woman answered. "Not precisely. The support structures are impregnated with explosives in case we need to destroy the building and the sensitive information contained here, but the password to access the initiation sequence is kept secure."

Penance shot the woman a critical look. "You're telling me this building can self-destruct? And it's just a password away? Listen, I've cracked a lot of locks -" She broke off, alert to something Kail couldn't perceive.

A deafening blast rocked the walls and floor.

Kail moved faster than he thought possible of in an instinctive attempt to shield the women from the onslaught of shrapnel. He took the dark-haired woman to the floor but Penance remained standing. She flung her arms wide and threw up a plasma shield around the three of them, similar to the containment field he'd had set up around the stadium. Even a shield as small as this would need stabilizer rods, however. As he watched, energy coalesced at an impact point on the shield and a bolt of energy shot out to lash at Penance.

She screamed, her voice hoarse, choking with pain. The bolt burned through her clothes and seared welts in her skin, racing down, splitting again and again until it grounded from her bare foot. Her outstretched hands convulsed, but the shield did not waver.

More debris hit the plasma shield, and with each impact, lightning lashed Penance. She screamed again and again. Kail's chest ached with the desire to protect her. He couldn't make it stop, either the desire or the attacks, and he couldn't break his eyes away from her agony. She had not acted as his enemy, and now she endured unimaginable pain to shield them. It was worse than seeing her blasted in the stadium. Though he had believed her dead then, he could also believe she had not suffered as she suffered now.

The blasts stopped.

Penance held the field a moment longer and then dropped it. She wobbled and Kail lunged to catch her as she fell.

Her clothes hung from her frail form in scorched shreds, still smoking. Blackened, bloody streaks spread across her skin in elaborate fractals, traveling along the wet streaks of the chemicals that soaked her. Her hair... Kail touched a burned wisp with one finger. In the stadium, her reddish-brown hair had caught the light like new copper, streaked with bronze. Now, half of it had burned nearly to her scalp, and the remaining locks crumbled to ash in his hand.

The ceiling groaned ominously.

"Hurry," the other woman said, her voice completely calm as she bent down to retrieve a book from the floor. "Those are not the only charges set."

Kail gathered up Penance's limp body in his arms and got to his feet to follow her as she strode out. Chunks of concrete and other debris littered the larger, open area, and the huge pillars that held up the ceiling had several large chunks missing. A huge piece of one, already blasted apart, lay in their path.

The woman changed direction, her brisk pace increasing to almost a run. Kail had difficulty keeping up. Though he had the longer stride, his injuries made him weak and slow. They climbed a ramp and came to a large metal door. The bent frame wedged the door tightly shut, and it took both of them to shove it open. They hurried through to a narrow stairwell and climbed.

Behind them, another round of explosions began.

The stairwell shuddered beneath them, but they kept running.

Kail's lungs labored, ready to burst, and his calves burned, but he'd been through worse in training. Not immediately after nearly dying, of course, but he hadn't reached his physical limits yet. He hoped.

At last the woman opened a door that led to fresh air. Without hesitation, she produced a weapon from somewhere in her clothing. She stepped outside and shot a man standing with his own weapon drawn - at a window in the building across the street.

"Don't worry, it's non-lethal," she called back at Kail as she crossed the street and went down an alley, ignoring the explosion behind her as the entire structure collapsed.

He hadn't been concerned about whether her weapon was lethal, but it did confuse him that she knew the man would be there. Of course someone would be guarding the exit to shoot any survivors, but how had she guessed exactly where he would be?

Mentally, Kail stepped back from the pain in his body and pushed back his confusion. He only had to follow. He could do that. He'd drilled countless times as a boy.

A few more alleys and streets later, as sirens began to scream toward the disaster area, she stopped, holding up her hand for Kail to stop as well.

She turned to him, her face still unnaturally calm. She still held the book.

"I am Mariposa Ramirez, Technical Command of Planetary Justice Headquarters, and Acting Justice of Earth. You are Supply Officer Kail *ip ibak* of Hylinek?" she asked.

Kail froze as a sudden, horrible realization swept over him. Penance had been right. They had thrown him away. The Emperor had severed him from military service, formally denounced him for treason, and sentenced him to Death so that his soul would drift for eternity.

He was nothing.

Which made her, by default, superior.

Though she was alien. And the enemy.

But he was nothing. He no longer had a people, a planet, an Emperor to fight on behalf of.

Without a people, what was left of him? Without an identity to anchor him, he could almost feel himself dissolving.

She waited for his answer. He didn't know if he had one to give.

Finally his conditioning won out and he dropped to his knees.

"I...I used to be, Commander," he said, bowing his head. His gaze rested on Penance, still unconscious in his arms.

The girl had bargained for him, he thought. It had gone badly and there was no telling how much debt she carried now. And now she was injured and needed treatment. More expense. He hadn't asked for it, but the idea that she'd considered him worth salvaging sent warmth to his bones. He wanted to prove that she hadn't wasted her efforts on him.

"Please call me Tech," the woman said.

"Yes, Commander Tech," he said automatically.

"Will you consent to questioning under a device to monitor the truthfulness of your responses?"

"Yes, Commander Tech."

She pulled a device from her pocket and unspooled a wire to plug into the end. The other end of the wire split into several strands, each ending in an electrode. He submitted, perfectly still as she fixed them to his head and swiped her thumb across the device's screen.

"Hello? Path. Code Black commencing in six minutes. Interrogation track eight. Alien," she said. A sleepy voice protested, and then spoke in an alarmed tone.

"Oh," Tech said in response. She turned to Kail. "You are not being tortured," she informed him. She spoke to the small screen again. "Is that better?"

The finer range of Kail's hearing had recovered somewhat from the explosion, and now he could hear the other voice. Another female. Were all the men of the Justice's unit eliminated?

"Not really. He's been through a lot and he's relying almost entirely on conditioned responses to avoid panicking. Mostly it's standard military training but some of this is... cult-like... aaaaand he can hear me now."

The female's tone changed. "Hi there," she said. Her tone radiated warmth and reassurance. In spite of himself, he stopped bracing against the expectation of pain from the electrodes. "It's going to be okay. I'm Path, I'm just going to make sure you understand the questions as asked because Tech's a bit lacking in the context and expression department." She laughed a bit at his skepticism. "And I'll be able to tell if you lie, of course."

"I won't lie," Kail said. Penance's life depended upon his trustworthiness.

"Very good. What are you looking at?"

He blushed. "Penance Copper," he mumbled. He shouldn't be staring at her, but he couldn't help it. He wanted her to look at him again, her green eyes alight with teasing mischief. He missed her abrupt, naked honesty and the shocking, flattering error of the way she pronounced his name. And now, he feared that she would never wake. He was stranded on a planet of strangers and she had been, if not a friend, an enemy he had enjoyed fighting.

"Noted. You got this from here, Tech?"

"Yes, Path," Tech said. "Kail, do you pose a threat to the sovereignty of Earth or the wellbeing of its people?"

He barked a laugh. It hurt his ribs.

Before he could answer, or apologize for insolence, she moved on to more questions, firing them so rapidly that he had difficulty keeping up. More than once, he accidentally answered in his native language instead of English.

Abruptly she stopped and he held his breath, anxious that he had failed the test. He feared that she had questioned him with the intent of finding some charge to hold against him, as the interrogators had done when he was arrested.

She detached the electrodes from him and listened to her device. At last she pocketed it and wound the wires up again into a neat ball. She turned to him and smiled slightly. "Your desire to protect Penance has been noted. Please be aware that her safety depends upon the security of this planet and act accordingly."

"Yes, Commander Tech," Kail said obediently, and then wondered when he had said anything about wanting to protect Penance.

He realized that it didn't matter whether he'd said it out loud or not. It was still true.

"We need shelter and resources," Tech said. "You may not have noticed, but there was an attempt made to erase my memory as well as take my life and Penance's. We are all in need of medical treatment. Also, it's nearly dawn and we are too conspicuous to be out in daylight."

She closed her eyes, concentrating. "Medical. Vehicle. Proximity. Improbability. Code Black initiated." She opened her eyes again. "Let's go."

Kail fell in behind her as she set a brisk pace through the city. As he followed Tech through alien territory, Penance lay light and limp in his arms. Tech did well at keeping them away from people. It seemed she had some extra sense of when and where to stop to avoid detection.

Soon the surrounding structures became shorter, the spaces between them wider, and there were areas bare of concrete. They passed through what appeared to be a residential area, rather than industrial.

Commander Tech headed directly for a shelter and rapped on the door. Prudently, Kail positioned himself against the wall beside the door, out of the immediate line of sight, and knelt down.

Footsteps approached from within, and a voice said, "John, if you've forgotten one more thing you're going to be late!"

The solid inner door opened and a woman peered through the mesh outer door. "Oh! Can I help you, ma'am?"

Tech held up her badge. "You are Shandra Mark, emergency medical personnel?"

"Yes, I'm a paramedic, but I'm on leave..." She squinted at the badge.

"Pursuant to the form you signed upon employment, I am requesting your assistance on behalf of Planetary Justice Headquarters for a period not exceeding twenty-four hours. You will be compensated appropriately for your trouble."

"I can't leave my son home alone..."

"Leaving will not be necessary."

The woman caught sight of Kail. Her eyes went straight to Penance, still unconscious. "Oh my. Of course, come in." She unlatched the flimsy mesh door and gasped as Kail rose to his feet. Recovering her composure quickly as the giant alien maneuvered through the small doorway, she led him through a seating room. "These are chemical burns... and electrical? Looks like... lightning? Incredible that she's still alive," the woman murmured as she assessed Penance's condition. "Come this way."

Kail followed her down a hallway to a small room equipped with a trough along the wall and a washstand. The woman flipped a switch set in the wall, bathing the room in light.

"Set her down in the tub so I can wash the rest of that chemical residue off."

Penance remained unconscious even while he lowered her into the trough. He extricated himself from the tiny room with difficulty and made his way back to the first room. A moment later, he heard water running – a lavish amount.

He attempted to stand at attention, but he was so exhausted he trembled.

Tech regarded him soberly. "At ease, soldier."

He sank to the floor and closed his eyes.

# First Aid and Abetting

## CIVILIAN HOME, UNITED STATES OF AMERICA, EARTH

He listened as Tech walked down the hallway to join the woman tending Penance.

"This is one of the worst burn cases I've ever seen. I'll need to call an ambulance..."

"No," Tech interrupted. "Our presence must remain secret. We will accept whatever help you can offer and then we must leave. I personally will contact you when it is safe to disclose your involvement."

A door opened down the hallway and small feet came running toward him.

"Hey, you're that supervillain! Are you here to fight?"

Kail opened one eye to see a small boy aiming a lightweight, brightly colored weapon at him.

"Devon!" the woman shouted from the bathroom, panicked. Water sloshed. "Devon, no!"

Kail raised his hands. "I surrender."

The boy looked disappointed. "Aw, that's no fun. Here, you can have this one, I got another." He offered Kail the little gun.

"I think it's against the rules for me to touch it," Kail said. He nodded toward the bathroom. "She's captured me already."

The little boy took back his gun as his mother came up and grabbed him. "He's all surrendered already, Momma."

She turned him around and shook him by his shoulders. "Devon! You can't just..." She stopped and hugged him. Tears streaked down her face. "I don't even know how to explain it to you."

Kail looked away as the small boy reached up to pat her face. "I'm sorry, Momma," he said, contrite. "What's wrong?"

"He's lucky it was me," Kail said. "Deyn also is accustomed to small children. But the rest of the men in my unit would not have reacted well. They would not play – they would fight for real."

Devon turned to him, eyes wide. "Where are they? Are they hurting people?" And he gripped his toy weapon like he would go now and make them stop.

Kail broke into a grin. The boy had good instincts, but little idea what to do with them. *A fine son who must be his father's pride*, Kail thought. "They are on a different planet. And to fight them you must grow big and strong first. Eat all your dinner every day, even if you don't like it."

The little boy made a disgusted sound. "Everybody says that."

"Because it's true," his mother said. "Go put your toys away and leave the man alone. He's hurt."

She turned to Kail. "We were all watching the game when you and your soldiers crashed it. It was all he talked about for days."

Kail bowed his head. "I'm sorry to have caused distress. I had orders to obtain supplies. I tried to ensure that no one was harmed."

"You look a bit harmed yourself," she said. "Let me get the kit and see what I can do for you." She returned in a moment with a case of equipment and medical supplies, similar to some he'd taken from the stadium. "I thought for sure that girl was a goner, when that beam came down on her like that. I expected to see nothing but a pile of ashes when it was over," she continued. "This is her, though. And I was right. She's the same girl I'd met earlier that day. She was running from somebody then. Must have been somebody pretty scary, since she was brave enough to walk right up to you and offer to kick your butt." Her voice dropped to the barest thread of a whisper. "You wouldn't happen to have heard of a man called Acid, would you?"

He shook his head, mystified. She held his gaze for a few seconds and blew a small sigh. Then she got back to work.

Kail set aside his combat vest, closed his eyes and endured the examination. Her hands were gentle and her manner as practiced as any skilled medic on Hylinek. She shone a light in his eyes, listened to his heart through a device of tubes and a very cold disk at the end, and directed him to breathe in and out.

"You're as jumpy as a cat," she observed. "What kind of accident was it?"

He flinched. "Execution. I was... I was... they... I think I was dead."

The medic stared at his chest. There were two burns he didn't recall – he'd been beaten, but not burned. She measured them against her hands. "That girl... she can make electricity with her hands."

Kail looked again. They did look about the size and shape, if the fingers were closed. "Why would she burn me?"

"She restarted your heart," the woman said. "We have a machine that can do that, it's called a defibrillator. Is this her book?" She pointed to the book Tech had left on the seat. "That's a good edition, I studied that one in college. There's a whole chapter on cardiac arrest and defibrillator use. How does your ribcage feel?"

"Cracked."

"All right, let's bind that up and then we can get you something to eat." She hefted herself to her feet with difficulty.

"Are you ill?" Kail asked, noting her distended stomach. That would explain why she was on leave.

She shook her head. "No, just pregnant."

"What does that mean?"

The paramedic woman stopped and gave him a puzzled look. He had evidently asked something strange. Or possibly inappropriate.

She pointed to her rounded belly. "It means that I'm carrying a baby in here."

Kail covered his face with both hands. "I shouldn't be here," he mumbled. That was not something he was allowed to see. His caste wasn't anywhere near high enough to so much as look on a man's wife during her vulnerable time - a man rich enough to have both a young son on the cusp of training age and another child so soon. Automatically he tallied the fines for breach of conduct in his mind, then stopped as he realized that the fine structure may well be different on another planet. Would it be better to ask now, or just concentrate on surviving, no matter what it would cost later?

The woman patted his shoulder. "You haven't done anything wrong. You'll feel better after some breakfast."

Surprisingly, he did. She brought him into the kitchen, which had a table with three mismatched chairs and a short bench sturdy enough for him to sit on. He was allowed to drink a good amount of water, though he knew not to drink too quickly, and the woman cooked a large pot of something grainy and filling, flavored with a little fat and salt. She called it "grits." He tried not to look longingly at the pot after he'd scraped his bowl clean, but she caught him. "I guess you're big enough you can have a bit more without it being too much. You look like it's been a little while since you've had square meals, so don't eat too fast."

The little boy sat across from him with his own little bowl, kicking his feet under his chair and chattering happily about his dad, who was a firefighter, and his friends, who he'd been playing alien invasion with. And his cousin, who was almost as big as Kail and played football, and did Kail play football? He really liked football.

Kail finished his second bowl, still short of having his fill, but wary of eating too much unfamiliar food after a week of quarter rations in the mines. He got up from the table to go back to the seating room. The woman had returned to tending Penance in the bathroom, and would probably need him to move her again.

Commander Tech sat at a small table with her hair pinned up to the top of her head, removing a panel from the back of her own skull. An array of small tools lay out before her, and she selected one to insert into the opening.

A tiny click, and she winced. "Ah!" She squeezed her eyes shut and moved her jaw, which popped audibly. "Ugh, finally," she said, and replaced the panel.

Kail blinked. This was the most expressiveness he'd seen from her.

She caught sight of Kail and pointed to the panel under her hair. "Brain augmentation," she explained. "There was an EMP blast as well as the explosives that destroyed the building. Fortunately, my skull is also a Faraday cage, and I had warning." She gave him a rueful smile. "I had been concerned that Penance would harm my information processing components, so I had built in additional precautions. But as it turned out, she wasn't the one I needed to be prepared for."

She fell silent, and packed her tools away methodically, seemingly lost in thought.

The splashing in the bathing room ceased, and the woman called Kail to help move Penance out of the tub. "If you can be careful and not strain yourself, I'd appreciate the help," she said, bracing her hand against the wall and hefting up from the floor. Kail eased around the woman and glanced down into the tub. He looked quickly away again.

The paramedic had cut Penance's clothes away for better access to her injuries, and draped a towel over her after draining the water. Covered was not quite the same thing as clothed. Kail knelt and slid his hands gingerly under the girl to lift her out. "Mind your ribs, you really should be resting," the woman fussed.

The attention to his injuries from the child-heavy woman was odd, but nothing the soldier had experienced in his life was nearly as awkward as lifting a naked, unconscious girl out of a tub. He supposed if she'd been conscious, she would be humiliated by this. In his mind, he canceled any debt she might have owed for embarrassing him with her pity. At least he'd been left the rags of his uniform.

As he held the slim alien girl, he counted the tiles on the wall and calculated the dimensions of the room rather than think about what his hands touched as the paramedic maneuvered around him. Once she slipped an oversized shirt over Penance's head and pulled her arms through the sleeves, he could bring himself to look again. The paramedic left to talk to Tech, and he stole a moment to check on the injured girl for himself.

In the bright lighting of the bathroom, he could get a better look at her injuries. Gently, he lifted a strand of hair from across her face and smoothed it back. Bruises and scrapes covered her face. Patches of her hair had burnt short in places. Purple shadows under her eyes contrasted with her death-pale skin. Her delicate eyelids seemed almost transparent, and her eyes moved slightly beneath them as he shifted her position in his arms. He could almost believe he held a ghost.

He'd seen men beaten, shot, and killed, but this filled him with grief. She'd been burned alive, her own strength turned against her in the most vicious way imaginable, and she'd borne it to protect him and Tech. That she was still alive was miraculous.

With great care, he stood and carried her from the room.

He caught the end of a hushed conversation between Tech and the medic. "I've had him thoroughly evaluated," Tech said. "Kail has deep personal convictions regarding the safety of children."

Well, of course he did. He'd had over a hundred little barracks-brothers to help look after, and they only had until they were twelve years old before they were taken away to be made men of. There was time enough ahead of them to face danger and cruelty.

Tech had arranged for them to borrow the paramedic's vehicle, and she and the woman unloaded everything from it and reloaded it with supplies. Kail set Penance down on the soft couch and went to help, but as the sun had now risen to full daylight, Tech sent him back inside.

Young Devon came in, carrying his little pack and some trash from the vehicle, and talked to Kail while he tried to make himself useful indoors. The boy was amazed that alien houses didn't have the same sort of fixtures as his own, and excitedly told Kail in great detail how things were done around the house and showed him how everything worked, from the light switches to the faucets. Once Kail finished working in the kitchen, Devon insisted on showing him an assortment of playthings, including a collection of brightly colored cards for a strategy game.

Devon grabbed Kail's hand and tugged him to the kitchen table to play with them, and was just going into a long and rather inconsistent explanation of the rules when his mother came in.

"Devon, you don't know how to play that. You can't read yet."

"I can too!" Devon said.

"Staring at the words and saying the first thing that comes into your head is not reading."

Kail stifled a laugh. It would be rude to laugh at his tiny host, and besides, it made his ribs ache.

The woman reached to turn on the water in the kitchen sink and stopped, noticing the pile of clean dishes stacked to the side. She turned around, puzzled. The stove sparkled, with no sign of dripped grits. The floor shone. A fresh dishrag hung from the cabinet handle. "The kitchen's clean?"

Tech entered. "That should be everything we need for a good start. I would wait until dark, but if you usually leave the house at ten, it may be less suspicious for us to keep to the same schedule. Once we leave, lay low and pretend you're not here."

Kail retrieved Penance from the couch. Some color had returned to her cheeks, and she wasn't as cold now. Death might not take her after all.

Tech waved him outside with her once she determined it was safe enough, and he brought her into the back of the vehicle and arranged her on a cot they had placed inside.

Tech gave the woman a slip of paper. "If anyone comes looking for us, contact this number. Don't use your home line."

The woman nodded and saw them out the door. Kail heard her murmur as she went back inside, "Come again."

Tech shut the back of the vehicle and climbed into the front seat. Kail settled down beside Penance's still-unconscious body as the commander started the engine and pulled away from their temporary haven. "Keep your head down," she called back to him. "It's going to be a long drive and as few stops as I can get away with. Sleep if you can."

"Yes, Commander," he replied. The familiar motion of the vehicle and Penance's soft, regular breathing by his ear soothed him, and soon he dozed off, dreaming of other missions under another sky.

# Soldier Out of the Desert

## LOCATION: UNDISCLOSED, THE SEQUEL

He heard it again – soft, eerily familiar on this alien planet. Kail opened his eyes and glanced up at the cot where the deputy justice lay. From his sleeping place on the floor, he could see her bandaged fist clenched against the pain.

In the barracks on his home world, it had been kindest to ignore a crying recruit and hope that the bigger soldiers-in-training wouldn't hear. Sometimes a young one required a nudge and a whispered reminder that it was only a dream, or in the later grades, to send him up next to keep watch if he couldn't sleep.

But here, secluded in this out-of-the-way shelter, there was no one to hear. No watch to keep, except reasonable vigilance against native wild animals. The enemy had little chance to discover them, since most of them were a galaxy away. Now Kail aligned with Earth's defenses, and his new commander, Tech, had assured him that she could deal with invaders for the time being.

He had orders to protect the deputy justice, Penance Copper, as she recovered from extensive plasma burns and to brief her on her new assignment as soon as she was ready for light duty.

Crying had not been covered in his briefing.

Abruptly the sound stopped.

Kail tensed.

"I didn't mean to wake you up," Penance said.

"I can look in the medical supplies Commander Tech left," Kail offered. "Though she said that with your unique biology, there isn't much that can safely manage your pain."

"Pain's not the problem. Lying here with nothing to do but think about what a screwup I am, that's what's gonna kill me." Disgust filled her tone.

Kail sat up, grunting as the motion ground into his cracked ribs and his own burnt hands. He avoided looking at her – he had carried her unconscious body to shelter, and it bothered him to think of the volatile powerhouse Penance as fragile and helpless in the wake of the disaster.

He had his own regrets, but the thought that she might wish she hadn't rescued him cut deeply.

"Commander Tech doesn't believe this situation to be a total loss," he said. "We aren't scheduled for termination, and she gave us assignments."

"Scheduled for... what are you talking about? The Justice and his team are the good guys. They don't go around *terminating* people. That's what people like Acid and whoever he's working for do. Auuugh," she struggled to sit up in her cot and thrust out a bandaged arm. "Acid's goons found out I went to the Justice's side and then they did this to me. It was gonna happen sometime, big freakin' deal. So why'd Tech plop us out in the middle of nowhere if she didn't just want us out of the way?"

Kail looked at her out of the corner of his eye. She'd regained some of her defiance, like she had been when she challenged him to leave her planet alone – but still vulnerable. His superior in the chain of command shouldn't be showing him weakness. Politely, he ignored the weakness and focused on the question.

"Commander Tech did tell me why we are here. Are you ready for your briefing on our assignments, Deputy Justice?" He hadn't expected to deliver the briefing in the middle of the night, but with both of them awake, anything was better than tears.

She blew a sigh. "Fine, tell me."

He pulled the folders the commander had given him from under the cot. "This facility was converted into a rehabilitation center several years ago but has gone unused and is not on the records. Since Commander Tech suspects information about your prior location leaked to your enemies, you are to remain here and recover from your injuries until further notice. In addition, your new assignment is to instruct me in Earth customs and other relevant training, and I have been commissioned as your bodyguard as you recover." He added,

"She also recommended I continue training appropriate to a translator." He smiled slightly to himself in the dark, proud to have his favorite skill recognized.

"You can read all that in the dark?"

"No. That's what Commander Tech told me."

"So she wants *me* to teach you about normal human stuff. And here I thought she didn't have a sense of humor." Penance gingerly swung her legs over the side of the cot. "I gotta pee. There a bathroom in this..." she paused and looked around slowly, "Facility?"

Kail nodded toward the doorway across the room, barely visible in the starlight from the windows. He had made a path through the junk that filled the main room to reach it, and then cleared and scrubbed the entire room. After that, he'd been too exhausted to do more than suck down a bottle of water and curl up on the floor beside the cot.

Commander Tech had been appalled at the condition of the facility when they had arrived, but he had insisted he was certified in habitation establishment, and she had been too tired to argue after driving for days away from the epicenter of the disaster. He would do whatever it took to keep that commission and the security it meant for him. When the commander or whoever she sent from headquarters came to evaluate their progress, the place would be improved beyond recognition.

Though right now he could see why Penance thought they had been abandoned. According to Tech, the building had been converted from a large animal shelter, finished with a kitchen, personal care room, and partial upper level as well, but now the damaged interior held nothing but stored junk. The trash-covered floor, interrupted by islands of broken furniture and appliances, provided cover for the small animals that lurked in the deeper recesses, squeaking and scratching. He would deal with them in the morning.

But the structure seemed sound enough, the generously high ceiling allowed him to stand comfortably, and the water ran pure and plentiful from the faucets. Commander Tech had left them with food, clothing, medical supplies and blankets that she had bought piecemeal at stops along the way. This could become a good place. If he had to excavate it first, so be it.

"Aaack!"

Kail leaped up, skidded down the path to the personal care room and slammed through the door to Penance.

"Eek! Out, out, get out getoutgetout!" Penance shoved him back out and shut the door. "Hey – normal human lesson number one, Kail – don't barge in on girls in the bathroom!" she yelled through the door.

It took him a moment to process the words and catch his breath. "What happened? Are you hurt?"

"Nothing happened! I'm fine."

"Then why did you scream?"

"Because there's a mirror in here. Ugh, what happened to my hair?"

"It... burned?" When Penance had been drenched in the chemicals that burned her skin raw, the bio-insulation that shielded her skin from her energy pulses had also been stripped.

That was another reason Commander Tech suspected a leak. Someone had infiltrated their base and sabotaged the deputy justice, rendering her greatest strength into a terrible liability. Tech and Penance could only be certain it wasn't him.

"Hey Kail?" Penance asked, interrupting his thoughts. "Do we have any scissors?"

Dawn came too soon, but Kail was used to interrupted nights and early mornings. He sat up and stretched, and immediately regretted it as his ribs shifted.

He looked down at Penance, the burnt ends of her hair now trimmed off and a few of her bandages gone. Much had already healed new and pink, though he didn't know if the insulating substance produced by her skin had replenished.

His doubts about the future lifted as he chose his breakfast from the cooler. Strange foods, but interesting and clean. They would have to be careful to ration it, of course. Even if he knew where to get more supplies, he doubted he could go anywhere unrecognized. Tech had explained to him that the people of Earth thought he was a new supervillain due to their cover story. On his own planet, he was an oversized freak but mostly unknown. Here, he was the giant who had held a stadium hostage until driven to a stalemate against an average-sized girl whose fists trailed plasma in their wake. *That* whole debacle had been televised, recorded and shown again and again. The paramedic's little boy had said as much.

His gaze traveled over to Penance again. She had first latched onto him as an enemy who could be reasoned with, and after his court-martial and execution for losing to her, she had found a portal to his world and brought him to her planet as a refugee. She had openly defied Commander Tech and defended him, then forced them to accept him.

Kail couldn't comprehend why she would do that for him. What if that had led to them sabotaging her?

First, he would let her sleep. Later, when she woke, he'd work on making the facility livable again. Maybe he could fix some of the equipment. And he'd found a problem with the plumbing – the waste disposal appeared to use drinking-quality water. He'd have to find the reservoirs and reroute the pipes. He hoped he could find some tools amongst the junk.

But for now, he should scout their location. He eased into a shirt from the supplies – though it was the biggest that Tech could readily purchase, it fit snugly. At least it would remind him to not move too suddenly and risk popping the seams - or his cracked ribs. The shorts fit comfortably enough around his waist, though not quite the right length. Finding proper clothing wouldn't matter until the cold season.

He slipped outside and stood still for a moment in the alien atmosphere. Small creatures flicked through the air and emitted musical sounds, tiny animals rustled through the vegetation, and everything blared dozens of shades of vivid green. The sky changed color as the sun rose, the blueness streaked with pink and gold clouds and probably-not-deadly rays of yellow sunlight.

Kail had flattened against the wall of the facility as if all this color concealed a threat. The countryside appeared even more alien than the city had been. At least he could recognize stone and concrete and metal and glass, laid out in rows and curves, roads and structures. This was... chaos. Open space and clumps of vegetation and the solid building behind him, and in front, the tracks of the vehicle they had arrived in, and another small outbuilding, all randomly scattered across the landscape.

Curious, he edged away from the main building and toward the smaller structure. It housed a large piece of equipment, likely some sort of vehicle. At least, it had wheels and looked like it contained the sort of combustion engine favored on this planet.

Beyond that building, a trail led through the open space over a small hill. Nothing interrupted his complete isolation, so he decided to follow the path. As he crested the hill, his nose twitched at the scent of water, even before he saw it.

A large pond, framed with tall, thick green grasses, glinted at the bottom of the hill. He'd never seen so much water. What kept it from soaking into the ground, or evaporating into the atmosphere? Was it toxic? Why so green, and how could green have a smell? Were things living in it? Dangerous things? Edible things?

Another structure – a narrow wooden path led a short way over the water, but stopped without crossing it. It seemed sturdy enough, though he couldn't bring himself to walk very far out on it. He dropped down and crawled the last few yards to look over the end. Insects buzzed around him, flying, crawling, some even skating on the surface of the water.

Lying flat on the dock, Kail could imagine that he lay in the bottom of an enormous bowl, with the water beneath him and the vegetation and tiny wildlife rising up all around him.

"Hey, there you are!" Penance's voice came from behind him. He started to get up but froze as her footsteps vibrated the dock, rapidly approaching. What was she running for?

"Cannonball!" she yelled and leaped over him into the pond.

He jerked back from the wave she created and then lurched forward. "Penance!" he gasped. "What ... where are you?"

She bobbed to the surface a few yards away and wiped her hair from her eyes. She looked up at him and burst out laughing. "What's the matter with you? It's water, not lava." She leaned back and flicked her feet up, splashing him again. "Pretty sure we're too far north for gators, so what are you looking so scared for?"

"What are you doing?" Kail snapped. "I haven't cleared this area. You don't know that it's safe."

She shrugged. "Safe enough. You coming in? I can check how deep it is – bet you can stand on the bottom though, big guy." She raised her arms over her head and disappeared beneath the surface.

"Penance!" Kail roared and lunged for her still-visible fingertips, stopping just short of overbalancing and falling off the dock.

She surfaced again, just out of reach, and gave him a puzzled look. "Hey, supersoldier, can't you swim?"

"I lived my entire life in a desert. There's no water for submerging in," he gritted through his teeth.

"Well. That's no good. Normal human lesson number one, you gotta learn to swim."

"I thought normal human lesson one was 'don't barge in on girls in the bathroom.'"

She made an amused snort. "You're right. Basic Earth survival lesson, then. Look, this pond has green plants and live bugs and frogs and things, so it's not deadly. It's shallow enough that you can touch bottom and small enough that you're the biggest thing that's gonna be in it. Still, it's deep enough that you can learn to float and wide enough that you can swim a few strokes once you learn. Watch me." She flipped over and glided through the water. Her arms and legs propelled her smoothly and quickly to the far side. Then she returned, this time lying on her back as she swam. "Come on."

*Why did she have to be right?* Kail knew water covered the surface of this planet.  And from what she said, this wasn't even very much water compared to what was out there. She offered training that would be considered highly specialized on his own planet, and very practical here. He edged over the side of the dock, flinching at the coldness of the water.

Penance cocked her head at him and he realized he'd done something strange... what, he didn't know. He hoped he wasn't meant to let go of the dock yet, or worse, simply jump in like she had. His feet hadn't touched the bottom yet and he was too tense to lower any further in.

"Usually guys take off their shirts when they swim," she said. "But if you're thinking about your scars, it's no big."

Well, *now* he thought about them.  Penance had caused some of those scars, and he considered them honorable enough as they were gained in battle. Most, however, were inflicted in the most dishonorable way imaginable, during the inquisition, torture, and execution that followed his court-martial and the sham of a trial he had stood on his own planet. She had revived him and brought him here. She had seen something in him worthy of saving. She still did – he knew because she was going to teach him.

He relaxed his grip and lowered into the water – his feet touched the bottom before he was more than shoulder-deep, just as she promised.

"Okay," she said, when he could look at her again. "Whatever you do, do not grab me or you will drown me. Got it?"

He nodded.

"First, you're gonna learn to float on your back. The water will hold you up if you relax and breathe. Don't panic if your ears fill up. You'll be fine as long as your face is out of the water, and I'll hold you up if you dip, 'kay?" She guided him to the middle of the pond and turned him to face away from her. "Remember, if you get scared, all you gotta do is stand up. No flailing. Now lean back and relax."

He flailed.

"Try again. I got you."

After several tries, at last he relaxed enough to allow the water to nearly close up over him, and then her reassuring hands cupped beneath his head. The fear and anger that had gripped him since his trial and near-death eased. His chest rose and he floated, perfectly at peace, beneath the intense blue of the sky. "I could sleep," he sighed.

Behind him, Penance laughed. "Don't sleep. Next you gotta learn to put your face in."

He jerked up, all peace forgotten, and flailed again before regaining his footing. "What?!"

The sun had moved directly above them and his stomach considered trying to turn and eat itself before she allowed a break, satisfied with his progress. He now knew how to float on his back, float on his face, hold his breath and blow bubbles underwater without panicking. He knew to never swim without a buddy. Also, never to drink open water without boiling it first, and that the ocean he had never seen was full of salt and no good for drinking even boiled.

He had also learned that Penance had a habit of leaping from one topic to the next as they came to mind. Frequently these leaps struck him as funny, but he pushed aside his amusement and took the lessons seriously. She taught well, not allowing her own pain to distract her from ensuring his understanding.

Kail hauled himself onto the dock, surprised how much strength it took. As if gravity had drastically intensified in the time he had spent floating. He glanced up to remark on this to Penance.

She stood on the dock, shaking out her hair. Her wet clothes clung to her body, and as she straightened, the curve of her waist and hip transfixed him. The uneven ends of her hair and the welts still evident on her skin did little to disguise her appeal.

Kail swallowed and looked down at the rough boards of the dock, clenching his hands until the warm wave of emotion passed. Commander Tech had granted him many new freedoms, but he didn't have permissions for this. She'd meant for him to guard the girl, not bond to her.

On the way back to the main building, he decided he'd merely experienced an inappropriate emotional reaction to the overwhelming sights and sounds. He would be fine once he became accustomed to all the green and water and weird little animals, and repaid her patient teaching by improving the facility. The sooner he got started, the better.

Penance reached the building ahead of him and turned on a faucet.

"More water?" Kail couldn't believe how commonly she wasted water.

"Yeah, I don't want to go around all day smelling like pond scum," she said, rinsing her hair and then her legs with the hose.

Kail looked away quickly.

"Neither should you," she added, and turned the hose on him.

He yelped and dodged. "Hey! Ugh, think of the waste."

She giggled. "It's well water, it's free. There's lots of water underground. Comes up through there," she pointed at a half-buried concrete cylinder in the ground several yards away – and sprayed him again when he looked.

He made to rush and tackle her, but stopped short and instead pinched the middle of the hose, stopping the flow. With his free hand, he reached around her and turned the faucet off.

Suddenly aware that she was nearly in his arms, he stilled. He inhaled the warm scent of her skin, now clean of the burning chemicals and beginning to gloss again with protective oil. She did smell a little of the greenness of the water, but that smell had already lodged in his mind to mean good things. Peace filled him, as it had when she had taught him to allow the water to hold him.

Leaning close, he studied the glitter of water droplets on her eyelashes and the chopped-short strands of her hair. Green eyes met his, as varied in shade as the vegetation on this alien world. Her lips quirked with a small, secret grin, as if she felt ready to burst with mischief.

He released the hose and she used the remaining pressure to spray him in the face. Spluttering, he backed away and laughed, mostly at himself.

Penance had nearly died in the disaster, just as he had nearly died on his own planet. Of course they would both act strangely. It didn't mean anything.

He needed to remember to not act like a complete fool, and preserve his chance for whatever status they chose to let him earn.

Kail brought the cooler outside so they could sit in the sun and dry while they ate lunch, and she told him the names of the foods and which went together, though she didn't know how to cook much.

"You don't cook?" he asked. "How do you manage supplies and maintain a base?"

Penance shrugged. "This barn is the closest thing to a house I've ever lived in," she gestured to the building, "at least that I remember. Acid took me when I was really young, we never lived anywhere, just slept for the night and moved on. Sheds, warehouses, train cars, caves, hunting trailers we broke into. All I really learned was how to..." she shook herself and broke off. "So yeah, not a lot of staying around long enough to get groceries and cook 'em."

They ate in silence for a while. "So," she said finally, "they teach home ec in the alien military?"

"Early on, I was not considered officer material, so the administration placed me in supplies and requisitions. Then I finally caught up my scores but it was too late to move me, so they made me commander of a supply unit. After that, they discovered an... error in my documentation. I'm actually three years younger than the rest of my class unit, so I had taken the tests three years early the first time. But by then I already had assignments for supply runs and I couldn't transfer." He shrugged. "A rival unit sabotaged my first mission, so I ordered my men to scavenge a portal drive from a wrecked ship to open the portal to Earth for the raid on the stadium. You know the rest."

"So seriously you really only wanted supplies."

He bowed his head. "And recognition for outstanding efforts. Supply Unit Officer is low caste. I'd never have advanced enough to get off planet or retire before death otherwise." He shifted uncomfortably. "It didn't turn out like I hoped."

"Sorry."

He dared to smile."Don't be. I think I like where I've arrived."

Penance grinned up at him. "Me too. Congratulations on the three years early. How old are you, then?"

He scratched his chin, considering."The years aren't exactly the same, and longer days... but roughly, eighteen years old. I think I've finally stopped growing, or at least slowed down enough to wear the same uniform an entire year."

Penance laughed. "Yeah, I can see how that'd be a problem. Don't tell Tech, but I'm not quite seventeen yet. I put down that I'm nineteen but I don't think she believes me."

"Why did you lie?"

"She wouldn't accept me if I wasn't old enough to join the military. The Justice isn't part of the military but they follow some of the same rules. I'll tell her next year, when she can't get rid of me."

"She won't get rid of you. She took care to be sure you live to recover and return to the field."

Penance shook her head. Then, slowly, "Does this... change things?"

He didn't understand. Which of the many things they been talking about might change?

She noticed his trouble translating. "I mean... we're almost the same age. Hard to believe because you're over eight feet tall, though."

Unconsciously, he touched the long scar on his left arm as he remembered what changed when his unit discovered that they had been placed under command of an *ibak* three years their junior. It seemed that betrayal by his own people held a large part of the pattern in his life. But Penance Copper was alien – no, here, *he* was the alien. Though she seemed to think that they were the same.

That must be it. She didn't want a potential rival for her rank.

"I won't give you any trouble," he said. "It doesn't matter that you are younger when you have more experience. And I need the training very much. There is no return to my own planet. There is no other offer from either government or rebels. I can't even fight you for control of the unit when there is only the two of us."

"So are you here until something better comes along?"

He stared at her. Did she suggest treason? Or had they not formally accepted their commissions yet, so this would be a theoretical discussion? Neither changed his answer. "I can't imagine anything better than this."

"Uh-huh." Her non-committal tone left him wondering what nuance he'd missed in her question. "So what's so great about this, then?"

He couldn't avoid a direct question from his superior, though he didn't know how to talk about his own preferences. Everything must be about the state, the Emperor, imposing order... Selfishly, he hated the way things were on Hylinek, how the state and the Emperor's order had convicted him in spite of his innocence. The supposedly omnipotent Emperor couldn't even charge him with crimes he'd committed, only generic treason and impurity. On Earth, he had no attachment to the state. As far as he knew, there was no Emperor. His only attachment was... he found himself staring at Penance and dropped his gaze.

Earth's strangeness unsettled him. He didn't know if he would be able to truly adapt to the alien world, no matter how long he lived there. Penance held all the charm he found on this planet, but he couldn't tell her so.

He jerked his head at the building – she'd called it a barn, though sometimes she called it a house. "It will be nice to live in once it's finished. It's a good long-term project and Commander Tech approved it to be added to my duties. More duties and projects applied to my permanent record will help secure my status. The training from you, anything you're willing to teach me, will raise my status. Culture, customs, language, swimming... I..." he swallowed and continued softly, "I ...want... to be more."

"More than what?"

"I am *ibak*. Very low... only good for hard labor, or war. But a skilled *ibak* can sometimes get special honors. Permissions. Commander Tech gave me important work here, opportunities that I never would have had on my home planet even if I had been perfect."

"But you're already more than that."

"No, you might think because I'm big and a good fighter, that I was bred to be this way, but it's only a... a... what's the word? I'm not like this on purpose. There's no documentation of my genetic suitability for anything. I'm a nothing... what is the word for *ibak*? The people, that aren't really fully people?"

"What, some kind of half-people? That do work or fight in wars? I don't..."

"*Ibak* exist to serve the government and the government leaders that own them?" He saw the recognition then — she did know the word after all — but her face blanched. Misery twisted his gut, and he stared down at his hands.

He shouldn't offer excuses, but he couldn't stop himself. "I thought you knew," he muttered. "I didn't intend to lie about it. I thought..." He broke off. He'd been stupid. Of course they wouldn't have offered so much to an *ibak* if they'd realized he was one. It was all a mistake.

Penance reached over the cooler and placed her hands over his. "What you were on your old planet, that was done *to* you, but that isn't who you *are*. You are just as much a person as anybody else, you hear me? You *are* a whole person. You belong to yourself, got it?"

Her hands trembled.

"You want me to lie to cover up your mistake in agreeing to teach me."

"No, I'm asking you to let go of the lie that some people are better than others and that they can *own* other people. And when I find whoever told you that you're less than anybody else, I'ma pound his face in."

*Riiiiinnnngggg!* The sound came from inside the house.

"I got it," Penance said, getting up. She jogged inside, leaving the door open behind her.

Slowly, Kail put away the food, trying not to eavesdrop. But his exceptionally good hearing didn't allow him to stop, and in any case Penance's voice rose.

"It shouldn't count if he didn't believe he really had a choice. When were you going to tell him? ... Because he thinks you own him! ...What? No! Don't you dare... You can't tell *me*..."

Kail stilled, sensing danger. Penance shouldn't be getting angry, not while she had imperfect control of her power. He approached the doorway.

Penance stood with her back to the door, gripping the phone as if she would crush it. Faint sparks began to gather around her as she shook her head furiously at something Commander Tech said. "You can't just drop us in this *dump* and not tell us anything, like we're too stupid to notice you don't have any backup! You can't save the world by yourself!"

The sparks coalesced , drawing closer to her.

Not a good sign.

Kail needed to calm her before she charged the air with too much plasmic energy and burned herself again. He edged nearer.

"*I am not a liability!*" she shouted – and the energy flared around her. She cried out and dropped the phone.

Kail threw up his hand against the vicious heat, and the wave of energy retreated from him. He wondered why the energy behaved as it did – Penance created it, guided it with her mind and will, and then it lashed out, as often at her as at her target. And yet it did not lash at him now.

He dove through the hot wave of plasma and it parted, allowing him through to where she huddled from the energy lashing from the cage of lightning she had made. He shielded her with his body and the bolts looped back into the net.

"Pen," he said, "please listen. You do have control. You are controlling this now. It's you – it's all you. Please stop hurting yourself. Make it stop."

"I can't," she whispered. The net roiled, but came no closer.

"You can. You don't want it to hurt me, and so it doesn't." He pressed his face against her hair. "Please. *M'lohn*... my... my friend, I don't want you to be hurt."

Slowly, the girl looked out from the shelter of his arms. Her tear-streaked face hardened in concentration as she reined in the energy. She lifted the dangerous net of heat and light and balled it into an orb above their heads.

He helped her stand and she waved the ball of energy through the open door, where it contacted the rusty remains of a fence and vanished, grounded.

She sank to the floor and he settled down behind her, letting her lean against his back. As he had done as a boy, keeping watch with a partner. They would protect each other.

Commander Tech still waited on the phone. He picked it up and held it to his ear. "*Ey-inh?* I mean, um, hello?"

"What is going on? Are you all right?"

"We're fine. I think we've discovered how the deputy justice can improve her control."

"That is excellent news." Commander Tech paused a moment. "Kail? I'm sorry, I didn't have a full understanding of your, ah, cultural context. Penance believes that you might be under the impression that you are the property of the government. I assure you, you are under no one's ownership and you will be appropriately compensated for your work. You have rights, the same rights as every other person, and we're working on getting you citizenship."

"Oh." Kail sat back, stunned. Penance had been insubordinate, but evidently the commander accepted her assessment despite that. "Thank you, Commander."

"You don't need to thank me. I'm only clarifying a misunderstanding."

"I'm sorry I misunderstood."

"Nothing to be sorry about either. I'll be in touch." She hung up.

"What'd she say?" Penance asked, her voice only a little shaky.

"She said... I'm going to get citizenship." He ducked his head. "I never thought I could hope for... Ah, also, it is excellent news that you are learning control."

"Why did you risk shielding me? I could've killed you."

Kail looked away. Would his answer "change things?" He wasn't sure he could handle much more change.

"Better to surrender to Death than to Fear, " he said finally, translating a proverb taught in the barracks.

"Thanks for having my back." She thought for a minute. "*M'lohn*," she added.

Startled to hear his own language, he realized she called him what he had called her. She really did think of him as an equal, as fully human as herself.

Moved by her sincerity, he nodded slowly.

"*M'lohn*," he agreed.

# Getting Out

## CIVILIAN HOME, UNITED STATES, EARTH

"And they're going to reimburse us for the van," Shandra finished telling John over dinner. "I had no idea when I signed that paper that the Planetary Justice Unit would actually show up at the door needing help."

"Still, loaning out the van was above and beyond what you were required to do," John answered. "I'm guessing that until they straighten out whatever mess they're in, we'll be a one vehicle family."

Shandra winced and rested a hand on her belly. These false contractions were getting persistent. "I don't mind that. But what I've been trying to figure out is if there's any connection..."

A knock on the door interrupted her.

"I've got it," John said, getting up from the table.

"I wanna see who it is," Devon said, but Shandra shook her head no and pointed to the untouched vegetables on his plate.

John opened the door to a middle-aged man wearing glasses and holding a folder, mopping his brow with a handkerchief. "Hello, ah, Mr. Mark?"

"Yes sir," John answered. "Can I help you?"

The man produced a badge. "Ah, perhaps. I am Dr. Robert Janus with the Planetary Justice Unit's research division. I wondered if you had any knowledge of the unfortunate explosion..."

"Yes sir, I was one of the firefighters on call. Very strange that a building would just collapse like that."

Dr. Janus mopped his forehead again. "Indeed, yes. I have been trying to locate a person who would know more about how that came about." He pulled two pictures out of his folder. "She may be in the company of a person claiming to be a representative of the Planetary Justice."

Shandra sat up and leaned over in her seat to peer around the corner at John and the man on the porch. That lady had said someone would come looking for them. Someone dangerous. This man didn't look terribly dangerous – only a balding bureaucrat – but she could see from a room away that he poured sweat and twitched restlessly. She narrowed her eyes. The sweat and twitching looked less like nervousness and more like some sort of substance withdrawal the longer she watched. She'd seen similar reactions in the emergency room all too often.

"Uh-huh." John rubbed his chin thoughtfully. "Well, I didn't see anybody like those two, but then, I was busy fightin' the fire down at the building that came down. Say, why exactly would you be here looking for them anyway?"

As the men talked, Shandra motioned for Devon to be quiet and sidled up to the window. Something familiar caught her eye about the man driving the black SUV that this Dr. Janus had arrived in. He turned his head slightly.

Recognition struck her.

She turned to Devon. "Honey, we're going to have to go soon. Go get your sleepover backpack and your favorite toy. Get your cards, too."

"But Momma..."

"Hurry, you don't want to leave anything important behind." She took her own advice, and hurried to her own room to add what she could to her hospital bag.

At the door, John still stalled Dr. Janus. "Well, now. That wasn't quite an answer to what I was asking. I'm not sure what our employment records have to do with the building coming down, or with these two ladies you're wanting to catch up to."

"If I could speak with your wife? Where was she at the time?"

"Not that it's any of your business, since she's on maternity leave. Due any day now. I'm not sure I want to bother her with all this until I'm certain I understand what's going on."

Dr. Janus lost patience. "Listen, you..." he began.

"John!" Shandra yelled.

John turned quickly to see what was the matter.

"John, it's time! We have to go! Devon, you got your things?" She staggered up the hallway, clutching her belly with one hand and the hospital bag with the other."John, we need to leave now! Right now!"

"Oh," John said. Then it hit him. "Oh! Come on, Devon, let's go get in the car. Why're you bringing all this stuff?"

"Momma said to."

"All right then, go get in the car. Shan, hon, let me get that." He helped her outside.

Dr. Janus followed behind, attempting to get Shandra's attention. "Ma'am, have you seen either of these two..."

"Augh! Oh, oh, I can't... I don't..." Shandra said, panting heavily. "Just let me go already."

Curious neighbors came outside, attracted by the ruckus. One shouted, "Can't you see she's in labor? Don't bother the lady!"

Dr. Janus got around in front of John as he opened the car door. "Why don't you let us drive you to the hospital instead?" he said. "I've got friends there, we'll get you in quickly."

John laughed to his face. "You don't have half the friends there that we do. Every nurse there has been waiting for this baby!"

Inside the car, Shandra screamed in pain again. "Ohhh, John, they're getting closer!"

"Devon, you buckled?" John asked as he climbed in the driver's seat. Dr. Janus tried to talk to him again but John only shrugged. "I'm sorry man, but we've got to go!"

Shandra leaned back in her seat and covered her face with her hand as they drove past the black SUV. She glimpsed the driver again between her fingers and became more certain that it was him, although she'd only seen him once before.

Lorie's boyfriend. The last man who'd seen her. She'd introduced him once as Jonah, but Shandra had investigated and discovered that he had another name he went by.

Acid.

John reached over and patted her knee. "You doing all right?" he asked. "Haven't heard you have a contraction in a little while."

"About that," Shandra said. "I haven't had a real contraction yet. But we'll be much safer in the hospital than we will at home."

"Why's that? Something shady about that doctor? Thought he acted twitchy."

Shandra shook her head. "Worse. It's his driver. That's the man I was looking for."

John turned to her, wide-eyed, and she waved for him to watch the road. "Lorie's boyfriend? The one who put a tattoo of his nickname on her back without her permission?"

"And what's more, that girl they're looking for has that same tattoo. It can't be a coincidence, that she shows up injured so badly with chemical burns, and the next day a man called *Acid* is looking for her." Her face crumpled with worry. There was no telling what that man had done to her sister.

John shook his head. "This is deep. We need to tell the police. That's got to be something to go on."

"The woman with the Planetary Justice Unit gave me a phone number, but she said not to use the home phone."

"I'll check you in to the hospital, and then I'll go buy you a burner phone," John said. "This is too important to let go." He reached over and grabbed her hand. "We're going to find your sister."

Shandra nodded, tears in her eyes.

Meanwhile, in Serenity City, a man gritted his teeth through withdrawal as he lay in a hospital cot. The gleaming ward on the topmost floor contrasted to the rest of the rundown, nondescript building. A sign out front declared the structure condemned.

Tech couldn't take credit for this safe house – Path had known immediately who would have such a place available, as well as a deep conviction about treating mentally injured Primes.

Adrian Cross, the Priest.

Finally, the man himself had returned, for the first time since installing the Justice in the ward.

"Well, young man," he said to the Justice, "I'm glad to see you no longer at death's door, but I can't say I like the side effects of the medication you're taking."

Justice mustered a grin through his pain. "Can't say that I do either, but it's the only thing that works after having my brain scrambled."

Adrian glanced from Justice to Path, busily taking notes on her patient's vital signs as he endured longer intervals between doses. "See that you don't forget your priorities while you're unscrambling," he said dryly. "Now, about this girl. She may have stayed at Hangman House for a little while, if she's the one I'm thinking of – but if she is, she hasn't wanted to contact anyone she knew from there, and she has a habit of wiping out electronic records of herself."

Path glanced up. "I'd hoped she had friends – some evidence of healthy attachments. Dr. Janus believes that she's irreparably damaged, and if so, I'd have to allow much more time to clear my own psyche before returning here."

"If all you need is information..." Adrian said, "I do know a journalist with a better memory than mine. I can send him this way, and if he's ever seen evidence of her existence, he'll know."

"Is his ability to keep secrets on par with yours?" Path teased.

The old gentleman smirked. "My dear, no one's is. But I will say that he's trustworthy."

After his departure, Path checked Justice's vital signs again. "It looks like our guest wore you out," she said. "That's enough pushing it for today. I'll get you another dose ready."

Path's phone rang right before she could replenish the medication in the drip. "That's odd," she said out loud. "Tech told me she was going dark." She brushed her fingertips over her patient's perspiring forehead as she walked past to grab her phone. The number was unfamiliar.

"Hello?" The voice on the other end was not Tech, but another woman. She sounded scared and worried. "Is this Path?"

"Yes ma'am, how can I help you?" Path spoke with warmth and reassurance. Even without the neural interface that allowed her to precisely receive or project her emotions to the recipient – provided they also had a neural interface – she could use her tone to some effect.

"Tech of the Planetary Justice Unit was at my house earlier. She asked me to call you if anyone came looking for her or if I found out any information. Today, a Dr. Janus came asking about her. He came in a black SUV driven by a man I know to be a criminal. You see, my sister was dating this man, and she went missing two months ago. The last I heard from her, she called me saying her boyfriend had tattooed his nickname on the back of her right shoulder without her permission and she was going to leave him."

Path gasped. This could be it, the break that the Justice had been searching for. "What was the tattoo?"

"Acid," the woman said.

"Acid," Path repeated. The same tattoo as the teenage Prime girl Tech had taken in at headquarters had. Then she realized what else the woman had said. "Acid is working with Dr. Janus?"

"It seems so."

"When Tech visited you, did she have anyone else with her?"

"Yes," the woman said. "Both the big villain who crashed the football game and the teenage girl who fought him were with her. They borrowed my van but I don't know where they went."

"Thank you so much, ma'am," Path said. "Are you somewhere safe?"

"Yes, I'm..."

"Don't tell me where you are, just stay safe, okay? And get rid of your phone as soon as you can." She hung up and found her patient sitting up, intently listening. "You need to lie down and recover," she scolded him gently.

"Dr. Janus was working with Acid?" he asked. Both he and Path turned to look at the medication that the doctor had brought. "That would explain quite a lot."

"It raises even more questions than it answers," Path said. "How could he deceive me? I met him in person, shook his hand, and he looked me in the eye and swore that this medicine would help you recover."

"Well," the Justice answered, "Perhaps it does, but the side effects are going to kill me." He started to get out of the hospital bed but nearly fell. Path helped him back into the bed and covered him as he trembled violently. He caught her hand and looked deep into her eyes. "Mercedes. It is likely that he's monitoring your phone. He may know that he's been found out. If so, he or someone else will be along to eliminate us soon."

Path nodded. "Just rest," she said, and reached to unplug the monitors. "I'll move you to another room."

The Justice chuckled. "I'm afraid it's going to take more than that," he said. "You should go and get yourself to a safe place. I'll be fine."

Path hauled the door open. "You are certainly not fine and I will not be leaving you," she insisted. She bustled around to the back of the bed and started rolling it out. "We need you too much."

"If this Acid is who I think he is, you need to get to safety. Penance is right to fear him – and you should know that his skin produces a corrosive substance. You can't touch him. You won't be able to defend yourself."

"We can't just let them -"

"And we won't." He reached back to catch hold of her hand again, but his expression shifted subtly, taking on a sinister cast. Path sensed the change immediately and placed her hands on his forehead to wrest his emotions back to normal, though the struggle for control left them both breathless and sweating.

He turned away from her, though she didn't have to look at him to know that he cried. "I... I can't be the Justice," he whispered. "Not like this."

"You are a good man," Path said firmly. "You will recover. Even faster now that you aren't being poisoned."

"You don't know that. The harm done may be irreparable."

"And you don't know that," she replied. "I choose to hope. And besides -"

The phone rang again. This time, it was Tech. "Path? My phone said you got a call."

"It does that? And yes, I took a call from a woman who says Dr. Janus and Acid are working together and visited her home after you left."

"I upgraded all the phones when I installed the trackers. You'll have to get rid of your phone and get somewhere safe," Tech said. "Dr. Janus' phone is heading for your location."

"Well then, he's not aware of the trackers yet either or he wouldn't have his left on. I'll keep my phone, thanks. How am I supposed to back you up if I can't get in touch with you? Do you have *any* backup? How are Penance and Kail doing?" Path said. She sidled to the window and peered out.

The Justice groaned. "How close is he?"

"Penance and Kail are untrained *kids*, Path, and not in any condition to fight an interplanetary trafficking cartel. Get out of there. I can only track Janus' phone – I have no idea how many operatives he may have converging on the area now," Tech said. "He won't be able to stay and look for you long – there's a large shipment that hasn't been able to go through for a few weeks while they build a new portal receiver. I found the warehouse but they moved the captives before I arrived. Janus will need to oversee the final steps of the build and he'll want to get paid."

Outside, a black SUV pulled up. "Tech, what are you planning?" Path asked, suspicious. The Justice slid out of bed and made his way over to her, bracing against the wall. She put his arm around her shoulders to steady him and led him downstairs as Tech spoke rapidly.

"He's there. I expect him to at least attempt to eliminate you and the Justice, and anyone else he might believe to be a threat. After that, he'll have to hurry to the new portal site. I should be able to follow him there," Tech said. "Please, Mercedes. Be careful. I'll call you later." She hung up.

Path turned to the Justice. "There are some things that worry me about all this."

He gave her a wry grin. "Only just now?"

The empath cocked an eyebrow at the hero. "I knew what Mariposa and I signed on for with you. And you've kept your promises. It's time for us to keep ours." She rested her fingertips on his forehead, pushing in all the confidence and courage she could muster, finding the points in his synapses where anxiety and craving gathered to clear them out. The Justice straightened, renewed, but Path held up her hand. "It won't last long. The toxin is still in your system. And... this shortcut may prove to be a setback in your rehabilitation."

The Justice nodded.

Below them, a door opened to the stairwell, and footsteps resounded on the metal stairs.

Swiftly, the Justice scooped up Path and leapt down to the next landing as quietly as he could. He opened the door to that floor and spun her through, holding a sharp, clear urgency in his mind for her to find an alternate escape. Obediently, she ran, not looking back, confident that he had the enemy handled. Even in the face of this dangerous, mind-altering addiction, she had an unshakable faith in him. He prayed that he would be worthy of it.

The footsteps came closer, and became quieter as well. The Justice could discern a distinctive cadence – step, scuff. Step, scuff. He frowned. Not even Janus would be so arrogant as to send a crippled man after him.

Even as he listened, the cadence changed, the scuff becoming less and less noticeable and the speed of the steps increasing again. Then, nothing. Not a step, not a breath, no sound at all echoed up the stairwell. The Justice widened his electromagnetic field to sense the newcomer's bio-electricity.

Directly below him, a man snickered. "There y' are."

A hand plunged through the bottom of the landing where the Justice stood, grabbing his ankle and yanking him downward. The edges of the hole popped and sizzled, melting away beneath him. Off-balance, the Justice dove forward onto the staircase, generating a strong magnetic field in his hands to cling to the metal stair. Anchored, he had enough leverage to kick free of his attacker.

"Interesting parlor trick," the Justice said, standing more warily now. "But I'd hoped for a fight, not a practical joke." His ankle burned where the man had grabbed him, but he ignored it.

"Oh, it's no joke," the man said, snickering again – this time from behind the Justice.

The hero spun with a roundhouse kick, but the man leaped easily over him, landing lightly as a cat to face him. The staircase swayed, the brace that anchored it to the wall melted through.

The man smiled and walked toward him, hand outstretched. "Y' see, I got first blood. Name's Acid, you must be Justice. I've heard so much about you." His hand smoked, burning off the traces of the Justice's blood before dripping a slick, colorless fluid to the floor. Each drip melted through the stairway and continued falling.

"I'm sure you have," Justice said, noting the increasing sway of the floor. "Hey, aren't you that slimy lowlife who's been herding girls off-planet?"

Acid shrugged, dropping his hand. "It's a living." He grinned, showing a few missing teeth. "Between the living and the dying, y'know? Every day, a little of each, walking the line." He nodded to himself, humming.

*He's stalling*, Justice thought.

"Been awhile since I seen one of our kind," Acid said. "I'd like a chat, catch up on the old home, and all. But I'd better get to killing you."

The Justice leaped out of the way of the sudden spray of acid, repelling the weakened floor beneath the insane villain to send it crumpling down the stairwell. He landed on his feet – upside down on the bottom of the stairs above, held there by magnetic force.

Acid moved faster than the hero had anticipated, flipping neatly away from the falling platform to grab hold of the railing of the same flight of stairs as the Justice. He vaulted neatly onto the stairs and lurched forward to corrode the stair the Justice stood on.

*That won't work again*, the hero thought, springing back further up the underside of the staircase as he generated a powerful electrical field. Arcs ricocheted wildly around the stairwell to shock his foe into submission.

Above him, Acid guffawed. "Cute, cute. 'Minds me of my little girl. Second generation, ain't you? Crazy how that turned out, both of you ending up with similar."

The Justice leaped from the bottom of the stair to the opposite wall, slinging static and electromagnetic fields to change direction in midair and propel himself upward. Acid straightened to look up at him, scratching his head, a delighted smile on his weathered face. "Y' fly, too? Don't that beat all. Wonder if Penny can learn to do that. She's a bright Penny, she is." His face crumpled with abrupt grief. "Can't tell 'er so. She'll get uppity." He jabbed a finger toward the levitating hero, anger replacing sadness in a flash. "You'd know all 'bout that – or at least, your turncoat *ibak* father would."

The Justice unleashed lightning upon the villain, blasting him through the bottom of the stairs. Molten metal dripped from where the man had stood. After a moment, the entire flight of stairs creaked free of the wall and crashed down the stairwell. Hastily, the Justice modified his fields to steady himself as he drifted slowly down, looking for the villain's body.

Horror filled him at what he had done – he should have let the man talk. His mind reeled at his self-betrayal. At the same time, the implications of the madman's ravings struck him. Acid hadn't been talking about second generation Primes. He'd meant second generation *aliens* - the *ibak* deserters of Hylinek.

Path dashed through the corridors of the derelict building, trying to remember which way led to the other staircase. *There – the main hallway!* It led right to the lobby, a once-elegant, three-story high room with a vaulted ceiling and a double staircase of broken marble treads and splintered balustrades.

She skidded to a stop at the railing, panting heavily, and looked down. The empath didn't see or sense anyone, so she picked her way down the better of the two stairways. From the bottom stair, she peered at the boarded up windows, wondering how best to get out without alerting anyone outside.

A hand came down firmly on her wrist, pinning it to the stair rail.

Dr. Janus smiled at her, his blue eyes twinkling behind his wire-rimmed glasses. Even with direct skin contact, Path detected no emotion whatsoever from him.

She smiled brightly back. "Oh, hello, Doctor. I didn't realize you'd be back so soon. I was just running out for ice cream." As she spoke, she pushed every emotion she could muster through to him, but instead of lodging in his brain to change his behavior, they simply disappeared.

"That sounds lovely," the doctor said, gripping her wrist more tightly. "I'll drive you there."

"No, really, that won't be necessary!" Path said, twisting to get out of the man's grip. When that failed, she balled up a fist and swung wildly for his face.

He ducked smoothly out the way and yanked her off the stair. "It's the least I can do, after all your help in developing some of the most powerful psychoactive drugs in existence."

"My help?" Path wrenched around, throwing her weight to the floor like a toddler throwing a tantrum. But the older man, much stronger than he looked, hauled her up.

Janus yanked her arm and she pitched ahead past him onto her knees, still trying to wrest her arm away from him. "Why, yes. It takes years of trial and error to fine-tune a drug to create a specific effect. Acid made an excellent test subject to increase the suggestibility in Primes, which makes them both more powerful and more biddable. However, to develop a means of creating the required ruthlessness in ordinary humans, I could only trust myself to test it. The neural interface records of our interactions provided all the data I needed to perfect my control."

The woman braced her feet against the floor, pounding and clawing at his hand on her wrist until she drew blood. Desperately she channeled guilt, fear, disgust – anything that could persuade him to release her – but he dragged her on, unaffected.

"What's wrong?" he asked. "I thought you were eager to leave." As he reached for the door, Path changed tactics and slammed into him as hard as she could with her shoulder. She knocked him back against the door, but still he didn't let go. He flung open the door and she clutched at it with her free hand, finally gaining purchase with her feet for an instant.

Setting her weight into her hips as if she hauled back a spooked horse on a lead, she gripped his wrist and pulled the doctor's arm back inside to slam it repeatedly with the door.

Still he retained his grip. He stepped back into the doorway, blocking the next slam with his side, and grabbed her other wrist as well. "It's a good thing for you that you'll fetch such a good price undamaged," the doctor gritted through his teeth as physical pain finally reached him. "My client has a preference for Prime women."

A motorcycle cruised up as Janus finally succeeded in getting her out the door.

"Help!" Path screamed.

The newcomer parked his bike and ran up the steps to them. Instead of tackling Janus, however, he grabbed Path around the waist and picked her up. Backing down the steps with her as the doctor kept tight hold of her wrists, he laughed cruelly. "Hey, I'm helping! Where d'you want her, doc?"

Frustrated, Path snarled, a noise she wouldn't have imagined herself capable of before today. She fell limp, panting. The abrupt change caused the motorcycle's owner to adjust his grip, and as his hands loosened, she bucked.

Dr. Janus stumbled and lost his grip on one of her wrists, and she slung her hand back to connect with the young thug's face.

"Don't let her touch you, you fool!" Janus howled, too late.

Path smiled with grim satisfaction. Here, she had something to work with. *Time to grow a conscience, kid.* She closed her mind to the ethical implications and raced through his emotions, shoving farther and farther back, recoloring his perceptions rapidly. The therapist in her still attempted to create the best approximation of healthy, normal development as she could manage in a fraction of a second. Even so, he had a massive knot of rage that she couldn't dissipate without real therapy.

Wincing, she directed it toward the nearest obvious target.

With an enraged roar, the young man dropped her and swung a wild punch at the doctor. Janus let go of her wrist to dodge it. The thug lunged over her for the doctor's throat and she rolled quickly out of the way. As the two men grappled behind her, Path crawled down the steps, eyes wide open for any more thugs coming to "help."

She reached the black SUV Janus had arrived in and eased up the side to peer in the window. Mercifully, no one else waited inside. Even better, keys dangled from the ignition. Hurrying to the driver's side, she swung open the door and climbed into the seat. Starting the car, she executed a three-point turn and careened around the building, ramming trash cans down the alley to the back staircase exit. *I'm sure the Justice has won by now. I'll pick him up and take him somewhere safer to recuperate...*

The exit door slammed open and the Justice staggered out, battered and bloody. Burns streaked his combat uniform. He looked up, his eyes wide and desperate as he recognized her behind the wheel.

Path hit the unlock button and opened her door, overjoyed to see him. "Get in!" But in the next instant she caught his emotions. "What... what's wrong?" She peered beyond him into the open door of the building, but could only see smoke. "You've won... let's go."

The Justice shook his head. "No."

Behind him, an ominous crackle echoed in the stairwell. The outline of a man appeared in the clearing smoke, climbing slowly down the pile of wreckage in the stairwell, glimmers of electrical arcs sparking around him. Mad laughter resounded, echoing.

"Demon!" the villain howled. "I knew it, that's what y' are. All 'un the same..." he slurred. An arc of lightning lashed out the door, conducted by a spray of acid. The Justice shielded Path with his body, hissing in pain as droplets struck his back.

The hero began to shut Path's door but she reached for him, wrapping her arms around his neck. "Hurry!" she whispered, frightened. "We can escape!"

He grabbed around her waist and set her firmly back in the driver's seat. "No. You can escape."

Path caught his intentions and gasped. "No, Justice..."

"Mercedes." He pulled her close and kissed her. Desperately she poured out her love to him with the contact, but it only strengthened his resolve. "I have sworn to sacrifice my life in defense of this planet. I'm not the Justice if I don't keep my word."

"Then I will fight with you –"

He shook his head, placing a finger over her lips. "But what I am really fighting for, is for your safety."

She pulled his hand away. "Fine, then. We will each do what we can, *and* survive. And when it's over, you can tell me exactly why it's taken you this long to kiss me." She sniffed. "As if it isn't obvious to *me* that you've wanted to." Tears filled her eyes as she reversed, peeling out of the alley as fast as she dared go, while the Justice faced a monster tailor-made to kill him.

# New From Old

## UNDISCLOSED 3: JUNKY BARN, EARTH

While Kail carried junk out of the barn to sort into piles of salvageable and trash-to-be-burned, Penance went through each of the handwritten folders of documents Tech had reproduced from memory and left with them. "Hey Kail, did you know that portals show up on the Lightning Detection Network up to an hour before they actually get through? I didn't even know there was such a thing. I just thought we had, you know, weather radar."

"You have radar for weather?" he asked, pitching mouse-ridden couch cushions out the door to the burn pile. "Weather on Hylinek doesn't move very much compared to Earth, so we mainly use radar for air vehicles."

Penance hesitated over the folder labeled _Chromatophoric Camouflage Replication_. She gently set it aside instead of flipping through it. "We'll have to get a computer... a laptop or something... so you can learn to search stuff," she said. "I always wanted one but let's face it, technology doesn't like me. I'm better off learning from books... speaking of books." She found her first aid book near the bottom of the pile of folders. "I didn't know Tech remembered to bring this." She smiled and picked it up. Underneath it was another book, with a plain black cover. "Oh!"

Kail paused as he carried out the old stove. "What is it?" He set the stove down and came over to see what Penance was excited about.

"It's a Bible!" she squealed. "She really got me a Bible!" She hugged it to her chest. Tech had listened to her after all. Maybe now she could get some answers about what to do next. She couldn't continue trying to be a good Christian based on nothing but half-remembered verses and a quick prayer. If she needed more to get in heaven, she'd rather not find out at the gates.

"What does that mean?" He sat down beside her to get a better look.

"It tells about God," she said, opening it. Kail sat back uncertainly and she looked up at him. "What's wrong?"

"It's a holy text?"

She had to shake loose of her first connotation for 'text' before his question made sense."Um, yes? I guess so?"

"Are we allowed to look at it?"

*Bless his heart, he looks so worried.* Penance grinned at him. "Why not? Are you scared I'll get struck by lightning?"

"Well...Considering that it's you..." he drawled, humor lighting his eyes.

She snickered. "From what I've heard, God's got nothing to hide. What kind of religion is scared to let you find out what you believe?"

"On Hylinek, the Emperor says that he is god, and that all belongs to him by right. He knows all and owns all, and must be repaid for the use of that which is his. It is unforgivable to question the purposes he assigns to us, for his will is perfect and must not be defied," Kail said. As if he recited a law, or the pledge of allegiance. He shook his head bitterly. "But the Emperor does not know all. His laws are not just. His orders sentenced me for crimes I was not guilty of. You should be careful of allowing *gods* to determine your fate."

Penance reached for his hand, but he avoided her and got up. Turning his back on her, he headed outside again.

"Well," she said to herself, "That's not how my God does. I've just heard He forgives, and man, do I need that." She looked down at the Bible and measured its thickness. "This is going to be a whole lot of reading," she said to herself.

Hours later, she still hadn't gotten very far. She couldn't concentrate with Kail coming in and dragging stuff out, and reading in front of him embarrassed her as well.  She had to follow the words on the page with her finger and sound out each word, and then go over each sentence again in a whisper to try to understand it. Her method had been great for memorizing the first aid book, but the Bible had so many thin pages of such tiny print. She'd never memorize them all.

"If it helps you feel better, I can't read it either," Kail said, coming up behind her.

Pen rolled her eyes at him. "Ha, ha. I bet you read in your own language."

"I was training to become an officer, so it was necessary. I read a few languages, not as many as I speak, because it's hard to find much written work." He regarded her curiously. "I don't know if any women read on my planet."

Pen sat up and shoved her hair out of her eyes. "Well, here, everybody reads. Every kid is supposed to do school and learn to read and write. There's even little kid TV shows with songs and puppets and stuff." A sudden feeling of guilt rushed in on her and she caught a bare thread of a long-ago memory.

Bright colors and songs on the TV, a fistful of sugary cereal right out of the box, one arm locked tight around a fluffy stuffed bunny as big as she was. Her father and his partner crossing back and forth behind her, hauling valuables out of the stranger's house.

The TV unplugged and carried out as well. She gave the bunny a sticky kiss goodbye and followed the men out.

They sent her in the houses first, to turn off the alarms, to open garage doors, to dismantle security systems. To make it easy to get in. The only thing she knew, and the only thing they valued her for. Until that wasn't enough for the man her father had become, and he began training her for... no.

Kail watched her, still and silent. He had no idea what she'd done. What her life was.

What it used to be, she reminded herself. That wasn't who she was anymore. Just like Kail wasn't a military slave, she wasn't a thief. And she wasn't the girl staring pitilessly down at the mark, while he lay at her feet and coughed blood...

*Little girl... help me...*

Penance shut the Bible and rubbed her eyes. "My mama taught me a little bit, but then Acid stole me. Reading wasn't on the list of stuff he wanted me for."

"I'd like you to teach me to read your language, when you have time," Kail said. "Also, I need to learn about the local currency. We're going to run out of supplies at some point and I need to know how much I can plan to buy."

"Do we have any money?"

Kail grabbed a rusty coffee can from under the cot and gave it to Penance, who accepted it with an odd look. "Money in a coffee can under the bed," she mumbled as she pried off the lid. "You sure you're an alien and not somebody's grandpappy? I gotta teach you better places to stash... oh my word." She pulled out a huge wad of cash. "Tech left all this?"

Kail nodded.

"Is she ever coming back?" Penance shook her head and began to count. Kail watched intently as she laid out stacks of bills. "Two grand."

"What does that mean?"

"Two thousand dollars. Which can buy... well, out of the kind of stuff we'd need to buy... like groceries and clothes..." She stopped, dismayed.

"What's wrong?"

She shook her head. "It isn't nearly enough. I can get clothes from a thrift shop for fifty bucks and be done for the year, but you, you're going to need custom." She groaned and hid her face in her hands. "Just... just decent shoes for you might be two grand. I don't even know."

"Is that all?" Kail said, amused. "Don't worry, I can make shoes. I've already gotten started."

Penance looked up. "You're kidding. How do you make shoes?"

He shrugged. "Everything is made somehow. I've had to make my own uniforms for years. Shoes included."

"Oh, this I've got to see," she said, shoving the money back in the can.

"I'll make you a pair as well, if you like," Kail offered as she watched him carve salvaged rubber of various thicknesses for the layers of the soles. "These are a modification of the style for desert soldiers of Hylinek. I haven't been anywhere else to learn what is regulation for other environments though."

He pegged salvaged leather from the old couch out on a board and sketched on it with a bit of charcoal. Evidently, he'd done this so many times that he didn't need a pattern, just his own right hand to measure the proportions of each piece as he drew them with his left. He picked up a box cutter to cut the leather smoothly into several pieces, which he arranged into two stacks. Then he grabbed an awl and hammer from a tray and punched neatly spaced holes around the edges of each piece to prepare them for assembly. Other pieces were already set aside, grommets and strapping and tacks.

Penance looked around Kail's workspace that he'd made under the lean-to against the back of the barn, realizing that she wasn't looking at arbitrary piles of junk at all. He'd stripped down everything that could be taken apart to its components, and had found trays and boxes to hold different kinds of screws and nails and cords and wire. She picked up a length of copper wire that had fallen out of its box and twisted it in her hands absently.

Kail had found some tools, and made others. In addition to boxes for sand casting, he'd built a forge and fashioned a crucible for pot metal. He'd poured and cast a bigger set of pliers already, and some other extra large tools she didn't recognize but which looked made to be used left-handed.

He'd taken his shirt off to work, and moved from one task to the next with equal skill, whether he wielded tongs to maneuver boiling pot metal into position to pour into wet sand casts or his deft fingers stitched together the leather uppers. Fascinated, she watched his methodical process for creating useful, quality stuff out of random junk. Since he'd healed up a good bit, she could appreciate how he *moved* again. Strength and power in everything he did, but every move also economical and... graceful. Like a tiger.

He caught her staring and she dropped her eyes to the wire in her hands. Not that looking at him embarrassed her. He had a lot worth looking at. But she didn't want to make him uncomfortable about his scars. Long stripes of thickened flesh wrapped his sides from his shoulders to his spine where he'd been flayed by – looked like cables. Acid had done that to a guy once, for getting uppity. Same pattern, but that guy had gotten off easy compared to this. Kail's marks went all the way down his back.

If she bent the wire a little bit more this way, she could make a cross. She borrowed a pair of needle-nose pliers out of the tool tray and and twisted it a bit more, making the ends of the wire spiral into the center of the cross. Just like her mother's necklace. She poked around and found a string to put through the top loop of the cross. "Look, I made something too," she said as she tied it around her neck.

Kail glanced up from attaching the soles to the uppers and smiled. "Very beautiful," he said.

Penance laughed. "Thanks, but I know it's not that impressive. Nothing like what you can do." She sat down beside him as he finished the first boot and set it aside. "I can lace it for you," she offered. She settled up against his back with the boot.

"Thanks." He passed her a ball of sturdy cord. "Don't cut it until you're sure it's long enough. We don't have much."

"Mm-hm." She stroked along the neat, even stitches. If she hadn't watched him hand-sew them, she'd have thought they were done by a machine. "This is made so good. All these parts are just fitted so perfect together. It does not even look like you made it from junk. I never would have guessed you hadn't bought this. Except that it's huge." She finished lacing it and put her own foot inside. "My *word*. I could fit *both* my feet in here."

Kail glanced back and grabbed it off her foot. "Please don't." He sounded a little strangled.

Penance sighed. "I wish I knew how to make stuff. But all I can do is train. Even my training's been getting slack lately."

"That's good," Kail said absently, back to sewing the other boot. "You train too much and you don't eat enough. You're too thin for your muscle and you have nothing to recover with."

Penance sat up. "Excuse me? Since when is my body your business?"

"I specialize in nutrition for the military. You can't continue to eat half rations with the physical load you subject yourself to, especially while you're supposed to be recovering."

"I know how to take care of myself!" Penance said, scrambling to her feet.

Kail looked at her coolly. Even sitting on the floor, he was still just about as tall as she was."Then why don't you act like it."

She spun around and stomped off, away from the house.

Long after sunset, Penance sat on the hilltop beyond the cattle pond, staring up at the endless sky.

*So many stars.*

Kail found her there and settled down to sit as well, saying nothing. His warm, strong back pressed against hers. Together, they listened to the cacophony of frogs and crickets, watching the fireflies wink in and out around them. After awhile, he shifted, and placed something beside her. A pair of boots, much smaller than his but otherwise identical. She picked one up and traced the fine stitches with her fingertip. "They're beautiful," she said.

Kail's shoulders moved with a smothered laugh. "Beautiful is a word I'd save for... ah, not desert boots."

"The way you made them is beautiful." She tried it on – perfect, of course, like everything he made. "How did you know what size?"

He shrugged. "Your footprints on the dock at the pond."

She put on the other boot and scrubbed at her eyes. "Ugh, I've cried more this past month than I have my whole life, I think."

Kail set something else beside her - a bottle of water. She picked it up, puzzled.

"What's this for?"

"*Oiv*, it's water. To drink," Kail said, teasing. Then his voice softened. "If it was the last water we had, I would warn you not to cry more than it contains, but there is plenty, and you can cry all you need."

"Oh." Water meant a lot to Kail. She wondered if it would be rude of her not to drink it. Then she realized he'd known she'd been crying all this time and had come prepared. She hugged the bottle, blushing in the dark. "Is your planet mostly desert?"

"Hm? No, I don't think so. Just where I come from."

"Where *do* you come from? I mean, who? In the prison mines, I saw all kinds of people, but nobody like you. Do you know anything about your parents?" Penance asked.

The big soldier shook his head. "No. My caretaker-general found me at the entrance to the compound. He brought me in, chose a name for me, and made a record of me. Before then, I didn't exist."

Penance scratched her head. *Paperwork made Kail exist? His brain has some weird flips going on.* "That doesn't make sense. You *existed* or there wouldn't have been anything to bring in. You had to come from somewhere. Don't you have any clues?"

Far off, coyotes yipped and fell silent again. An owl called in the distance.

Penance waited.

After a minute, Kail replied, "In the mines, the radiation didn't affect me. One tribe is known for immunity to radiation – the Laevii. So... I am of the Laevii." He paused. "Heh. Kail *ip* Laevii."

"Hey, that's really cool," she said. *Sounds nicer than Kail* ip ibak, *now that I know* ibak *means 'bastard slave.' Being radiation-proof is pretty sweet too.*

Penance rolled a blade of grass between her fingers, thoughtful. "It's strange to be out in the country like this," she said. "Hadn't been out this far from alarm systems and cell phones and static in ages. It's shaking some things loose in my memories."

"What kind of memories?" Kail asked.

Penance shrugged, but it became a shudder. "Stuff I'm not sure I'm ready to remember," she said. "A red truck. A guitar. I was little. Really, really little. Mama was there. She'd hold me on her lap and sing while my..." She broke off. She hadn't thought of him as that in a long time.

"What did she sing?" Kail sounded interested.

"Jesus loves me, this I know, for the Bible tells me so..." she sang, shyly. "That's why I wanted the Bible."

"Who is Jesus?" Weirdly, he sounded almost jealous rather than interested this time. But maybe she still wasn't that good at reading his tone.

"He's God. God is the Father, the Son, and the Holy Spirit, and Jesus is the Son part. God made everything there is, and it was perfect, but even perfect things get broken. People are broken, but God still loves us, and He sent His only Son to save us. Jesus will save anybody who asks Him." Penance rubbed her eyes with her wrist. "Anybody."

She sighed and looked back up at the stars. "I just don't understand how it's supposed to work. I know I'm broken. And... and damaged. And I know I'm safe – saved. Dying isn't the scary thing anymore. Living, though? I don't know what I'm supposed to do now."

They listened to the crickets chirp, and the frogs in the pond below. Kail shifted. "I remember songs from when I was small."

Penance tried to imagine tiny Kail and couldn't quite manage it. "You, small? I'd like to've seen that," she teased. "What kind of songs?"

"Marching, counting, teaching stories. My... the caretaker- general, Baos, raised us all, the *ibak*, in a barracks in the desert, far from the fathers who abandoned us, who couldn't afford us. He trained us and taught us... he had not been born an *ibak*, and he would sing the youngest babies a song he had learned from his mother." And Kail sang it to her, softly, as if giving her a forbidden gift.

Penance held her breath, listening. His voice rippled rhythmically, asking questions that hung in the air in expectation of an answer. "What does it mean?" she asked, as quietly as he'd sung.

He tensed behind her. "I don't think we're supposed to know it," he said.

She reached back and found his hand. "I won't tell," she whispered. He didn't respond.

They both straightened at the purr of the vehicle as it pulled up the driveway and stopped, followed by a car door shutting.

Penance and Kail exchanged a look. Kail indicated himself and the trail to the house, and silently directed Penance to go around. She nodded, and they both dropped low and split up, keeping to cover.

# Path

## THE HOME FOR INCONVENIENT PEOPLE AND CONVALESCENTS, EARTH

"Hello? Is anybody home?" a female voice called.

Penance circled around. The vehicle turned out to be a black SUV, and she saw no one but the driver, who now walked up the path, monitored by Kail.

"*Hola*, don't shoot," the woman continued. "I brought gifts. I know you... is it Kail?"

"Path?" Kail said. He'd broken cover.

Penance stifled a swear - and a quick apology to God in case He was strict on swears. She wasn't far enough in the Bible reading to know if that was a real thing or not. *What is Kail doing?*

She jogged up the track to find him having a nice conversation with the woman.

Obviously, the intruder was no threat. She carried a double armload of shopping bags and appeared soft... very soft. *Not remotely a fighter*, Penance thought with a shade of contempt, *though she's pretty, in a generously rounded kind of way. A bit plump, to be honest.*

Though Penance hadn't made a sound, the woman turned to her immediately. "And you must be Penance. You're so pretty! I'm glad you're feeling better too. I'm Path. I'm sorry I couldn't meet you earlier over the phone, but Tech said the neural interface kept malfunctioning. She's kept me up to date on your progress, though."

It took Penance a moment to sort through all this. Meanwhile, Kail accepted the pile of shopping bags from the woman's arms. He caught Penance's eye. "If we can't trust Path, we may as well be dead now," he said bluntly. "She knows everything."

Penance sighed. "Fine. Tech sent you?"

"Not exactly." Path looked downcast. "I just didn't know where else I could go."

"Oh," Penance said. "Welcome to the Home for People Tech Don't Want to Deal With." Path flinched, and so did Penance and Kail, now that the echo of it hung in the air. "Maybe that was a little harsh," Penance said, by way of apology.

Path shook her head. "No, I think that's a fair assessment. But she's honestly doing the best she can to protect you. Aren't you already much happier here than you were in the lab? Not nearly as... I don't mean to pry," she finished abruptly. "Speaking of the lab, you will never guess what I brought in the truck! I didn't even realize it myself until I got a few hours down the road..."

She led Penance and Kail back down to the SUV and flung open the rear door. "Look!"

Penance peered in under the dim interior lights and saw boxes piled high in the back, some familiar-looking computer components poking out of the tops. She sniffed, catching a vaguely familiar fishy smell. Climbing inside, she shoved a heavy box out of the way, rocking the vehicle. Water sloshed and she tracked the sound to a large fish tank.

A sinuous form slipped along the bottom of the tank, and an eye with a slotted pupil peered back at her. "No way. Oh my goodness."

Penance poked her head back out of the SUV, beaming. "Kail! They saved Squishy!" She scooted the tank closer to the rear doors and found a tote full of Squishy's tank accessories.

Kail bent to look at the tank. Squishy slid around behind her rock. "Is it food?" he teased.

Penance rolled her eyes. "No, it's my pet *sepia officinals*. She's mine now, anyway, right?" She grinned hopefully at Path, who nodded. "How did you get her out in time?"

"Oh, she was in the car when I stole it from Dr. Janus."

Penance burst out laughing and offered Path a fist bump, which the lady delicately returned. "Nice!" She turned back to Squishy. "Poor baby, hauled all over the country for days," she cooed. "Glad you didn't ink and suffocate yourself."

"Well, actually she did," Path admitted apologetically. "I couldn't bear to have anything happen to her, not after Tech told me how important she was to you.

But fortunately I found an aquarium on the way with the expertise to treat her and change the water. Wonderful people. Ecstatic to help."

"I bet they were," Kail muttered, passing the shopping bags to Penance so he could lift the tank out of the back of the vehicle.

"Have you had dinner yet?" Path asked, and opened the front passenger side door. "I brought pizza... though I don't think I brought enough." She indicated Kail, walking up the driveway ahead of them with Squishy's tank.

"He won't want any. Cheese and milk type stuff grosses him out."

Path blinked. "He's lactose intolerant?" She pulled the pizza boxes out of the seat and shut the door, and they walked up the driveway together.

Penance snickered. "No, he's got a cast iron stomach. But I explained cows yesterday and he says milk is the most disgusting thing about this planet."

"It's true," Kail called back. "There's something wrong about drinking milk meant for the young of another species. Fermenting it into solids is even worse."

"I... never thought of it that way." Path looked down at the pizza boxes and wrinkled her nose. "I did bring some other groceries, if there's a way to cook?"

"Yes," Kail answered. "I need to learn more cooking skills."

"More pizza for me!" Penance sang.

At the house, Kail set up the camp stove he'd repaired and gathered the pans and implements he'd found and refurbished.

Path organized the groceries on the table, considering what didn't require milk."Would you like to make empanadas? Oh, wait, those wouldn't be done until past midnight..."

Penance shrugged. "We got no place to be."

"Oh... I see. I suppose you are entitled to an update," Path said, selecting a pan. "Ground beef is really not my favorite for these but it's what we have and it should be cooked soon anyway... I didn't realize the refrigerator was broken when I bought all this. Would you please get a pan, Kail?" She set aside a jar of salsa and poured corn meal into a bowl. "I assisted the Justice as he recuperated from the fight with you, Penance. We had a hospital room set up away from the Center. The night the building collapsed, Tech called me and told me as much as she knew."

Kail nodded. "And you evaluated me as well."

The woman smiled up at him as she mixed dough. "Yes. Here, if that's browned you can set that aside and start heating the cooking oil." She picked up a small section of dough and made a ball. "The next evening, a lady called me and told me that your... handler, Acid, and Dr. Janus, had come to her house looking for you."

Penance choked on her pizza. "Is she okay?"

Kail watched as the lady pressed dough into rounds, and copied her exactly.

"As far as I know, yes. She recognized him as her sister's boyfriend before her sister disappeared, so she knew to leave with her family and call me. So when Janus and Acid came for the Justice, we had a little warning. He didn't have much strength, but he could confront them."

Path bowed her head over her work, not meeting their eyes. "Those look very good, Kail. I suppose we can take a shortcut on the filling." She finished a stack of rounds and added salsa to the pan of ground beef.

Taking a deep breath, she continued."He didn't win. But he delayed them so that they would have less time to track you down – or harm the lady who helped you before you came here. He insisted that I take the car and leave him behind." Path fell silent, filling the empanadas with exaggerated care.

Penance sank down in her chair, wide-eyed. "He... he isn't better by now? I'm sorry... I had no idea I hurt him so bad."

"Oh, no, honey, he had mostly recovered from the physical injuries. He would have gone back into the field sooner, but I found something strange about his emotional state. Whenever I gave him the medicine he did better for a little while, but then got much worse. I didn't know whether to try to keep him on it, or wean him off. His physiology is so different. But when it started causing his moods to change, I decided to wean him off. Dr. Janus told me that I shouldn't do that, no matter what... but the Justice became a different person. He... lost himself."

Penance gasped. Path gave her a questioning look. "What is it?"

"Did he..." Penance started, then stopped. "Was it like, he'd be fine, and then he'd just start being a little... twisted? Like he'd see something beautiful, and then go to touch it, and not stop until he'd mauled it? And then this little grin..." Penance rubbed her arms convulsively.

Path stared at her, wide-eyed. She nodded, slowly, as though that tiny motion filled her with pain.

"Oh shh... shoot," Penance whispered. "Janus gave you that stuff? To give to the *Justice*?"

Path nodded again.

"It's him. He's Acid's dealer. He makes the stuff. He paid for the hit. And I..." Penance buried her face in her hands and rocked. "I... oh dear God, what have

I done? I hurt the Justice in the first place... and now he's a switchhead like... like *Acid*..." Her shoulders twitched.

"Oh, oh honey, no, it isn't... you can't..." Path began. "I'm sorry, if I could, I'd help you straighten it out but I'm not holding together too well myself right now."

Penance slammed her fist on the table. Kail barely picked up the pot of hot oil in time as the rest of the cooking things bounced.

"You don't understand!"she screamed. "There's no coming back from that stuff. He's *gone*. Justice - *the Justice* - can never be trusted again. We have a freaking alien invasion coming and we don't have a Justice!" Sparks crackled in the air around her.

Kail set down the pot and gently placed his hand on Penance's back. Though he rested the back of his hand against her rather than his palm, the gesture eased her misery, and the sparks subsided. "You could not have known. This Janus has betrayed and used many innocents to carry out his plans."

Penance sniffled and wiped her nose on her sleeve. "Been awhile since I could be called innocent..." she began.

"You did what you had to do to survive," Path said. She sighed, thinking of her own recent compromises. "I have as well. So has Tech. So has the Justice, for that matter. None of us blame you... or if any of us thought we should, that's long past. You've proven yourself already. The Justice... before he had that drug in his system, he said you chose to try to protect Earth rather than run, and he will always remember that. And you protected Kail and Tech, even though generating and holding that force field hurt you badly. You've done so much more good than harm. I hope you can see that." Briskly, Path resumed cooking.

"But the Justice..."

"Will be fine. He realized what was going on and... well, he left. To protect me. And I thought it wasn't a good idea to be alone, so when it occurred to me where Tech had put you, I came here." Path dropped the last empanada into the oil and watched it brown.

"How did you know where we'd be?" Kail asked, as he cleared away the camp stove and cooking utensils. He sat down at the table, turning over the new food with interest.

Path glanced around the barn, sadness in her eyes. "This is where we had to house our brother. He was like me, but... he couldn't let things go. Other people's emotions hammered at him all the time and he didn't know what were his feelings and what weren't. We found out too late that he'd started trying to medicate himself. He died of an overdose, thirteen years ago." She shook herself and said briskly, "That was before the Justice found me and Tech. So of course this place isn't on any of the official records."

Kail turned back to Penance. "What is a switchhead?"

Her shoulders jerked involuntarily under his hand. "Switch is a drug that makes you switch off what holds you back. You get everything you're capable of, one hundred percent. It sounds wonderful, right?" She laughed, in pain and sadness.

"No fear, no pain, no God, no devil. No love. Nothing at all to stop you. And then when it wears off, it... it wasn't you. So there's no guilt. It feels like it was all somebody else, nothing to do with you." She shuddered again. "One switchhead has an edge on me without even being a Prime. Two or more could tear me apart."

"What does it do to a Prime?" Path asked.

"Primes burn through it faster. It makes them stronger in body, but weaker in will. They give in to the worst of themselves. If they been on it long, you can tell when it's about to burn through because they start seeing demons. Watch out then. They turn quick."

Kail had been gently stroking her back, but now his hand stilled. Both he and Path stared at her in silence. Penance flinched under the weight of their pity and horror, and Kail removed his hand. "It is late," he said, picking up the dirty dishes to put in the sink. "We can continue talking in the morning. You can both sleep in the upper level."

"Oh, is that where you put my bed? Where are you going to sleep?" Penance asked.

"Where I've been sleeping. I'll be able to guard you both better from here."

Path looked from Kail to Penance and back again as the atmosphere in the room changed. "Thank you so much!" she said brightly. "I do feel much better with you around to keep things secure." She turned to Penance. "Would you show me around?"

"Oh, sure," Penance said. "G'night, Kail."

Kail nodded. "Good night."

# Last Ditch

## INTERSTATE, UNITED STATES, EARTH

*The mission is in shambles*, Tech thought as she downloaded the new emergency emotive protocol and set her driving to autopilot. While she had called to be certain that Path, Penance, and Kail all still lived and they had copies of the key documents for the Planetary Justice Department, the same couldn't be said of the Justice.

For the second time in as many months, he had disappeared, compromised and possibly dead. The department he had founded to protect the ideals of Sovereign Earth against alien threats, now stripped to an untrained skeleton crew of two injured teenagers and a therapist. Over a hundred citizens of Earth abducted with no way of recovering them from a hostile planet. Precious little of what the Justice protected could be salvaged now, but she would give her all for what small victory she could claim. Even if all she could do was stave off the inevitable.

She had been concerned that Dr. Janus headed to the recuperation facility to eliminate Penance and Kail, but the tracker on his phone indicated that he had turned off the interstate, well away from their location. She left the interstate at the exit before the one he had taken and continued cautiously down the frontage road.

Tech didn't have the natural intuition that Path had, but she did have the ability to subconsciously analyze thousands of tiny clues and arrive at a conclusion. And this road and direction pinged a few promising connections. A quick scan cross-referencing her memory found the answer – Dr. Janus' resume, before he had joined the Planetary Justice Department, included work from a nuclear power plant in this region. At the time she had considered his record there as corroboration of his excellent mental health and trustworthiness, but now she suspected that he had some means of beating psychological tests. Something that would even work to obscure his true intentions from her sister Path's empathetic abilities.

If so, Janus' plan had been in motion for much longer than she had first thought. If he had begun laying the groundwork thirteen years ago when he worked for the nuclear facility, he could very well hijack the power generated to create a portal from Earth to a focus device on Hylinek. That would make it much more difficult to prove to the Interplanetary Council that Earth hadn't voluntarily entered into an agreement with the foreign planet.

Sovereign Earth as a whole had done no such thing, but some aliens on the council were already baffled by the concept that one planet could have several independently ruled countries.

After this debacle, those aliens would insist that they were correct in declaring that Earth could not defend itself and could well appoint themselves as guardians, taking control of Earth's resources and distributing them as they saw fit – among all the planets in their coalition.

For all Tech knew, Dr. Janus worked for them as well as selling women to Hylinek's Emperor. If he could substantially discredit the Justice himself, the entire department might be next, and then factions on Earth would be free to push the rest of the planet into servitude to foreign powers. Already rumors of alien invasion reached the mainstream networks, despite her best efforts to pass Kail's indiscretion at the stadium off as the work of a local supervillain. A worldwide panic from a large-scale, undeniable invasion could push the whole planet into the arms of the Council. The Interplanetary Council had the power to declare Earth incompetent and place it under the rule of a more established planet. For its own good, of course.

Path would find Penance and Kail – perhaps by now she already had – and someday Penance's raw power and talent could be tempered by Kail's steadiness and discipline. Kail especially showed promise as a diplomat, if he could overcome the harmful elements of his programming. Tech had no idea if that would be enough to salvage Sovereign Earth.

She could only buy them time.

For that, she had her own plan. She set her internal computer to finding and downloading a map of the power facility. Within moments, she figured out how she would take over a nuclear facility if she had begun thirteen years ago and could reliably evade psychological testing. As she had thought, routine maintenance had shut down the plant today and tomorrow. Janus might well have the entire facility staffed with his people. She would have to assume that she was going into hostile territory.

She finished downloading her new emotive protocols and incorporated a heads up display of the map of the facility. Pulling the rearview mirror over, she applied a fresh coat of lipstick. She hated the display, as it made her right eye seem to wander. But since she needed to change her appearance significantly for this plan, perhaps that would help.

She wrinkled her nose at her reflection. She'd straightened her hair and forced herself to cut her own bangs less than perfectly. There was little she could do about her bone structure, but she had de-optimized her diet over the past two days of monitoring Janus' actions and her face showed traces of water retention. She would just have to cake on makeup, wear clothing typical of the targeted women, and hope for the best.

Her hand hovered over the cell phone on the console beside her. *Not yet. Path will guess the plan as soon as she hears my voice - and she won't like it.*

# No More Hiding

## HOME FOR INCONVENIENT PEOPLE AND CONVALESCENTS, EARTH

Over breakfast, Path divided the packages she'd brought into two stacks, one each for Kail and Penance. "Well? Open them!" she said, smiling. Gifts were a nice icebreaker, and she'd been careful to purchase useful things with two such pragmatic souls. They had both gotten up and begun working on their respective projects hours before she had awoken. Their busy contentment in the back of her mind had caused her to wake up happy for the first time since... since the Justice...

She picked up the burner phone Tech had left with them and found the phone number for it so she could update her contacts on her own phone. Penance and Kail had done very well for themselves out here, but taking care of them made her feel better about the whole situation, at least.

*Such sweet kids. A bit stubborn. Rather hormonal.* Probably just as well that Kail's discipline prevented him from acting on his impulses and Penance's self-esteem issues kept her oblivious to his interest for the moment. Not that they'd be a bad couple, but they seemed so young, and it wouldn't be healthy for them to use physical intimacy as a crutch to avoid doing the work of becoming well-adjusted. She breathed through a sudden pang of grief and longing for the Justice, releasing it quickly before it could disturb the two teenagers.

"What's this about?" Penance asked, pulling a box at random and using her nails to carefully break the tape without damaging the box. Kail followed her example, but he used a knife. She'd have to remember that he favored tools. And was left-handed.

"I thought you could use some nice clothes. Something a little more durable. Tech told me your size but... I'm afraid Kail will to have to have his tailored still." She shook her head. The young soldier was so much bigger than she'd been able to comprehend over the phone.

"Oh, that'll be no problem," Penance said, still picking apart the tape on her box. "You should see the boots he made yesterday... ohhh." She had opened it at last and stopped mid-thought, gazing at the contents. "New clothes, really new... for me?" She reached to stroke the material and stopped short. "They're so *clean*."

"Go on, open the rest," Path said, reassuring. "They're for you. I tried to pick things you'd like... I didn't realize..." *Goodness, I can't finish a sentence without potentially embarrassing the girl.*

"Oh, thank you," Penance said, trying to act normal instead of completely blown away, like she knew all about gifts and nice clothes. She opened the next few packages faster. "I love the green. And I needed some jeans so bad. Love the pockets." She looked up at Path and Kail. "Um. Are y'all going to need the bathroom for a bit? I should probably take a shower, get ready for the day and... and stuff."

"No, go ahead," Path said, and flicked her fingers in a little shooing motion. Penance gathered her gifts up and dashed into the bathroom. A moment later the water turned on.

Kail watched Path's expression change from a bright smile to tears, flowing as if they would never stop. He offered her a napkin.

"Hm? Oh, thank you. I'm... having a little trouble compartmentalizing, sorry. I had no idea she'd feel so strongly about getting nice clothes as a gift," Path said, dabbing at her eyes. "I should have started her therapy right away but things were so busy..."

"I made her boots and she yelled at me," Kail said. He grinned mischievously at Path's shocked expression. "No, that isn't quite how it happened," he admitted. "She yelled at me for caring about how she pushes herself. The boots were more of an apology afterward." On the surface, he made light conversation, giving her information to help with her patient as well, but beneath that, he tested her. Measured her. Her tears stopped and she caught her breath, dizzied by the change.

Detached, balanced between risk and reward, debts and merits, rules and permissions, Kail held still and watchful. All the broad uncaring universe rested on a scale, and that held him as well. Within him, a storm of needs and desires roiled, kept in check until reward outweighed risk. Path shrank from Kail's anger at his own betrayed loyalty. Who would be next to hurt him? Even as his assignment slaked the desire to protect the girl, it grated against the desire to protect himself. Now, in the face of her pain, he fell short of that duty as well.

Path reached to pat his shoulder but decided against it. Her own emotions might transfer with contact, and she didn't want to escalate his emotional state. "She'll come around. You're doing her a world of good. But she needs to allow herself..." she broke off and winced. "Oh, poor child," she whispered. She clutched the edge of the table, and she made herself let go and breathe through the pain. She deeply regretted not coming in person right away to help Penance when Tech had first brought her in. Lost in so much turmoil even a day longer than necessary, believing that no one cared whether she lived or died... waiting to be thrown away the moment she became inconvenient. And even neglect was preferred to affection, and its associated dangers.

Kail looked from Path to the bathroom door. He half rose from his seat to check on Penance, but she'd been unhappy with him the last time he'd done that.

Path shook her head. "No, don't. She needs privacy right now. I'll..." She paused and took a deep breath. "I'll let you know if she's in any danger."

Kail nodded. "Thank you for mine as well," he said, setting his boxes out on the table and rapidly categorizing their contents. "Will it be all right with you if I take these apart and sew them again?"

"Yes, I bought them for you to use, after all."

"How much do I owe?" Kail said, pulling a tool out of his pocket to pick the seams.

"Nothing. These are a gift... you are not in debt. Not a cent. You don't have to pay any of this back... why don't you believe me?"

He shrugged. "Perhaps you simply don't know. Or perhaps the totals aren't tallied yet. There has been a lot of upheaval in the administration of the Planetary Justice's department. Perhaps it's some other department that I owe." He really wasn't insulting her. To him, it was simply the way of the world that repayment must be made and every point of every transaction created an excuse to add to the price. The foreign concept of material gifts made little impression on him.

How had she managed to end up with the only two people in the world who were so odd about gifts? Penance grieved in the bathroom, trying to come to terms with layers of memories of abuse, while also wrestling with the safest way to show gratitude for gifts but not get attached enough to be manipulated by the threat of taking them away. Terror at losing her place because she didn't know how to receive gifts swung rapidly to nausea at drawing attention to herself. And Kail simply added his to the mental tally he kept about everything.

"Life is not built entirely on debt," Path said. He registered her words, evaluated them, and discarded them as well-meaning but ultimately empty. He didn't mean it as an insult, but it stung nonetheless.

"Good luck getting him to see that," Penance said, coming out of the bathroom with her face red from scrubbing and her toweled-off hair still damp. She had chosen a snug white cotton cami with a short-sleeved, patina-green shirt over it, unbuttoned. A wide leather belt held up dark wash carpenter jeans, and she'd put on the combat boots Kail had made for her. Around her neck, she still wore the copper wire cross she had made.

"You look lovely," Path said, turning her attention to evaluate Penance's state. *Oh, good, she's found a nice focus point with some pleasant memories. She's certain of... her mother's love.* She smiled as she noticed the cross. *There it is. She's made a memento of her mother.*

"Thanks, I needed good sturdy clothes. These ought to wear good." *Not quite ready to think positive things about her appearance, however.*

Kail, on the other hand, froze in place. He'd become used to seeing Penance in baggy t-shirts and oversized shorts with double-knotted drawstrings over a ragged collection of bandages. As long as they both recovered from injuries, they had relied upon each other as equals. He had gotten comfortable. But now... the temporary shared vulnerability came to an end, and his assignment with it. Attraction and longing knocked Path's breath from her lungs and she struggled to set Kail's emotions in their own compartment, separate from her own. *Oh yes, now I remember why I don't like to work directly with people*, she thought wryly. *Without the neural interface, everything is personal.*

The war among Kail's desires renewed now that Penance appeared to outclass him, further out of reach than when she had met him in the stadium. Now, potential competitors suddenly expanded to include the known universe. She wouldn't need him much longer. And then what? Path's fingers twitched in sympathy as Kail tried to grasp an alien concept – would she want him, as he wanted her? Or would he have to stand aside to see her choose another?

Penance passed her hand in a slow wave in his direction. "Earth to Kail. You okay?"

He nodded. "Lucky you," he said gruffly, dropping his eyes to his work again. He nearly stabbed himself with the seam ripper. "I have some work before I can wear mine."

Path's expression changed from hurt, to suspicion, to embarrassment before she looked over in alarm to see Penance's carefully blank face slowly warm to pink. She'd accidentally mirrored the emotions Penance tried to hide. *And now I'm getting echo, and that's always a bit muddling...*

"I'm sorry my control isn't very good right now, but I swear I'm not trying to intrude. You don't have to feel so naked..." Path clapped both hands over her mouth as soon as she'd said it.

Penance crossed her arms over her chest and avoided looking at her, and Kail had already been carefully not looking at anyone.

Path sighed. "I'll... just go see what's left of my garden." *Teenagers*, she thought. *They'd complain all day that you didn't understand, but the moment they realize that you do, they'd rather you didn't.*

After she left, Penance stole a glance at Kail. "Oh. My. Goodness."

"I think we'd have been all right if..."

"Yeah, if she hadn't come out and said it." Penance snickered. "Just *feeling* like it is plenty embarrassing."

Kail cracked a smile. "She made it worse."

"Sooo much worse," she giggled. "Wait, you knew before I did! You didn't warn me?" She planted her palms on the table and tilted her head up at Kail.

"I tried to but..." he shrugged. "Right in front of her? While she's been so kind?"

"Mm. I guess I should've picked up on it sooner. For all the good it'd've done. How do you block something like that? Tin-foil hats?" She scooted dishes away from the clothes and material he had laid out on the table.

Kail chuckled. "Do we have any tin-foil?"

"No, if we did I'd cover my whole body to try to keep myself..." she paused and folded her arms across her body, "... to my*self*. Eek."

"And if you did, there wouldn't be enough for me," he said, falling into a playful rhythm. He stopped, uncertain, but she didn't notice and continued stacking breakfast dishes in one hand.

She waved her free hand in his direction. "Ah, you got nothing to be ashamed of. I mean, *dang*." She snorted and dumped the dishes into the sink to scrub. Outside the window, Path found a pair of gardening gloves and ripped weeds out of the old vegetable garden.

Penance's hands slowed and her shoulders slumped. "Still, nothing's solved. Everything's a mess and we're just supposed to wait and see some more." She finished washing the dishes silently, and Kail found a rag and began to dry them and put them away.

"I'm going to go see if I can get any farther with reading," she said. "Let me know if... anything." She climbed the ladder to the loft and looked around again at her room. She hadn't been able to appreciate it much last night in the dark, but now she could see how hard Kail had worked on it. Fresh morning light shone through the windows on the east wall, and below them, Kail had built a seat and shelves for her books – all both of them. He'd built a real bed, too. Better than the cot, though she'd let Path have it last night, as the guest. All the best blankets were on it – the new ones from the supplies Tech had left, and the one Kail hadn't had to patch much after he washed it.

*That man could clean*, she thought. The rough pine boards under her feet practically gleamed as she walked to the bed and sat down on it. Compared to this, she'd hardly done a thing in the past few days. She felt awful about it, but she didn't know what she could do. Being hurt didn't excuse her from doing her share. Injuries never stopped Kail. Every time she looked at him, he was working.

Also, it seemed like every time she touched something to start cleaning it or moving it, in the next minute he'd taken it over and she wasn't even sure how. And if she started feeling restless and decided to train, he'd catch her in the middle of pull ups or crunches or deadlifts before she got more than halfway through her reps and ask her for help with some easy thing. He definitely coddled her. She didn't know what to think of it, but heaven help her, she liked it.

It didn't mean anything, though. As kind as he was, as charming as he could be when he pulled work out from under her hands or asked her to teach him, as beautifully and thoughtfully as he made things for her, it was just his job. Taking care of her was part of the assignment and to be safe, he'd spoil her rotten. He just did things that way.

*It isn't personal to me*, she thought as she stretched out on the bed.

He'd built the bed only slightly wider than the cot.

Obviously, he had no plans to join her there.

Downstairs, the phone rang.

Path dashed inside, clattering garden tools by the door. "About time," she muttered as she picked up the phone. "Tech?"

Penance rolled off the bed and crept to the edge of the loft. Below, Path paced with the phone.

"You've found the women? How many?... Oh. They're in a transfer truck? Of course, just tell me what you need. Where?..." Path paused and listened intently. "Tech. How can I back you up if I don't know where you are?"

The woman listened again, tense. "What aren't you telling me? Why won't you... Mariposa! No! You can't..." Path sank to the floor and stared at the phone in her hands.

Penance leapt down to the main level and rushed to Path. "Path? What's going on?"

The other woman folded into herself, shuddering. "Mariposa... Tech. She's tracked the transfer truck with the shipment of women on the way to the new portal location. She guesses they'll be transported off-planet tomorrow."

Penance sat back on her heels. "But that's great! There's time! Where are they?"

Path shook her head. "She won't tell me. She says she'll send an automated message... triggered when she completes the mission."

"That sounds kinda like..." The girl didn't want to finish the sentence.

"That's exactly what she means." Path's voice broke. "She plans to sacrifice herself to destroy the portal. She wants me to come after the danger is past, to take care of the women." Tears dropped onto her phone. "Oh, Mari, I can't lose you too."

Penance reached to touch the woman's shoulder, but pulled back, remembering Path's powers. "Sit tight. We'll think of something." She got up and jogged outside to Kail's work shed.

He waved at her from where he sat on the floor of the shed. He had lost no time getting ready – he already wore his resewn jeans, a snug short-sleeved shirt, and his old combat vest from his upper body armor.

"Hey Kail? Guess what now."

Kail looked up from the parts and pieces arranged in a neat semicircle on the floor around him. "I don't have to guess. I heard."

Penance shoved her hair back behind her ear. "Oh. Wow. So... Tech's gone dark because she's trying to tackle this on her own. But she can't. The Justice is gone, Janus is a traitor, and Path... well, what's she gonna do? Emote?"

Kail fitted a couple pieces together as he listened. Hands always fixing a thing, every time she talked. She'd learned that didn't stop him from listening.

"I'm the only one who's got a shot. I know Acid. I know what he'll do. And even though I've never won against him... I'll last longer than anybody else. Maybe I can distract him while Tech gets the girls out of there." She fiddled with the cross at her neck. "He... he's my problem. If anybody's gonna die trying to beat him, it should be me. Not Tech. Earth's got to have a Justice." She looked back to Kail, her heart in her throat. "So that's why I have to go."

Kail added a tube to the end of the thing he was building. It started to take on a familiar shape.

"Is that a gun?"

Kail nodded. "*Eyh*. The rebels make these, since ammunition is scarce on my planet. I guess the translation for it would be 'slag gun.'" He picked up an aluminum rod from a pile of them he had cast and angled it to an opening in the gun. "Put scrap metal in here and this melts it, then this action stamps and fires." He smiled slightly. "No recognizable 'ammunition' to carry, and easy to reload from whatever is around."

"What, cock it manually for every shot?"

Kail nodded.

"Hot scrap metal instant bullets? How uniform are they?"

"Not very."

"No powder?"

"No powder."

Penance wrinkled her nose. "I'm sorry. Your gun's gonna suck."

"I know. But I'd rather not show up without some kind of gun."

She stared at him for a moment. "Show up..."

"To help you and Tech stop Acid and Janus. Thanks for not sneaking out, by the way. I'd have had to come along with just a blade." He nodded to the newly sharpened machete leaning in the corner.

Penance threw her arms around his neck, overwhelmed with gratitude. "Thank you, thank you, thank you," she whispered. She turned to kiss his cheek but remembered just in time that he didn't like to be touched. He'd gone still as stone already.

She let go hurriedly. "Sorry, I didn't mean to get in your personal space." She clasped her hands together and bounced on her toes, unable to contain her happiness. "When can you be ready?"

He wouldn't look at her. "A few minutes. Test this first," he said gruffly.

"Okay, I'll go get ready!" She turned and dashed back in the house, and Kail tightened the final few screws on his weapon before sighting it in on the targets he'd placed out back. Satisfied, he slung it over his shoulder and sheathed the machete at his side before heading in to pack water and meals for the trip out.

Path staggered up from the floor, desperate to feel anything but the familiar, crushing despair. She could be angry. Mariposa would never dare to shut her out like this in person. If she could just find her and slap some sense into her first... Her fingers curled around the phone.

*The tracking application.* Path pulled out a chair and sat at the table. Her hands trembled as she scrolled through the apps.

Penance came dashing back inside. "Path! Kail and I talked, it's gonna be okay!" she called as she rushed past and climbed the ladder to the loft.

Path nodded, still scrolling. She found the tracking app in a submenu of the GPS and paused to scrub tears impatiently from her eyes. *I should take a lesson from Penance. Excited to get going on a course of action...*

She sat up. Her eyes widened with realization.

Kail entered and set the cooler on top of the table, rapidly swapping out items and repacking with military precision. He glanced over to the phone as the map came up on the screen, pinpointing Tech's location.

Penance came back downstairs, a first aid kit slung over her shoulder.

Path jumped up from the table and grabbed the car keys from the hook by the door. "Don't even think about it," she said. "You're going to stay..."

"It's okay, we don't need keys to start the car," Penance said, grinning on her way out. "Don't forget to feed Squishy!" She snapped a spark from her fingers and disappeared out the door.

Kail smiled apologetically at Path as he shouldered his weapon and swiped her cell phone off the table into his own pocket. "Keep the doors barred," he advised, before he picked up the cooler and left too.

Path heard the car start in the distance as she stared at the keys in her hands. "Well," she said aloud. "I suppose I ought to start getting a little tougher if I don't want to keep getting left behind for my own good."

On the other hand, she'd had a hot day of working outside, and a pint of ice cream had just been taken out of the cooler and left on the table.

Decisions.

# Road Trip

## DEPARTING HOME FOR INCONVENIENT PEOPLE AND CONVALESCENTS

"**P**ay attention, normal human lesson... whatever number we're on," Penance said as she scrambled up into the driver's seat. "Learning to drive is like, the thing that makes you an adult in this country."

Kail cautiously wedged himself into the passenger side seat. "It doesn't seem nearly as frightening as what I had to do to be considered an adult," he said.

"Yeah? Is it something you can tell me about sometime?" Penance asked. That sounded like the start to an interesting story. "Check the side of your seat, there should be a lever to give you more leg room. And buckle your seat belt, it's a stupid thing to get pulled over for on the way to a..." She stopped, hand halfway to the steering column. "I guess it's kinda like a heist, except we're the good guys. Usually you put the key in here and turn it this way, but we don't have the key. So my... Acid taught me how to drive, and before I could do this..." she felt along the steering column and gave it a quick zap. "He taught me how to hot-wire, too." The SUV purred to life, but Kail caught her right hand and turned it palm up in the light.

She jerked her hand back. "It's okay. Just a little scorch."

"Your field isn't out of control, but you still can't protect yourself from it," he observed.

She adjusted the rearview mirror and put the car in reverse. "Always check your mirrors before you move. This is the gear shift, you use it to take the car out of park and put it in drive, reverse, or neutral. We already know that neither of us is up to fighting weight. Like I haven't noticed you ain't got your condition all the way back."

He regarded her for another minute as she finished turning the car around. "Where are we going, exactly?"

"I figure we can head somewhere with a computer, a library or something, and figure out how to do the Lightning Detection Network thing to see if there's a portal opening up anywhere. We'll have about an hour to get there once we spot something. When we get close enough, I'll be able to pin down exactly where it is." *It isn't a good plan, but there's a lot less wait-and-see involved*, Penance thought grimly. *If we don't end up being too late.*

"Or..." Kail grinned, pulling Path's phone out of his pocket, "we could probably use this device to track the matching one that Tech has."

"What? You..." Penance veered a bit on the road as she looked over at Kail's prize. "Yes, they are totally set up to track, even when they look like they're off. It's not tracking us now, though." She grinned over at Kail, who had set his seat back as far as it would go. His knees still touched the glovebox, and the seat didn't quite contain the rest of him. "Nice work, Kail."

He turned on the phone and found the app Path had opened. "This picture looks like a map." He frowned at the screen. "It's tracking two devices," he said. "Which do we follow?"

"Shouldn't matter. One's Tech, and she's tracking Janus. They'll both end up the same place." Penance turned on the blinker and checked both ways before turning  onto the main road. "We just got to keep an eye out, and not get seen first." Janus and Acid might be driving another black SUV... but then again, they might not be. And for all she knew, some extra thugs might be converging on the spot too. "The women are being shipped in a transfer truck – but those are everywhere. No telling which one it'll be."

She glanced again at the map on the phone and found the interstate. "What if the women aren't getting shipped to your planet, though? It's a big universe."

Kail shrugged. "They aren't likely to be going anywhere else. It is against the Interstellar Charter to abduct people from their planets or to invade foreign planets. The Emperor of Hylinek publicly supports the Charter. He devotes most of the resources of the planets under his control to his military, which is in space enforcing it." He glanced over at Pen, one eyebrow raised. "Selectively."

Penance made a disgusted noise. "So he's a crooked cop and his base is Hylinek. Everybody there knows this? Let me ask a stupid question. Isn't there somebody to report him to, and if there is, would you testify against him?"

Kail gave a short, surprised laugh. "What? Yes, there's the Interplanetary Council, but no, he's on it. He's *most* of it, I think. As for testifying... how many executions do you think I can survive?"

The girl glared at the road ahead. "Your whole planet is screwed up, you know that? All this Emperor does is prop himself up by stepping on everyone else." She blew a sigh. "At least now we're on our way to stop any more from going." Reaching over the console, she flicked her knuckles against the big soldier's arm affectionately.

"You're confident," he said. She couldn't tell if he thought that was a good thing or not.

She shook her head. "Nah, it's just got to get done. You get one life, spend it slow or spend it fast, but you got to spend it, so I'd rather buy something good with it. There's no pretty way to die."

Kail straightened. "I'm not going to let you die."

"Good, I won't let you die neither," she replied, sass creeping into her tone. She didn't know if she could do this if they let it get too serious. For all she knew, an army of switchheads waited for them... plus Acid.

They drove in silence for a little while.

"Pen?"

"Mm?"

"Since we've agreed not to let each other die, what will we do when the mission is complete?" Kail stretched as far as he could and leaned back, arms crossed behind his head. Penance guessed he was trying for casual. His seat creaked.

"I dunno. Want to go to the beach, see the ocean?" She laughed, remembering how impressed he'd been by the cow pond. "It's gonna blow your mind."

"Sure," Kail said, smiling. "Sounds fun."

# Close

## INTERSTATE, UNITED STATES, EARTH

"You really need a license to drive," Penance teased as Kail swapped seats with her at dusk.

"Where's yours?" he retorted. "Besides, I'm authorized to drive eight classifications of vehicle on Hylinek."

"I guess this'll be ninth, then." The girl yawned. "Just try not to attract attention from the highway patrol. If sirens come up behind you, pull over and wake me up." She stretched out in the passenger seat, which remained laid as far back as it would go. She suspected Kail's weight had broken it.

"What attracts their attention?" Kail asked, adjusting the seat and the mirrors.

"Driving too fast, driving too slow, wobbling all over the lane, getting too close to other cars, taillights or headlights out... or if they suspect the car's stolen."

"What then?" He pulled off the shoulder of the road back onto the interstate, checking their destination on the phone again.

"Let 'em arrest us, walk back to the patrol car, then I'll EMP their car and comm and then we get back on the road." Penance shrugged. "Done it a hundred times." She snuggled into the seat, pulling Kail's combat vest over herself like a blanket.

Kail glanced over at her. *Already asleep. Borrowing my gear again.* She'd tried on his boots, examined his armor, borrowed tools and – most shocking of all – worn his spare shirt to bed. On Hylinek, he trusted no one to touch his few possessions. He made an exception for Pen, who remained oblivious to the intimacy of her appropriations. She could keep the shirt – he didn't know if he could wear it again without constantly picturing her in it anyway. But he would need his armored vest back.

He turned his attention back to driving. Another skill added to his record. Perhaps he could modify the vehicle further now that he knew more about how it worked. There must be some way to increase the leg room.

A transfer truck blew by, going much faster than the speed limit. Kail eyed it suspiciously as it disappeared over the next hill. Pen was right – big trucks like that one were common. They had passed hundreds over the past six or seven hours of driving across country. Still, he couldn't help noting each one.

The soldier shook his head. Even if they did stumble across the truck with the captives, they would have to allow it to continue to the destination. Janus, Acid, and the rest of the ring had to converge where they could be caught with the evidence, before they sent more captives through. He hoped that taking a shift driving through the night would be enough to catch up in time.

Penance yawned and stretched, the late morning sun finally waking her. "Kail! Why didn't you wake me up?" She struggled to sit up in the seat, peering out the window at the thick pine woods and power lines."Where are we?"

"Our target slowed down on these back roads. I think we're getting close." He glanced away as he made a turn, but reached over and brushed the knuckles of his right hand against her arm. "You need more sleep than I do."

The girl stared at his hand, confused. *Kail touched me – and it's not an emergency?* She checked her field. No sparks, no anxiety, nothing but peace about doing the right thing for once. *Maybe he thinks I'm scared?* Kail suffered through letting *her* touch *him* sometimes, like an exceptionally dignified cat. He never initiated contact, except when protecting her from her own sparks and, rarely, to sit with his back companionably against hers. She'd picked up on his rules and tried to follow them, though occasionally she still mortified him by impulsively grabbing his hand. Now the back of his hand rested against her elbow and she didn't know what to do.

"We need a plan beyond finding Tech," he continued, his voice deep and warm though he avoided looking at her. "We need to carry out the primary objective, no matter what, even if Tech is already dead. Can you sense where she is?"

"What? I can sense electronics, not people. People have an EMF sig too, but it's really weak unless they're like me, or... or the Justice... and even then they have to be using it."

"Commander Tech has a computer in her skull."

"What? No sh... uh, how? I'd notice something like that."

"She shuts it down when she's around you."

Penance sat back and thought this over. It could be. It explained a lot. She wasn't sure whether it made being ignored and avoided by Tech hurt more or hurt less. Maybe it hurt the same amount, but for different reasons. "Okay, there's a lot of signal everywhere but if it's unusual, or moving around like a person, I can try to sense that. I'll probably have to be a lot closer, but I shouldn't have any trouble pinning down where she is."

Kail nodded. "Good. Our primary objective, however, is not Tech."

"It's not?"

"No. You're the Deputy Justice, you should know this."

"The missing girls?"

"Close. But there is something else that we must accomplish, no matter what it takes, or else this will simply happen again and again. We'll be chasing new locations and new sellers for the rest of our lives if we don't. And that's if the Emperor doesn't mount a full invasion."

Penance nodded slowly. "We have to shut down the portal. But... I know you're talking about permanently. We can't, not yet."

"Do you not have the technology?"

"I have no idea what we do and don't have right now. It doesn't matter. Because I'm not leaving all those people already stranded on Hylinek. We will be going back there. I don't care how long it takes or how much trouble it is. Every last soul on that planet is worth it."

Kail slowed the car to a crawl and nodded toward the window. She sat up and craned her neck, looking for what he had seen. A burgundy minivan, mostly hidden in the scrubby pine woods off the side of the road. "That's the vehicle Tech requisitioned from the paramedic," the big soldier said, and pulled off to the side of the road.

Tech wasn't in the car, but she'd left behind a tablet rigged to her phone, which had a timer counting down. Two hours and twelve minutes were left on it. "What is it?" Kail asked.

Penance turned her palms up. "Could be a bomb, could be set to make a recorded phone call." She backed out of the van and dusted her hands on her jeans. "Best leave it alone," she said. "She's got some kind of plan going, and we're better off if we can find her and get in on it rather than take the chance we'll work at cross-purposes."

Kail nodded, and together they found the trail Tech had taken through the woods from the van. They followed it down an embankment, over a narrow creek, and up again to a chain link fence along the top of the next hill. Two security cameras guarded this section of the fence. Penance gestured Kail down as they approached, and edged ahead to see what the fence contained.

The air hummed with power to Penance's senses, too much to tell whether an active portal was nearby or not. Past a field and parking lots, three immense silos rose from the ground in the distance, towering over the adjacent buildings. Transformers sent electric lines overhead.

Penance backed up to check the fence line again and estimated how much ground each camera covered. She guessed they didn't quite overlap. Sure enough, in the gap between the cameras' fields of vision, she found a shallow trench scooped away under the fence. Just big enough for a petite woman like Tech to get through.

She crawled back to Kail to report. "It's a nuclear plant. Tech told me that I'd used nuclear energy to boost the portal when I went and got you, so I guess that's how they're going to get enough power to open portals from this end instead of from Hylinek."

Kail nodded. "With the risks opening this planet has posed recently, the Emperor is probably not pleased about wasting Hylinek's limited energy on ground-based portals."

"There's another thing," Penance said. "There's no help for it, we're going to have to split up. I can follow Tech but you can't. I could fuzz cameras and get you in that way, but there are lots of cameras and a whole string of them gone to static looks suspicious."

"I'm not going to hide out here while you go in alone and get killed."

"Ain't nobody gonna see me to kill me."

"Pen." The massive soldier placed a knuckle under her chin and turned her face to him. His violet-blue eyes darkened seriously as he regarded her. "Will you promise to wait for me?"

*He's gonna kiss me*, she thought. "Yes," she whispered.

Kail relaxed and reached to a pocket on the back of his vest to draw out a pair of bolt cutters, which he presented to her. "Good."

*Oh. That works too, I guess.*

"All right, you remember how I showed you?" Penance asked again as they watched a transfer truck drive in the front entrance of the nuclear facility. The gates swung shut behind it.

"To hot-wire? Yes. You remember not to try to take on everyone before I can get in?" Kail replied, teasing.

"I promised, didn't I?"

"Signal me if you get in trouble," he said.

"What kind of signal are you going to be looking for?"

"Knowing you? Probably an explosion."

Penance rolled her eyes. "I don't cause that many explosions."

"'That many,'" he mocked.

She punched his arm. "Let's just go." They split up, Penance sprinting for the breach in the perimeter fence and Kail heading back to the SUV.

Penance cut a long line in the chain link fence above Tech's trench, and clipped two carabiners to each side of the break. Then she crawled through and dashed over the open field to the first building. Dust rose from her feet. Ahead, the tractor trailer they had seen pulled into the inner parking lot and backed up to a loading dock. Penance cast around, checking for cameras and any other electronics, but the fields generated by the plant itself made it difficult. Pinning down Tech's location might be tougher than she'd thought.

"Just come this way, ma'am, and I'll take you by the security office so you can make a report," the security guard said as he led Tech down past the loading dock. He glanced over to the back of the truck that had just pulled in. "And where did you say you got away from these people?"

Tech saw what he had seen — a still-intact padlock and chain on the back of the trailer. She reached for her gun but not fast enough. The man lunged and grabbed her wrists, throwing her up against the wall by the loading dock. "Well, well," he said. "No harm in adding a little extra to the pot."

The next moment, he crumpled to the ground. Penance stood behind him, shaking out her hand. "Oh, just a regular guy. I guess I hit him harder than I needed to," she said.

"Penance Copper!" Tech hissed furiously. "What are you doing here?"

"Rescue mission, Commander Tech," Penance grinned, finally recognizing her. "What the heck are you wearing?" Instead of an immaculate cream colored suit and matching stiletto heels, Tech wore distressed faded denim shorts, a red halter top, and tennis shoes, all grungy like she had slept in her clothes for a week. She looked like a college student who'd gotten lost on spring break.

"I allowed myself to be captured so that I could be the first to go through the portal and sabotage it," Tech answered.

"Sabotage it how? As you go through it..." Penance suddenly realized that she sensed quite a lot of energy emanating from Tech's skull. What did she have juicing that computer? Plutonium? "Yeah, that plan sucks. Can we go with the plan that sees everybody out of here *without* you blowing up your freaking brain?" Penance asked. "Did you find out where the other women are?"

Tech pointed to the trailer and Penance applied her bolt cutters to the padlock. "Watch out for the driver, I didn't see him leave the truck."

"Yeah, already got him," Penance tossed back over her shoulder, and pulled the chain loose from the doors. Frightened women huddled on the floor inside the trailer. "Hey, ladies, y'all okay? Can everybody walk?"

"We're with the Planetary Justice Department," Tech added. She turned to Penance. "Do you have a plan for getting them out?"

"Straight back the way you came in," Penance said, helping a weeping woman down from the trailer. "Here, stay on this side. I clipped the fence, should be able to pull it open wide and get everyone through. Kail's waiting on us, once these ladies are out we can go take down the ring and disable the portal rig."

Tech nodded. "Since we have found the captives, the first priority should be to get them to safety," she said. "But then we must find and shut down the portal, and we are running short on time."

They herded the women together, Tech in the lead. Penance brought up the rear, fuzzing multiple cameras at the same time to conceal them all. Coupled with the constant, distracting hum of energy from the plant, she failed to notice the trap until one of the women screamed.

Instinctively, Penance pulled energy from a nearby transformer and laid out two high arcs of plasma energy, one on either side of the group. Gunshots popped from every direction, but a curtain of energy from the arcs to the earth shielded the women as they hit the ground. Penance couldn't keep up the arcs long, but at least this configuration sent the bolts straight down to ground instead of lashing out at her. Tech remained standing and fired shot after shot, even though she couldn't see her targets. She guessed correctly at least twice, marking the invisible attackers in their own blood as she took them out.

Pen divided her concentration, struggling to hold two different forms of energy in her mind as she pulled a new arc from the transformer. Fuzzing the energy broadly into static, she flicked an opposite charge across the dry dust at their attackers' feet. The dust clouded thickly over the armed thugs as she and Tech dropped to the ground with the rest of the women. Gunfire sounded overhead. Behind them, the abused transformer blew out with a loud crack and caught fire. The plasma shields, unsustained, collapsed.

Chaos broke out behind them as a vehicle roared down the drive. Penance stood up from the dissipating dust cloud as the black SUV careened around the corner, ramming through cars at top speed as all the camouflaged gunmen turned their attention to it. It caught a high curb badly and crashed, rolling several times before it skidded to a stop, greasy side up, peppered with gunshots.

Penance froze in horror, and then realized about the same time as the gunmen that Kail wasn't in there. With a relieved sigh, she turned back to the battle. Her dust cloud had done its other job well, and the formerly invisible gunmen stood out starkly in the bright sunlight, their camouflage clogged and useless. Tech resumed firing as the women behind her picked themselves up and ran for the widened opening in the fence. And there, providing surprisingly rapid cover fire for the women as they escaped, Kail with his homemade gun. He'd done something clever to rig the SUV to steer itself in. She'd have to ask how he'd got it to turn corners.

Things looked pretty good after all, until she caught a whiff of a familiar smell.

That was all the warning she had before Acid struck her.

The blow caught her across her ear, knocking her to the ground. She landed on one hand and flipped out of the way, but Acid moved quickly, pressing in. *He's had a fresh hit*, Penance thought. *Gotta keep him moving until he burns through it – and he'll get more dangerous as he goes.*

Behind her, the distinctive crack of Kail's weapon sounded, and Acid flinched back, dodging just in time. "You stay outta this," Acid snarled at the big soldier. Corrosive liquid dripped from his hands.

The distraction allowed Penance to snap a kick at Acid's crippled leg, but her target moved, avoiding the full force of the strike. The villain returned his attention to her, slinging a spray of acid. She leaped backwards but her opponent had no trouble keeping up. As Acid closed in, Penance glimpsed Kail's frustrated face. The massive alien kept a bead on the villain but didn't pull the trigger. *It's not accurate enough at this distance! He can't shoot Acid without possibly shooting me, too.*

Penance dodged the next spray of acid and kicked again, unwilling to risk getting close enough to throw a punch. As Acid retaliated with a kick of his own toward her head, she dropped to a crouch. Before his foot hit the ground again, Penance jumped as high as she could over him. She hit the ground with a forward roll and kept low as she spun around.

She'd gotten out of the line of fire, but now Kail had four switchheads converging on him. He struck at them with the butt of the gun, saving his ammunition for Acid as he plowed through the battlefield. Bullets struck his armored vest, miraculously missing his head. Blood streaked his arms.

*Kail will back me up when he can.* The thought drove back the chilling terror of defying Acid. *I just gotta keep Acid between us so his next chance won't be wasted.* Hope kept her moving as her old tormentor lashed at her again and again, driving her back.

Kail barreled through the battlefield toward Pen, trying to get close enough to get a better shot at Acid. Bullets whistled past him and he returned fire, dropping a man. Another leaped at him, hacking at his armor with a knife. Kail flipped his gun around and clubbed the man's arm. The switchhead dropped the knife but kept coming. Kail grabbed the front of the man's uniform and lifted him from the ground, swinging him into another attacker before throwing him away from the battlefield.

A bullet grazed his arm and he searched for who had fired it – anyone with ammunition still left could shoot Pen. He leveled his weapon and fired, his own bullets spattering erratically around the gunman. A lucky hit to the trigger hand took care of that one, but Kail's homemade weapon neared the end of its usefulness. Melted metal built up inside it, throwing off the accuracy. It would only get worse.

Behind him, Tech stopped her steady rhythm of shots. Kail glanced back as she fell, blood pouring from above her ear. "No!" he gasped. Too late, he tackled the man who had shot her, picking him up and throwing him into the next switchhead who aimed a gun at him.

*I've let my commander down*, Kail thought. *I've endangered the mission. I'm no soldier. I'm nothing at all.*

The empty, uncaring universe yawned open before him, as it had when he was dead...

Another switchhead bore down on Tech's still body, unarmed but with his hands twitching madly as if he longed to rip her to pieces. *Pen said they see beauty and mangle it...* Kail leaped between the man and his fallen commander, striking a left uppercut that sent him flying. Of all the aliens Kail had met on this planet, Commander Tech had been the strangest. But she had been a good commander, and he would not allow her body to be desecrated.

"Uhnn," Tech groaned, sitting up. She blinked up at Kail and touched her bloody scalp. "It's okay, he got me in the plate." She picked up her gun to check the magazine. Finding it empty, she discarded the gun and unholstered two more from inside her clothing. "Recalibrating."

Stunned, Kail shielded her as she completed her calibrations. *Evidently she has much more strangeness left.*

The man who had shot Tech staggered upright and turned back to them. He bellowed in rage, brandishing his gun like a club as he charged them. *Probably out of ammunition*, Kail thought, as he grabbed the barrel of the weapon and pointed it up. *Still, best to not take chances*. Casually he ripped the gun out of the man's hands and knocked him out with a punch to the head.

"Thank you, Kail," Commander Tech said, standing up with a gun in each hand. "I've put in a call for backup. They should be here soon. Go help Penance. I'll cover you."

"Thank you, Commander!" Kail said, relieved. He had orders again. He hadn't lost his place after all. Behind him, Tech resumed firing – the rhythm of the shots twice as fast as she alternated between her weapons.

Still, switchheads outnumbered them.

*These switchheads don't stay down!* he thought. *They don't feel pain. I'd have to rip their limbs off to neutralize them. And Earth is not like Hylinek – even the powerful face scrutiny over the perception of excessive force.* Enemies charged him like maddened animals and he knocked them aside.

His weapon had one, maybe two shots left before it became useless. He had to get close enough to his target to make them count.

Penance danced back lightly, warily watching Acid's face for the change in mood that signaled "seeing demons." So far, he had nothing but plain anger. She preferred that to the sudden maudlin sentimentality that whipped just as quickly to murderous rage.

He lunged and she dodged again, but she chose her direction wrong and he caught her.

Knocking her back hard toward the power plant, he followed up with a right hook that connected with her ear and left her head ringing. She flinched away from him and he kicked her, catching her stomach unguarded and flipping her to the ground. Breathless and stunned, she fought against terror as he bore down on her. *Don't spark! You know what happens!*

He always had been stronger than her. She'd always known that.

One day, he'd kill her.

Maybe today.

Far away, Kail yelled her name, but suddenly a massive wave of energy overwhelmed all her senses. Roiling overhead, it slammed into the gap between them. It blasted in her skull, leaving her disoriented and sick. Worst of all, she knew this energy.

It was *hers*.

She had done this to the Justice.

She had done this to her mother.

It was all her fault.

She deserved to have it done to her.

"Pick up your brat," Janus said, somewhere over her head.

Acid grabbed her jacket and she flailed, slipped out of it and scrambled away, but he kicked her stomach again and sent her rolling. She retched on the ground and he caught her up and threw her over his shoulder like a sack of potatoes.

Her head lolled and she squinted through tears as Kail bashed the force field with his gun, unleashing bolts of plasma to lash at him with each strike.

All those tests Janus had put her through. Those weeks when he had been evaluating her abilities. The way he'd lost interest as soon as she'd come to the end of her tricks. He'd used her. He'd copied her. And now he had a machine that would do exactly what he wanted and not ask questions or get attached to specimens. She couldn't take it. The feedback from her natural field and his too-similar, artificially-generated one screamed in her skull, in her skin, in her bones. Taking her apart.

She had to let it go.

In the midst of the two people she hated and feared most in the world, she had to release her only protection. Her only comfort.

*Jesus. Save me*, she whispered in her soul – and let her energy field die. Her sense of all the energy fields around her broke away, and left her in a cold, empty void, occupied only by pain and the taste and smell of her own bile.

She slumped, limp and nearly unconscious, over Acid's shoulder as he carried her into the plant.

"Pen!" Kail roared, slamming the plasma containment field with the butt of his weapon. An arc of energy lashed out but quickly reabsorbed into the dome. He reached toward it with his bare hand, but unlike Pen's field, it did not part for him. He backed away, looking up at the dome that now covered the entire nuclear facility.

Heavy, rapid breathing and thudding steps approached behind him. The switchhead leaped on his back and Kail threw him over his shoulder into the plasma shield without a second thought. The man screamed as he contacted the field and the resulting arc of energy threw him off. He landed some distance away and lay limp on the ground – finally, something worked to neutralize them.

The sirens came closer and stopped in the part of the parking area still left outside the dome. Kail glanced back at Tech. "Commander! What do you know about plasma containment fields?"

She came jogging up to him, picking her way among groggy, injured switchheads. "Not much. Dr. Janus never submitted his report on the one you used. I did see those black posts in the footage from the stadium – they seemed to attract the energy."

Kail nodded. "Stabilizer rods. Deyn said that competition from a strong enough signal could take down the dome."

"How do they work?"

Kail shook his head. "I'm not sure."

Tech narrowed her eyes at the facility within the dome. "This is bad. They've isolated the nuclear chamber – if the core overheats while the dome is in place, there's no way to cool it. We could be looking at a nuclear meltdown."

"Are you sure they've isolated it from the safety mechanism? How do you know where it is?"

Tech pointed to her right eye, still staring at the building. "Map."

"I see you've had most of the excitement without me," a newcomer said, striding across the battlefield from the parking lot.

Tech turned away from the building, smiling in relief. "Justice. I'm glad you're all right."

"I wouldn't go that far. Acid and Janus left me for dead at the safe house. And I would've been, if Mr. Plutarch hadn't arrived and found me." He gestured to the spectacled driver of the vehicle, who lifted a hand in modest acknowledgment.

Path ran up, glancing around anxiously. "Where's Penance?"

"Taken inside," Tech answered.

The Justice approached Kail, giving the former invader an appraising look. "And you must be Kail."

Kail nodded, returning the man's interest. So this is the Justice for Earth. Pen said he was compromised by the drug, forever. But she had also told him that this man's abilities were the nearest to her own she had ever encountered. "Can you take down the dome?"

The older man shook his head slowly. "I don't think so – and even if I could, it may not be wise. If the core goes critical, we'll want it there - there's a chance the dome will absorb and convert any radiation before it blasts the area. Still a disaster, but at least it won't render the county unlivable for the next hundred years."

Tech broke in. "Penance is in there. We have to get her out. If you can make an opening in the dome, I'll go in for her."

The Justice frowned at her. "You aren't insulated well enough from either the force field or the potential radiation. The power source for your computer will not tolerate it."

"But I am the one going," Kail said.

Tech and the Justice turned to him. "You can't," Tech said flatly. "We can't get a radiation suit big enough for you."

"Then it's a good thing I don't need one. I am *ip Laevii*. Radiation didn't affect me in the mines, and it won't affect me now."

Once inside the nuclear facility, Janus turned to snarl at Acid. "I've done everything I've promised you. See where it's gotten us? In debt, behind schedule, what good is your precious little freak now?"

Step, scuff. Step, scuff. Acid limped behind Janus, letting the man rage at him.

"Everything I've done! It's all given away now! Years, decades of work and planning destroyed! All because you wanted to keep your illegitimate little brat! Now he's coming and he'll take everything. We're more trouble than we're worth and he will destroy us both unless you do what you should have done years ago!"

Step, scuff. Step, scuff.

Janus opened a door and brilliant white light poured out. A portal, Penance knew. A big one, that needed all this energy from the power plant. But she couldn't feel it. She'd let her field go entirely for the first time in her life, and she didn't know how to get it back, or even if she could.

Janus grabbed her hair and wrenched her head back to look at her. "The Emperor pays more for Primes. I've failed too often now. But you, you freak accident!" Janus said, shaking her. "You will pay the debt. You should be more than enough."

A voice boomed from the portal, and Acid dropped her on the floor. She saw Janus hurry to the portal and kneel, hands above his head in a strangely familiar pose. He spoke in another language, begging. She couldn't quite make out what he said, but she had heard that rhythm before.

Penance looked up at Acid, his harsh features blurred and softened through her tears. For a moment, he almost looked like himself again. His real self, before all the tragedy began. The switch had to be burned nearly out now. Maybe she could remind him. Maybe, for once, he would see who the real demons were.

"Daddy," she whispered. "You and me and Mama, we lived in a red truck. You worked on a farm. Had a guitar you'd play." Her voice grew stronger. "Why won't you be that man again?"

Acid grabbed her hair and hauled her to her knees. His fingers burned through her hair, leaving a chemical stink, and he snatched a new handful to drag her to the glowing portal.

But it seemed to Penance that the hesitation in his step wasn't only his limp.

He stopped and rocked down to his knees, and Penance lifted her eyes to see through the portal open before her. A huge figure, a man bigger than Kail, waited for her. He wore golden armor, gleaming so bright it hurt her eyes. *This is him*, she thought. *The one running the trafficking ring. I have to know -*

She found his face and gasped.

Her stomach turned.

His face was handsome, noble even. His perfect lips curled cruelly. Beneath dark straight brows, his brilliant violet blue eyes pierced and held her.

Penance looked at the devil himself.

It was as though, for a final insult, he had stolen Kail's face. And then she remembered that Kail didn't have a father – only an Emperor he'd believed in, until he'd been betrayed and sentenced to death.

She lifted her chin and glared at him. "You've got a lot of nerve."

The Emperor laughed. Even his laugh sounded like Kail's, but with an ugly edge to it. "Little girl, I am the Emperor of all. I only reclaim what should be mine." His gaze swept down her body and he nodded slowly. "Including you."

"She's a stubborn, insolent girl, but strong," Janus interjected. "She is the most powerful Prime I could capture for you – a plasmic reactor in a human body. Worth much more than our paltry debts."

"Silence!" the Emperor boomed. He directed a feral grin at Janus, who cringed. "Your payment is weeks late and your carelessness has lost the rest of the shipment. One girl for my personal use is considered a gift – you still owe me."

Penance scoffed. "That's what I thought. There ain't no getting out of debt to the devil."

"Devil?" Acid mumbled beside her. He squinted at the Emperor through the portal.

The Emperor found this amusing. "You call me a devil, a demon, little girl? You will be entertaining to break." He laughed again. "Very well, I accept your pathetic gift. I will even grant you a month's extension to deliver a new shipment."

The Emperor reached for Penance.

Beside her, her father took a ragged, gasping breath. Acid looked down at her and released his grip on her hair. His expression changed, abruptly childlike, trusting. "Pretty Penny," he whispered. "Always were a bright one. Know one when you see one, don't you?"

"What are you doing?" hissed Janus. "Push her through!"

Acid growled at his dealer. "Why don't *you* go through!" He lurched at the doctor, grabbing the man's collar and hurling him through the portal to land sprawling at the Emperor's feet.

The Emperor kicked away the man and lunged toward the portal. "*Ibak!* Do not forget that you belong to me!"

Fear and resolve crossed Acid's face. He thrust one arm through the portal. "Penny, collapse it," he shouted.

"I... I can't. I can't control that much power... I need a conduit..."

"Use me!" he bellowed.

Startled into obedience, she groped blindly, relying on will and memory to pull electricity from the equipment. Her efforts rewarded by a solid arc, she slung it to her father, where it raced in spirals along his skin and shot from the fingertips of his outstretched hand. The turbines whirred madly and arcs skipped over and lashed her exposed skin, faster and faster until she couldn't guide them anymore and let them go.

The arcs lashed at the Emperor, causing him to falter, but the portal remained unchanged. She'd made the devil blink, but already he gathered himself to grab for her again.

Penance realized that there was nothing she could do. It wasn't up to her. It wasn't her burden, to find and use more and more power to fight against bigger and bigger threats. The Owner and Creator of the universe and everything in it could be trusted to take care of this... this demon.

Her entire being changed from panic to calm. She lifted her chin and spoke directly to the Emperor. "In Jesus' name, keep your filthy paws to yourself."

The massive alien emperor roared in anger, lunging for her.

But in that moment, a connection clicked together in Penance's mind. Dreamily, she linked to the familiar feeling, a field like her own, and pulled on it to cover herself. Her mind slipped down it to find its source, metal and magnets and whirling electrons dancing in a cold, fixed mockery of her own. She brushed against Janus' plasmic reactor with her mind and dissolved it. As the atoms were dismantled, she directed the electrons to race to her father, who guided them inside the portal to burst in irregular waves. Overwhelmed and disrupted, the portal skewed and ripped apart.

As did Acid's arm inside it before he collapsed.

Matter-of-factly, Penance ripped the hem of her shirt off to make a tourniquet on Acid's arm. Her head rang – no, that was a siren. Red flashing lights and loud blaring alarms made it harder to think. She tightened the tourniquet and stood, trembling. Somewhere, there had to be an emergency button or something. She wiped her palms on her torn, scorched jeans before grabbing Acid under the armpits and dragging him to the door.

Two steps toward the door, she fainted.

# Final Connection

## OUTSIDE NUCLEAR FACILITY, UNITED STATES, EARTH

Strong arms wrapped around Penance, holding her safe and close. Warm breath tickled her neck. Men shouted terse instructions about stretchers and an IV nearby, but they didn't bother her.

"Kail?" she murmured.

He made a curious growling noise. "Arrrrgggghhh, you worry me."

"Sorry?"

He nuzzled behind her ear, his breath ragged. Several minutes passed before he loosened his grip, and even then he only pulled back just enough to look at her face. He paused, studying her as if he would memorize every freckle.

"What is it?" she whispered. She looked away from his intense gaze and rubbed an itch on her face she suspected was dirt. "I'm a mess."

He nodded solemnly. "*Eyh.*" He broke a grin and nuzzled her again suddenly, baffling her with the onslaught of physical affection – she'd thought he hated to be touched?

A man in a radiation suit jogged up. "Here's that blanket you called for, sir," he said, and dropped it with a quick salute before he hurried off. Kail let go of Penance with one hand long enough to catch it and tuck it around her, still shielding her with his body.

Penance clutched at the blanket, wondering just how badly her clothes had gotten shredded in the fighting.

"I promise I didn't look," Kail said. But he grinned so big she wasn't sure if he joked with her or not. He looked entirely too pleased with himself to be completely innocent.

Tech approached, scanning her phone. "I'll need a statement from you, Penance, on everything you witnessed. Where is Dr. Janus?"

Penance blinked. Oh yes. "My father... Acid tossed him through the portal."

Tech raised one eyebrow and tapped something on her phone. "I see. So you did see the portal in operation? Could you see anything through it?"

"Yes. The... the Emperor. In gold armor, designed like Kail's, but shiny. Big guy. Bigger than Kail, a bit."

"Really?" Kail asked, impressed.

"Yeah really. He's a jerk. Said he'd accept me as a gift for his 'personal use.' I was gonna be 'entertaining to break.'"

The massive soldier's arms hardened around her and he growled deep in his throat. Tech and Penance both stared at him until the sound subsided. He glanced away and swallowed. "Continue?" he asked.

"I dunno if it led right to Hylinek, though. Looked like a big nice hall, a throne room maybe. But... Janus and my father both did the *ibak* thing. Kneeling, hands up, talking about debts." Disgust colored her tone. "Biggest con I ever saw, getting people on a whole other planet to stay slaves."

Tech scowled at her phone and tapped on it some more. She nodded. "Well, that's enough for the Interplanetary Council to open an investigation, at least. I'll want you both to help me develop a new interference device to prevent new ground-based portals, and Kail, I'll need you to study a few more languages if you can handle it." She shook her head. "These aliens would jump at the chance to trade us a little protection, in exchange for all our freedom."

Penance shifted and Kail tucked the end of the blanket around her again. "It's a racket," Penance said. "The Emperor who's kidnapping people and threatening us is on the Council."

Tech nodded soberly. "Yes. We will need to be careful. And of course there are still the earlier shipments of captives to save."

Two paramedics whisked by, bearing Acid on a stretcher. He lifted his remaining hand at Penance as he went by. Justice stumbled behind, holding his head, freshly wrecked after forcing a gap in the energy dome for Kail to enter. "Both of them need rehabilitation," Tech added sadly. "Path is nearly done counseling the women we rescued today. I need to check on her and then we can go."

Kail waited until Tech was out of earshot before he whispered, "Did you know her skull is bulletproof?"

"No! Really? Full of surprises from the neck up, isn't she." Penance laughed, incredulous. Sliding off his lap, she wobbled upright and turned her back to him. She peered inside her blanket to check how indecent her clothes had gotten in the fight.

Her jeans had holes ripped in the knees and her midriff showed from where she'd torn a piece for the tourniquet, but other than that, her clothes covered her. She turned back to Kail and smacked his shoulder. "You troll!"

He shook with silent laughter, wiping tears from his eyes. "Ready to go home?"

Home? She had one of those? She grinned right back at him. "Yep. Let's go."

# Epilogue: Penance's Diary

What is wrong with the way I say -C-a-l-e K-a-l-e – no that's a vegetable – Kail? How bad is it? Is it like if somebody says my name really, really wrong and it comes out 'Pants?'

I am so glad that Kail's decided my nickname is 'Pen.' Could be sooo much worse.

It's funny that now sometimes I wake up singing songs in my head.

*I fall too far and*
*I ask too much and*
*I take it too hard and*
*I know you think I'm crazy*
*but*
*I've seen the most beautiful light*
*I've dreamed the impossible*

*and it doesn't make sense at all,*
*but I really think he loves me.*

Kail is really unhappy about my training. He's right, I should rest. But if I slack off too much I'll get my period and I am just not ready to explain that.

I'll have to dig a hole to bury my dead of embarrassed self in first.

*He told me truth*
*He washed away your lies*
*He gave me hope*
*and never compromised*

It's frustrating that I can hear the music in my mind but I don't know how to write it down.

---

Found a tattoo artist who says she can cover up my tat, no problem. I won't have to go around branded like a cow anymore. I can get whatever I want!

I think a cross. I want it pretty, though. Wonder if she can make it like stained glass?

---

I'm only on the first bit and I did not see that coming. What do you mean "Adam was with her?" Standing right there the whole time? She <u>didn't</u> trick him? He just watched the whole thing and he was ok with that?

Whole world got broke because boy don't know what to do with a poisonous snake. They were in there doing gardening, you'd think they'd have invented a hoe by then.

Kail would have.

I have homework now. So does Kail. I'm going for my GED and he's studying for citizenship. He says other people in his class talk to each other about him in their own language. I told him on the last day, he needs to say something back.

Ac--- my father is going to live after all, it looks like. They've found something to alkalize his skin and stop it weeping. In a few months, if they can get his stump to heal over, they might let him have supervised visitors before they transfer him to the prison.

He's been asking after me, they say.

---

*Standing*
  *in the gap*
  *Down in the trenches*
  *Carrying me*
  *when I couldn't stand.*
  *In all my heart*

*All my soul*
  *With all my strength*
*I am home.*

—◆O◆—

The Justice called today. He says he knew my mother. She was trying to get help for me.

He wants to know if he can visit.

# Epilogue: Kail's Records

E nglish Writing Practice 1

    Kail ip Laevii

As part of my training, I have been instructed to learn to read and write in English, and have been given a notebook and a supply of pencils.

As my schedule, duties, and projects are listed elsewhere, I have no idea what I am supposed to write about.

I will ask Path to clarify her instructions.

English Writing Practice 2

    Kail ip Laevii

Path tells me that the notebook is for my personal use and she will not be inspecting it, nor will anyone else.

I am not comfortable with the idea of setting my inner thoughts outside of myself onto paper.

English Writing Practice 3

    Kail ip Laevii

Today I have finished moving my sleeping quarters to the outbuilding.

I have seen Pen making marks and drawing in her notebook. She is not concerned at all that she will be caught not adhering to her assigned writing. She claims that doodling, as she calls it, helps her think of what to write about. She also mocked me and called me the straightest of straight arrows.

She has no idea how many regulations I'm breaking by existing.

English Writing Practice  4

Kail ip Laevii

Pen has brought a tiny feline in to live with us. I am familiar with the desert felines of Hylinek, but this feline is not even as big as one of their cubs, and it doesn't have large fangs. It makes a noise pitched almost like a baby's cry.

It is terrified of me if I'm standing, but will insist on sleeping on me as soon as I lie down. Pen has named it Jezebel.

My hammock broke last night; Jezebel chose an escape route across my face, with all of her claws extended for traction. I will make a sturdier hammock today and see if Jezebel trusts it enough to sleep on me again tonight.

# To My Wonderful Readers

Thank you for reading *Penance*! I hope you've loved this story as much as I have.

It's taken a lot to get here, from the beginning when a single chapter was included in the *Paragons* anthology from Silver Empire Press as the short story "Soldier Out of the Desert," to the first edition as part of Silver Empire's Heroes Unleashed shared universe, until now.

When Silver Empire Press closed down, I had a lot of things to figure out. I didn't want to abandon Pen and Kail's story, since I still had two books of their adventures left to tell. I had the option to find a new publisher, or I could have simply republished it as-is, but I wanted to relaunch with something more for my readers. Besides, I had discovered a typo. Obviously the thing to do is to tear down and rebuild completely, with bells, whistles, tinsel and glitter! Or, you know, a new cover, illustrations in every chapter, an extra epilogue, and an audiobook edition. Surely most of this is well within my capabilities as an artist – after all, who knows how these characters and this story look better than I? I may as well take full control of the publishing process while I'm at it. And then the next two books in the series will be produced to the same standard – or even beyond, since by then I'll have had so much more practice and opportunity to grow as an author, artist, and publisher!

Yeah, there truly is no end to the amount of work I will set for myself. (Well. Future Paula drew the line at also learning to become a narrator, at least.)

In any creative endeavor, there is creating to perfection, and then there is creating to completion. In order to create to completion, you have to set limits to create within. For example, as much as I would have loved to give you all full color, full page illustrations, I'll have to save that kind of extravagance for the graphic novel. Though the illustrations here are mid-sized black and white, I've tried to keep the imagery and composition fresh and interesting in each one. What I've learned from painting these will make the ones for the next projects even better.

As an author, I can only do my best to write a satisfying story – and then the next, and then the next. I hope you continue on this journey with me.

If you have enjoyed this story and would like to read more from me in the future, please write a review and post it somewhere! On any site that carries the book, on your own blog, or even a quick mention on your social media. Reviews raise the profile of a book more than anything else and increase its chances of being seen by more readers. This would be a huge blessing for me and OtherRealm Studio and would help ensure that I can continue publishing.

For more of my stories, art, artifacts, and other endeavors, please visit www.OtherRealmStudio.com.

# About the Author

Paula Richey is a person who dislikes writing about herself in the third person. From the evidence you hold in your hands at this moment, you already know that she is a writer and artist.

She loves other worlds and larger-than-life legends, and is plagued by a sense that she can't yet communicate to you JUST HOW EPIC the story *really* is. This has led to a lifelong mission to create stories in every feasible media, to better illuminate different facets of each story. Time and budgetary constraints apply.

Find out more about her current projects, books, comics, art and more on her website, www.OtherRealmStudio.com

# Who Is Thomas Plutarch?

I was there from the beginning. When the Event happened and the Primes first came, the wave hit me, too. I didn't realize it at first. My own powers developed slowly, and they were never any good for combat. Yes, I tried my own hand at heroing. But let's not talk about that.

Superhuman memory - truly perfect recall - doesn't help much in a fight. But it did let me piece it all together, to figure out what really happened.

It took me a while to find the perfect authors to help me tell the tales. They had to be told right - because Lord knows nobody else ever did.

Achilles, The Banshee, and Pendragon. You know the names, but you don't know the story. You only think you do. The government has some explaining to do when it comes to Matthew White and Jason Vermilion. But that's nothing compared to the story on Adam Song. Hah, what a crock you've been fed there. Joe "Overlook" Smith? They tried to bury that story deeper than the truth about JFK. And Deckard Riss? That tale will keep you up all night - and tomorrow night, too. Some things, maybe you don't want to know.

But I know. I remember them all. That's why they call me The Historian.

*Thomas Plutarch is a writer who exists within the Heroes Unleashed universe. Transmissions have been interrupted and the initial point of contact has been lost. However, you may be able to find more stories from the universe from these authors:*

*Morgon Newquist*
*Paula Richey*
*Jon Mollison*
*Richard W. Watts*
*J. D. Cowan*
*Kai Wai Cheah*

*O*therRealm Studio is creating stories, art, and artifacts of strange and beautiful worlds in multiple media formats. Explore the OtherRealm's illustrated novels, light novels, comic books, graphic novels, ebooks, audiobooks and more!

**Series:**

### *SoulBound*

*Adventure. Romance. Psyche.*

Lost in a realm of monsters, myth, and magic, Becca must find a way to return home – before her soul breaks away from her body and falls into the void between realms.

Torrin's first test as the leader of his people has failed, leaving him scarred beyond recognition. Can he withstand the curse placed on him long enough to fulfill his oath to the foreign girl from the Other Realm?

### *Teen Heroes Unleashed*

Penance Copper is a superpowered runaway, desperate to turn her life around.

Kail is a young soldier from another world, devastated by betrayal.

Can these two lost and broken souls find the strength to save the world?